DEAD EYES

ALAN BROWN

World Castle Publishing, LLC
Pensacola, Florida
Copyright © Alan Brown 2021
Paperback ISBN: 9781955086462
eBook ISBN: 9781955086479
First Edition World Castle Publishing, LLC, July 19, 2021
http://www.worldcastlepublishing.com
Licensing Notes
Cover: Karen Fuller
Editor: Maxine Bringenberg

CHAPTER 1
THE CREMATORIUM

His eyes were fixed on the concrete ceiling, where the paint was peeling. There were cracks in the ceiling, most tiny and thin, but one was bigger, thicker, and longer than the others. Small drops of water were dripping from it slowly, about every thirty seconds. A wet spot, about three inches wide, surrounded the crack. The water seeped through the opening and slowly formed into a drop. When the weight of the drop was too much to be supported by the ceiling, it fell to the floor into a blue plastic bucket strategically placed to capture the falling drops.

It was storming outside. He could hear the thunder and the rain pounding against the building.

Dennis Glenn had known this day would come. He'd hoped he would not be able to prevent it. But, some fates were impossible to alter. Now, all that he could do was wait for it to end. "Will it be painful?" he wondered. "Of course, it will," he said to himself. He, of all people, knew that. He had been there countless times when others had gone through what he was experiencing now. He had seen the pain in their eyes. Dennis had heard their cries. He had thought he just imagined it. All logic told him that what he saw and heard could not be real. But now he knew it was real.

Dennis tried desperately to move any part of his body. He couldn't. Whatever they had given him completely paralyzed his body, every inch of it. His mind was fully functioning. He could see. He could hear. But he could not talk, and he could not move. It was terrifying. Dennis knew what was going to happen, but he was completely powerless to stop it. Damn, he wished he had chosen a different direction for his life. He wished he could go back in time and change just one of his decisions. That's all it would take, just one different decision, and he wouldn't be where he was now. *It's strange how one choice a person makes in their life can have such dire consequences*, he thought.

Now, all he had left were memories, most of which were painful. He remembered when it all began when he started down the dead-end road of his life. It was nearly six years ago that he started working in the crematorium. That was the beginning of his end. That was the beginning of his never-ending nightmare.

Dennis learned soon after starting his job in the crematorium that a human body is made up of about seventy percent water. At 1650 degrees Fahrenheit, the water boils from within. It bubbles and expands the skin, causing ripples on the surface that looked like ocean waves. Body fat sizzles like bacon in a frying pan until it gets so hot it explodes through the surface of the skin, projecting pieces of flesh outward. The inner walls of the cremation furnace were coated with small pieces of flesh. They cook and stick to the walls like pieces of overcooked meat to an uncoated frying pan. But the worst part of working in a crematorium was not cremating the bodies. The worst part was cleaning the inner walls of the furnace at the end of the day.

It took Dennis months before he stopped getting sick to his stomach when it was time to clean those furnace walls. When he finally did get used to it, he learned to enjoy the slow pace and solitude that working alone in that crematorium brought him. That was until the day Gloria Jean Booker showed up on the gurney in the refrigeration room of the crematorium.

***

Gloria Jean Booker had spent most of her adult life trying to please her husband. The man was never satisfied. In her twenties, she had breast implants. In her thirties, she began Botox injections. In her forties, she had a face lift. Gloria Jean wasn't a vain woman — she was just trying to keep her husband from straying. She dieted, exercised, and applied every type of anti-aging and wrinkle-eliminating treatment she could find. She wore flattering clothes and did everything she could to keep her husband interested. None of it worked. Her husband was a scoundrel, going from one affair to another. Gloria Jean forgave him more times than she could count. She told herself that she loved him and that he loved her. Her husband wanted a son. His devoted wife gave him three. He complained that she wasn't a good mother. He berated her for not tending to his every need. Her husband was emotionally and, toward the end, physically abusive to her. She stayed through everything. Gloria loved her husband. She wanted a stable home for her children. When she was fifty, and their children were grown, he divorced her. Six months later, he married a young, petite blonde-haired, blue-eyed woman, twenty-five years her junior. She had looked like his new wife once, many years ago.

The divorce was nasty. Her husband was a successful businessman who made a lot of money. But he didn't want to share any of it with his ex-wife. She hired the best attorney she could find. He did the same. The attorneys went back and forth, dragging out the inevitable. She got the house and a monthly alimony check, enough so she didn't need to work, but not enough that she could have a comfortable lifestyle.

Single life was not easy for her. She was an attractive woman at fifty, but there were a lot of single, attractive women, many much younger, much firmer, and much more desirable. The bar scene was not kind to her. The men that spent time with her only wanted to use her and had no interest in starting a long-term relationship. They didn't want to get to know her—they were only interested in immediate satisfaction. After a string of one-night stands, Gloria Jean Booker found more comfort and satisfaction from a bottle of gin than in the arms of a stranger. The gin numbed her reality and dulled her senses. It made life a little more tolerable.

She was tolerating life a little too much one cold, December night. She knew better than to drive herself home, so she called a friend to pick her up. Home was only eight blocks away. She almost made it too. But two blocks from home, her friend took an icy curve in the road a little too fast. The car went off the road and down a steep hill, colliding with a large oak tree. Gloria Jean Booker was killed instantly.

The ideal temperature for cremating a body is 1650 degrees Fahrenheit. It takes approximately two hours for a body to burn completely at that temperature, and it will produce an average of three to nine pounds of course gray material, like fine gravel. But, of course, the temperature can vary depending on the bone density of the corpse. Gloria Jean Booker was a small-framed woman, thin and tiny-boned. "Fourteen-hundred degrees Fahrenheit will burn her body completely in about two hours,"

Dennis Glenn figured. He set the temperature and then walked into the refrigerated room at the back of the room. Inside were three bodies, tonight's work.

Gloria Jean Booker occupied the first metal table on the right. Dennis removed the white sheet covering her and checked her toe tag for identification. It was just a part of his process to insure the correct body was being cremated. He didn't need to check—Dennis knew her. He had seen her a handful of times in the past. But in his three years working in the crematory, he had never cremated the wrong body, and he wasn't about to start now.

Gloria Jean Booker, 4214 Bloomsdale Road, Kansas City, MO.

"Yes, that matches up with the cremation order," he said to himself.

Dennis looked over her body. "She was very attractive." He had always thought so ever since he met her, but he'd never had the ability to study her facial features so closely before. The accident had not damaged her face. She looked alive, almost as if she could jump up from the metal table at any time. Her eyes were wide open and focused directly at Dennis as he looked down into her face. If eyes could talk, Dennis wondered what they would say. "Eyes are a reflection of the soul.". Her eyes were sad and dark. *They had been crying shortly before she died*, he thought. He leaned down to within a few inches of her eyes. "What are you trying to tell me, Gloria?" he asked in a quiet voice.

Gloria Jean Booker was his first "special order." There were instructions left on Dennis's desk to tell him how to dispose of her remains. Every bit of her body needed to be ground down to ashes. Nothing that could possibly identify her could remain.

Dennis focused his attention on her breasts. She had implants. He had speculated that her breasts were not totally natural many times before, but he didn't know for sure until now. They would need to be removed. Breast implants implode when exposed to the intense heat of a cremation furnace. They will not completely burn down, resulting in a sticky, slimy substance that lines the inner walls of the furnace and can mix into the ashes. He could not put her in the cremator with implants. Dennis sliced open the breasts, removed the implants, and placed them inside a large trash barrel. He wheeled the barrel out the rear door to a large trash compactor, emptied the contents of the barrel into the machine, and pressed the button. The huge metal jaws squeezed the contents together into a flat wall of trash. Then he returned to the refrigerated room.

Dennis rolled the gurney that held her body out to the cremation furnace, then rolled her body onto a metal lift table connected to the outside of the furnace. After that, he put on the protective cover and gloves and goggles hanging next to the furnace. The heat from the cremation furnace was intense. Without protective clothing, his flesh would begin to burn within a few seconds. When he got to the cremator door, he opened it, lifted the metal table to a forty-five-degree angle, and slowly rolled the body onto a metal shelf into the furnace. Fire shot up immediately, consuming the body in a wall of flames. He could see her skin begin to bubble before he closed the furnace door. An hour and thirty minutes later, he checked the furnace. Parts of the skull and some larger bone fragments had not burned down to ashes. Dennis took a long metal bar and beat down on the bones to mash them into smaller pieces. Thirty minutes later, he removed Gloria Jean Booker's remains from the cremator.

After letting the remains cool for an hour, he poured them into a metal container about the size of a coffee can. He used a flat, metal rod to mash down the bone fragments that remained.

Then he mixed them into the remaining ashes, poured them into a cardboard cremation container, labeled the remains, and placed the container on the shelf. Someone would pick them up in the morning.

***

Dennis Glenn was a soft-spoken man in his late twenties. He had only worked at the Kansas City Cremation Service since he graduated from mortuary school six months earlier. The quiet and solitude at the crematorium suited him well. Being socially awkward, he didn't particularly like people. His voice was soft, and he talked with a bit of a stutter. Conversation did not come naturally to him. He tried to hide his social weakness behind constant smiles and a periodic nod of the head. "People like to talk about themselves," his mother had once told him. "Let them talk, and smile and nod your head when they look you directly in the eye. They will think you are interested in what they have to say."

Her advice had done him well in adulthood, but it had been of little value during his childhood. Kids saw right through that façade. Maybe because they hadn't developed a big enough ego yet to want to monopolize an entire conversation—or maybe they were just smarter.

The first time he tried his mother's advice was in the boy's bathroom at Somerset Middle School. He had been cornered there by three boys that had threatened him in the past. They were bullies, and Dennis was their latest target. They always picked on the weaker, less popular kids. They wanted a fight they could win. Although one could argue that in a fight between three boys on one side and one on the other, the group rarely had to worry about losing.

The larger of the three boys got within a few inches of his

face. "Do you know who I am?" he said in a loud, strong voice.

"No," said Dennis shyly.

"I am the owner of this bathroom."

His two friends began to laugh. They were a little shorter and a little less boney than their leader.

"Did you get permission from me to use my restroom?"

"No," Dennis said, his voice cracking just a bit. That's when he remembered what his mother had told him. *Smile and nod.*

He smiled. They did not.

"What the hell are you smiling at?" the leader said with an angry look on his face. "I'm going to wipe that fucking smile off your face."

Dennis continued to smile. When the bully looked directly into his eyes, Dennis nodded just like his mother had taught him.

The first blow to the face removed his smile, just like the bully had promised. The second and third blows knocked him to the ground. He laid there in pain, his lip bleeding and his nose aching. His stomach was spasming in pain. But he did not show it. He did not cry and did not scream. Dennis did not utter a word. That took his attackers by surprise. Their other victims cried. They screamed. They could hear and see their suffering. That was normal. Dennis Glenn's behavior was not. There was no satisfaction in beating up someone that didn't seem to care. Their victims' sense of fear was what motivated their attacks. Dennis did not show fear. He didn't fight back. He didn't try to run. He just didn't seem to care. There was no thrill in beating up someone who didn't seem to care, who didn't show any outward emotion. The bullies never attacked him again.

The crematorium had become his sanctuary. He worked alone during the graveyard shift. No one bothered him. He could work at his own pace. He was never rushed. His only company was the dead bodies in the refrigeration room. Occasionally, when he felt the need for conversation, he would go inside the refrigeration room, pull down the white sheet of one or more of the corpses, and start talking. "They are great listeners," he told himself. "They don't judge me. They don't care about my stutter. I can tell them anything."

Dennis didn't mind that his conversations in the refrigeration room were one-sided. He liked to finally be able to talk and not be judged for what he said or how he said it. Besides, sometimes the corpses would talk back to him through their eyes. He could read their souls through their eyes. He heard their voices talking to him inside his head. Not all the time, but some of the time.

About once or twice a week, Dennis would receive one visitor to the crematorium. That was Alvin Pinera. He worked at the Pinera Family Funeral Home directly across the street from the crematorium. The Pinera family also owned the crematorium. Alvin was one of three sons of Lou Pinera, who was one of two brothers that ran the family business. Andrew Pinera was the other brother.

Alvin was a young man in his early twenties, two years out of mortuary school. As a new addition to the family business, he drew the least desirable job, doing body pick-ups during the hours of 11 p.m. and 7 a.m. Until recently, there would only be an average of one or two pick-ups a night. But, a few months earlier, the Pinera family had signed a contract with the City of Kansas City to do the body preparation and burial for unclaimed bodies. There was a large homeless population in the city. When they died, most of those bodies went unclaimed. There were also a surprising number of other people that went unclaimed by relatives, or their relatives weren't known. The city became responsible for their burial if no one claimed the body. So, the city bid the disposition of those bodies out to local funeral homes. The Pinera family was the lowest bidder.

The new business resulted in an uptick in the number of body pick-ups that Alvin needed to do at night. His only responsibility was to pick up the body, deliver it back to the funeral home, put it on a gurney in the refrigeration room next to the embalming room, tag the body, and leave the paperwork on the desk of the embalmer.

Every so often, there would be a special order. Those were the bodies that were taken to the crematorium in the middle of the night. They rarely had paperwork, just a special tag marked special order. Sometimes they would involve a pick-up, and sometimes the body would already be in the refrigeration room when Alvin came to work. When he saw the red label on the body marked special order, he knew the body needed to be taken to the crematory that night.

Alvin never alerted Dennis when he had a special order. He just showed up at the crematorium. He had a key to the front door and would enter as quietly as possible. He got a kick out of sneaking up on Dennis and trying to scare him. He succeeded in doing so several times until Dennis hung a bell on the inside of the door to alert him if anyone entered. He never did like Alvin much, and Alvin didn't like him. They had to tolerate each other because they were family, but they were not friends.

Dennis had married into the Pinera family. He wasn't Italian, and he wasn't a man's man like most of the Pinera men. The family considered him weak. His personality was nearly the exact opposite of the other Pinera men. They liked to party. They like to drink. They were loud. They were boisterous. They cheated on their wives. Dennis did none of those things. He was outside the inner circle of the Pinera family. They didn't trust him, and they didn't let him in on any of the family business.

After he married Elise Pinera, Andrew's only daughter, the family helped put him through mortuary school. Once he obtained his funeral director's license, they gave him a job in the crematorium. He had been there ever since. He had no aspiration for doing anything else. The solitude of the crematorium suited him just fine.

Dennis conformed well to the rules of the Pinera family. He never discussed what went on in the crematorium. He did exactly as he was told. Special orders were handled exactly the way he had been instructed. When one arrived in his refrigeration room, they would be the first body cremated. The cremation furnace temperature would be set at the ideal temperature for disintegrating a body into ashes, usually between 1400 and 1650-degrees Fahrenheit, depending on the bone density of the corpse. The skull and bone fragments that would not totally burn down to ashes were broken down with a steel mallet and mixed into the ashes. There could be no remnants of the body remaining. Nothing could be left to identify the corpse.

Dennis never questioned his instructions—he wasn't one to cause waves. Still, he couldn't help but wonder about the increase in his workload recently. Ever since the cremation of Gloria Jean Booker, there had been a steady amount of special order cremations. The refrigeration room was nearly always full. He found himself working six and sometimes seven nights a week.

He didn't mind the extra work. The Pinera family paid him well. With overtime, he made a very good living. Elise was frugal—her family was not. The many parties and social events that required attendance by all Pinera family members required nice attire. The extra pay helped. Besides, the workload made his nights go by a little faster. Every night he followed the same routine, finishing his work first if there was any work. In his early days of the crematorium, they rarely had more than four or five cremations a week. That was before the city contract, before the uptick in business, before the special orders began arriving.

During his early days at the crematorium, when business was slow, he would read, normally a McNally mystery by Lawrence Sanders or something by Agatha Christie or Truman Capote. At exactly 3 a.m., he would open his lunch pale and eat. He had the same lunch every night; a bologna sandwich with American cheese, a tomato, and Miracle Whip on soft white bread, a bag of potato chips — plain, no ridges — and an apple. He would wash his meal down with a thermos of black coffee. After lunch, he would close his eyes and rest for an hour or so. Lately, he had not had time to read or to rest his eyes. Three bodies were about all he could cremate in one night, and most nights, the refrigeration room had three bodies waiting for him when he arrived for work.

While he worked, Dennis's mind often wandered to Gloria Jean Booker. She was Lou Pinera's ex-wife — Dennis had seen her several times at family events and celebrations. She was friendly — a bit quiet, but always smiling. Lou's wife was gorgeous, with long, flowing blonde hair, blue eyes, and thick lips. Gloria Jean always dressed as if she was going to a dinner party — dress, high heels, and a strand of pearls around her neck. She looked a bit like a Stepford wife.

She loved her husband. Dennis could see that. *But the love seems one-sided*, he thought. Her husband belittled her a lot. He was verbally abusive to her in front of people. She never argued back. There were times her make-up seemed a little more heavy than normal. Dennis suspected that Lou Pinera was physically abusive to his wife, also.

When they divorced, the news came as a big surprise to the family. It was the first divorce ever within the Pinera family. That just didn't happen. No matter how bad the marriage was, a Pinera wife would always turn the other cheek. They would cover up their marital problems and never consider divorce.

So, when the divorce was announced, the family turned their backs on Gloria Jean. She became an outcast. No one in the family would talk to her except for Dennis. He considered her a friend. She would call and talk to him from time to time. Dennis felt like a bit of an outcast in the Pinera family too. He felt empathy for Gloria Jean. Life on the outside of the Pinera family was difficult for her. Family members she had known and loved for so many years turned their backs on her. It was as if she had never existed to many of them. She had to fight for her divorce settlement, and when she finally got it, the one condition that was required of her was that she change her last name back to her maiden name, Booker. The family was adamant that they didn't want her to retain their last name.

Dennis had heard the rumors. Lou Pinera had a lot of women. He couldn't be faithful. It wasn't in his DNA. Dennis had been at a family picnic once when an attractive young brown-haired, ivory-skinned woman in her late teens or early twenties showed up looking for Lou. She was wearing a short, cream-colored dress with a low-cut neckline that accentuated her breasts. She was not wearing a bra, and her nipples were bouncing freely against the soft, silk dress. With make-up applied too thick for anything but seduction, she asked for Lou. Everyone at the party saw her. Everyone knew what she was there for. Lou took her into the house, walked her up the stairs, and gave her what she wanted. The lovemaking was loud. The window in the master bedroom was open. The sounds of their excitement echoed through the backyard. No one said anything, not even Gloria Jean. The party went on, and about thirty minutes later, Lou joined the party again. His friend had left. Dennis often wondered why Gloria Jean didn't throw a fit, yell, and scream at her husband that day. He asked her one time after her divorce. She smiled and told him, "I knew it wouldn't make a difference. It would have just brought me down to his level."

No one suspected that fifteen months later, Gloria Jean's remains would be chiseled off the inner walls of the cremation furnace at her husband's crematorium.

Chapter 2
Young Love

Elise Pinera was a beautiful girl even back in seventh grade. She had long, flowing, straight black hair that flowed down to her waist, an olive complexion that looked like a perfect suntan, and big, brown eyes and long, dark eyelashes. She always wore a dress. Her legs were long, brown, and slender. From the moment Dennis saw her walk into English class, he couldn't stop thinking about her. He watched as she took a seat in the front of the class.

Elise Pinera was out of Dennis's league. He had grown up in a blue-collar family that lived on the wrong side of Prairie Village. Elise lived on the north side of Prairie Village. The two parts of town were as different as night and day.

Most of the homes on the south side of town were built immediately after World War II, financed by the VA to give returning veterans a slice of the American dream. They were wood-frame homes, for the most part, with three bedrooms, one bath, and a carport or a one-car garage. Simple and inexpensive, they were the perfect homes for blue-collar workers beginning a family.

The north side of Prairie Village was much different. That was where the well-heeled families lived. They had large houses with wraparound porches, nice cars, and three-car garages. Prairie Village offered a dramatic contrast in social-economic classes. The differences in wealth became apparent when one crossed over 75th Street south to north. On the south side of 75th Street lived the families that struggled from paycheck to paycheck. Their cars were older, their lawns were small. Their children wore secondhand clothes and only dreamed of attending college. North of 75th Street was a different world. Families drove nice, new cars. Their children were dressed in designer clothes, went to private schools, and then on to college. Families didn't struggle to pay for their basic needs.

Elise lived on the north side of town, but she never flaunted her wealth. She never acted like she was better than anyone else. In fact, she reminded Dennis of himself. She was quiet, shy and rarely talked to others. Elise kept to herself. When talked to, she smiled and nodded to set people at ease. She was a person of few words, just like Dennis.

She was easily the smartest person in class, but she didn't act like it. She never raised her hand to answer questions and never talked about her grades. But when test scores and final grades were passed out, she was always at the top of the class.

Dennis and Elise became friends out of a common bond. They were loners. At lunch, they sat alone. Dennis approached Elise first and sat with her at lunch. They got to know each other. Together, they didn't feel awkward. Together they were normal. Dennis began walking Elise home after school. They could have taken the school bus but chose not to. He walked her the sixteen blocks to 75th Street, watched her cross the road, then he turned and walked the five blocks back to his house. Dennis never crossed 75th Street. He didn't feel comfortable on the north side of town.

Their friendship blossomed in high school. Sometime during the spring of their senior year, the friendship evolved into more. On a stormy prom night in 1984, they made love for the first time in the backseat of Dennis's '72 Volkswagen Beetle. Neither had made love before. It was awkward. It was impulsive. It would change both their lives forever.

Elise was accepted to Columbia University for the Fall of '84. This would be their last summer together. They planned to spend every day together, seventy-two days until it was time for her to leave for college. Her parents had other plans. They had never met Dennis. They were concerned about the amount of time he was spending with their daughter and that their relationship was getting too serious. She needed to focus on completing her education and finding a smart, well-educated Italian boy from a well-heeled family. Columbia would be full of those types of boys. She needed to focus her attention on the future.

Thirty-four days until she would leave for Columbia, Andrew Pinera requested that his daughter invite her friend to a family gathering over the fourth of July weekend. Elise was anxious to introduce Dennis to her family. She had fallen in love with Dennis, although she had not told him yet. She was shy and was waiting for him to profess his love first.

***

Dennis was shy and was waiting for her to give him a sign that she felt the same way he did. When he arrived at the Pinera house, he entered a long circular driveway. Near the entrance to the house, a valet opened his door, took his keys, and parked the car. Dennis was wearing a blue sport shirt, jean shorts, and tennis shoes. *Even the valet is dressed better than I am*, he thought. The men gathered at the front door wore slacks, button-down shirts, ties, and sports jackets. He wished he could go back home and change, but it was too late. Even if he had the time to re-dress, he didn't own any clothes as nice as what the other men were wearing.

The Pinera home was huge, two stories, with a red brick exterior with a large wood porch and white pillars that rose from the porch to an overhang expanding from the roof. Inside there was an entryway that led into a parlor more spacious than Dennis's home. At the rear of the parlor was a grand staircase that flowed in a circular motion up to the second floor. Servants guided the guests to the backyard. Outside was a large stone patio, and behind it was a manicured lawn. Two large tents were set up for guests to relax, eat, and avoid the hot summer sun.

Dennis expected a small family gathering. There must have been forty people in that backyard. He felt about as comfortable as a fly caught in a spider web. Luckily, Elise spotted him as he entered the backyard. She ran over to him.

"Hi, Dennis. I'm glad you came. My family is anxious to meet you."

"I wish I could say the same, but right now, I'm nervous as hell. Are all these people your family?"

Elise smiled. "No. We have a big family, but Father always invites some of his business associates too. Only about half of the people here are in our family."

"What does your father do for a living?"

Elise smiled again. "I'll tell you, but you have to promise that you won't freak out and leave."

"What?"

"Promise me."

"I promise."

"My family owns a funeral home."

"Okay. That's not so bad. I thought you were going to tell me something awful about them."

"No. It's just that some people are turned off by what they do. I don't tell many people about the family business."

"Well, your family must be very successful. This is the nicest house I have ever seen."

"I hope you don't think any differently of me now," Elise said, still smiling. "I'm still the same girl you've known for the last five years."

"Nothing could make me think any differently of you, Elise. You are beautiful inside and out."

"Why, thank you, Mr. Glenn. You're not so bad yourself."

With that, Elise took Dennis's hand and walked him around the backyard, introducing him to various family members. With each introduction, they smiled, shook hands, and exchanged brief pleasantries. Then, Elise took his hand and moved on to the next family member. Elise was shy too, and she empathized with Dennis. She felt uncomfortable in social situations. Elise moved quickly from one family member to another, not allowing for a moment of awkward silence. Dennis knew she was a special person—caring, gentle, loving, and the only girl Dennis had ever dated. She was the only person he was completely relaxed around and was the woman he wanted to marry someday.

It was on a wood bench between two large oak trees at the rear of the Pinera property that Dennis first told Elise that he loved her. He spoke softly and timidly when he told her, but he looked directly into her eyes when he uttered the words, "I love you." Elise had no doubt that he meant those words, but she wasn't ready to profess her love to him. Those words carried so much weight. They meant so much. Those words weren't meant to be used flippantly. She smiled back at Dennis, moved her lips to his, and gently kissed him. But she did not reciprocate what he had said to her.

Later that evening, after most of the guests had left, they sat down with Elise's parents, Andrew and Elizabeth Pinera. The meeting was cordial. On the surface, Dennis thought the conversation went well. Mrs. Pinera greeted Dennis with a smile and hug. Mr. Pinera smiled and shook his hand. The conversation was light, and the mood was welcoming. But that was how Andrew and Elizabeth Pinera were. They had grown up in a family of funeral directors. They were used to hiding their emotions. They knew how to put people at ease. Everything on the surface was a façade. Inside, they were determined not to allow their daughter's infatuation with Dennis to interfere with the plans they had set for their daughter. Elise was their only daughter. She was not going to get involved with someone in a lower social class than them.

Andrew Pinera was convinced that the relationship was no more than a June to August romance. "When Elise leaves for Columbia in August, that will be the end of their relationship." That's what her father thought anyway.

Elizabeth Pinera thought otherwise. She had looked into her daughter's eyes. She had seen that look before. It was the same look she had when she first fell in love with her husband many years earlier. It wasn't a June to August romance. They were in love.

Dennis and Elise spent every day together that summer. Dennis was not going to college—his parents couldn't afford to send him. Besides, he was tired of school. He would look for a job, maybe go to work at Bendix, where his father had worked for the last twenty-three years. But not this summer. He was determined to spend every day with Elise. This would be his summer of relaxation, his summer of love. He had saved enough money from mowing yards and shoveling snow to put gas in his car and have spending money to get him through the summer. He would look for a job after Elise left for college. Besides, both he and Elise enjoyed the simple pleasures of life. That was one thing he loved about her. She grew up on the wealthy side of town, but she didn't have expensive tastes. She was happiest holding hands, exploring the park or the zoo, and watching an old movie on the couch at night. They talked. They laughed. They tried to forget how fast the summer was going.

The final two weeks before Elise was scheduled to leave for Columbia, Dennis sensed a change in her. She talked less and smiled less. She seemed more distant. He asked her about it, but she didn't want to talk. She didn't want to think about the end of summer, although those thoughts were constantly on their minds.

Three days before she was scheduled to leave, they sat on the front porch of Elise's house. The silence was deafening. They held hands but said nothing. Her mind had drifted someplace else. When he tried to pull her closer to him, she pulled away.

"What is the matter?" he asked her.

"Nothing," she said. "I just have a lot on my mind."

Dennis tried to be understanding. He thought Elise was sad about leaving. He thought she might be confused about their future. They had not talked about plans after she left for Columbia. Neither wanted to think about the end of summer. But now, it was just a few days away. It was time to face what they had been dreading all summer.

"I love you, Elise Pinera."

That caught her by surprise. He had only said that once before, and then it sounded a bit timid. This time he said it with confidence, and he said it looking directly into her eyes.

"I love you too, Dennis Glenn."

That brought a smile to his face. She had not told him that before. He'd felt that she loved him, but it was reassuring to hear her finally tell him.

"Elise, I want you to know something. There is no one in this world I would rather be with than you. I would never stand in the way of your dreams. You need to go to Columbia. But, know that I will be waiting for you. I want us to build a life together someday. I am willing to wait until you are ready too."

Elise said nothing, but her face said everything. Her tender smile and the dampness in her eyes told him how much she cared for him.

She took his hand and stood up. They walked to the wood bench between the two large oak trees in the backyard. That was the first place that he had told her he loved her. She sat on the bench, and Dennis sat down beside her. She turned her back to him.

"Please unzip the back of my dress."

His right hand shook nervously as he did what she asked. Slowly, carefully he pulled the zipper down, exposing the back of her silky, white bra. She took his hand, moved it to her shoulder, placed it underneath her dress, and lifted it. One side of her dress fell to her side. Then, she took his other hand and moved it underneath her dress on her left shoulder. She lifted his hand until the other side of her dress slipped down to her side. With the dress laying at her waist, she stood up, turned around, and kissed Dennis. Her lips were soft. The kiss was tender. When she moved her lips away from his, she stepped back and looked into his eyes. They didn't say a word. Everything she needed to know was written in his eyes.

She bent down and removed her dress. She stood there looking at Dennis with the most wonderful smile.

"I love you, Elise."

"I know."

They made love on the ground in front of that wood bench. This time it was so much different than before. This time it wasn't lust. It wasn't a physical attraction that brought their two bodies together. It was an emotional bond that connected them that night. It was a thousand times stronger than any physical attraction could be. It was love.

The night before Elise was set to leave for Columbia, neither could sleep. They stayed up all night and talked on the porch behind the large pillars at the front of the Pinera house. They held hands. They kissed. They talked about everything and nothing. But, they didn't talk about tomorrow.

Dennis helped load her bags into her father's Cadillac. He cried. She cried. He promised to write her every day. She promised the same. Then he watched the car slowly pull away.

Dennis had never felt so lonely before. He had never been this sad. He told himself, "It is best for her." He said, "She will be back at Christmas." Their love was strong, and they would have a great life together soon.

But in the back of his mind, he couldn't help but think she was moving forward with her life, and he wasn't. They were going in different directions. Elise was in a different class than him. She was too good for him, and she would find that out. She would meet someone better suited for her, someone, that could provide her a nice home and financial security. The more he tried to think positive thoughts, the more the negative thoughts surfaced.

Three days after Elise left, Dennis took an assembly line job at Bendix. It was an entry-level position, but it paid fairly well. He hated the monotony of his work.

"Anyone could do what I do," he told his mother. "But they pay me well, so I'm not going to complain."

Besides, the work kept his mind off Elise, at least a little. He showed up on time, didn't use his sick days, and put in an honest day's work. The job was easy, and it helped life go by a little faster.

He wrote to Elise nearly every day. For nearly two months, she wrote him back with the same frequency. But by November, her letters came less often. By December, they stopped altogether.

He tried calling her dormitory. She would not take his calls. He went to her parents' house. He begged her mother to send word for Elise to call him. Nothing worked. So, he waited. Christmas would be here soon. She would be home for Christmas.

Dennis just needed to talk to her. He needed to know what was going on. He needed to know if she had moved on with her life. A week before Christmas, when he knew she had to be home for Christmas vacation, he began calling the Pinera home. The phone rang and rang. There was no answer. He drove by the house. Lights were on, and he could hear voices in the house, but no one answered the door.

Christmas was miserable that year. His heart was broken. He had never been so depressed. He kept telling himself that she must have a good reason for not talking to him. But, in the back of his mind, he thought otherwise. He tried to move forward with his life, but with every step he took, his past was right there beside him.

It was New Year's Eve night when the phone rang. He was

watching an old Alfred Hitchcock movie, *North by Northwest*, and trying to relax enough to fall asleep.

"Hello."

He heard the sound of a woman crying on the other end of the phone.

"Elise, is that you?"

The crying became louder.

"Elise, is that you?"

Through her tears, he could hear her softly say, "Yes."

"What's wrong, Elise? Why are you crying?"

"Dennis, I need help. I need to see you."

Her voice was soft. It was cracking. It was difficult to hear through her sobbing.

"Where are you?"

"I'm in the hospital. Menorah Hospital on Grand. Room 842."

"You're in Kansas City?"

"Yes. Please come tomorrow morning."

"I'm coming right now."

"No. They won't let you see me. You need to come during visiting hours."

"I'll be there in the morning. Okay?"

"Yes"

"Elise, can you tell me what is going on?"

"No, not on the phone. We can talk tomorrow. Come at 9 a.m., and don't tell my parents we talked."

"Okay. I'll be there at 9. Elise?"

"Yes."

"I love you."

"I love you, too." Then, she hung up the phone.

Dennis wiped a tear from his eye. He had been hoping to

hear those three words from Elise for a long time. He had almost given up. But now, she was in trouble. There was no way he was going to be able to sleep that night.

He was in the hospital waiting room at eight. Sixty minutes later, he walked into room 842. Elise was curled up in bed, covered in blankets. She had IV tubes running into the vein on her left arm.

"Elise, are you awake?"

She rolled over, opened her eyes, and smiled. "Yes, thanks for coming. I missed you."

Dennis moved to the side of her bed, lowered his head, and gently kissed her on the cheek. Her eyes looked swollen. She had been crying.

"Elise, what happened?"

She began crying. Her voice cracked as she talked. "I was pregnant. I lost the baby, our baby."

Dennis began to cry. He reached down and put his arm around her. Then he lowered his lips to hers and gave her a soft, gentle kiss. "Why didn't you tell me?"

"I couldn't. My father wouldn't let me contact you."

"You could have answered my letters. You could have got word to me somehow."

"I'm sorry. When I found out I was pregnant, I wanted to call you. I wanted you to know. But the doctor contacted my father. He thought my father should know. My parents got on a plane the next morning. They were at my dormitory later that day. They packed up my clothes and brought me home." Tears began rolling down Elise's face. "Dennis, they made me get an abortion."

Elise paused, waiting for a response from Dennis. She expected a look of anger, maybe a look of disgust. Instead, he put his arms around her shoulders and hugged her. They both cried, holding each other tightly.

"Why are you in the hospital, Elise?"

"I had complications from the abortion." Her sobbing intensified. Her body began to shake. "Dennis, I can't have children anymore."

CHAPTER 3
BUILDING A LIFE TOGETHER

Three days after Elise was released from the hospital, she sneaked out of the Pinera house to meet Dennis. They were married later that day at the courthouse in downtown Kansas City by a justice of the peace.

"Are you sure that you want to marry me, Dennis? I can never bear children."

"I don't care, Elise. I love you. We can always adopt, someday."

Dennis's father, Ron, and his mother, Susan, were the only witnesses. It wasn't the huge, Catholic wedding that Elise had always dreamed of, but she didn't mind. She was marrying the man she loved. Her parents had done everything they could to keep them apart. All their efforts just strengthened their love for each other. Elise defied her parent's wishes. The couple had the support and blessing of Ron and Susan Glenn. They would spend their honeymoon in the basement of the Glenn home.

Years earlier, Ron Glenn had built a family room, a small

bedroom, and a bath in the basement of their house. He intended to use it for guests. The small frame house only had two bedrooms on the main floor. The basement apartment wasn't much, but that didn't matter to Dennis or Elise. They were together. That was all that mattered. Dennis's mother welcomed Elise like she was her own daughter. The arrangement would be only temporary. Dennis and Elise would look for an apartment soon, but for now, it worked just fine.

The night of their wedding, Elise phoned her mother. She knew her parents would be worried. She didn't want them to call the police. She told her mother that she had married Dennis. He could hear Elizabeth Pinera screaming at her daughter over the phone. Then he could hear the crying. He saw the tears roll down his wife's face. She had disappointed her parents. Her father would tell her that.

Andrew Pinera demanded that the marriage be annulled. Elise refused. For months, Elise had no contact with her parents. It was her mother that made an attempt to reconcile. She came to see Elise and Dennis, saying she loved her daughter and would support whatever she wanted in life. Eventually, her father's position toward the marriage softened, too. Elise's parents did not want to lose their daughter completely, so when they realized she wasn't going to leave the marriage, they reluctantly chose to accept Dennis as their son-in-law.

They offered him a position in their funeral home. He would need to go to mortuary school and become a funeral director. It wasn't the type of career Dennis had considered before, but his wife wanted it for him, and it was a good opportunity, so he decided to do it. The Pinera family paid for his education. It took him two years to graduate. During that time, Elise worked as a receptionist at the Pinera Funeral Home, and Dennis worked several part-time jobs to make ends meet.

When he graduated, Anthony Pinera put him to work on the graveyard shift in the new crematorium he had built across the street from the funeral home. It was the worst job with the worst hours. In Anthony Pinera's mind, it was the worst possible job he could give his new son-in-law. He expected him to fail. He expected him to quit. That would have reinforced his opinion that Dennis was not worthy of being a member of the Pinera family.

But Dennis neither quit nor complained. The job suited him well. Working the graveyard shift took a little while to adjust to, but he learned to embrace the quiet and the solitude once he did. The most difficult part of working those hours was sleeping during the day. The phone rang. The sun poured through the window curtains. But after a while, he got used to it. Still, it wasn't much fun sleeping alone. Elise worked the hours he was sleeping. They would eat breakfast together, and then Dennis went to bed, and Elise went to work. They saw each other again at dinner. For the first year of their marriage, they continued to live in the basement of Dennis's parents' house. Susan Glenn treated Elise like the daughter she never had. They became good friends.

Every night, her mother-in-law made dinner. Helping Susan in the kitchen was something Elise had always wanted to do with her mother when she was growing up. The Pinera family had a cook on staff seven days a week. Elise had never even seen her mother cook. In fact, Elizabeth Pinera had never learned to cook. Nor had she learned to clean the house or do laundry. She had staff to do those chores. Her mother was not a mother in traditional terms. She was cold and distant. Elise and her mother never had deep conversations and rarely talked about anything of substance.

What Elise learned about cooking and taking care of the

house, she learned from staff members. Elise was inquisitive. In her teenage years, she befriended Janie, the cook. Janie was an overweight woman on the downside of forty. She started working for the Pinera family when Elise was ten years old. Her husband had left her and her three children two years earlier. He was a drunk and a philanderer. One night, he left the house to go to a bar and never came home. Janie found out later that he had emptied the family checking account just before he disappeared. Janie had no money and no job. She and her kids were evicted from the house and spent the next couple of months on the streets going from one homeless shelter to another.

But Janie was determined to make a life for her and her kids. She took any and every job she could find. She started cooking at one of the homeless shelters. It was there that she befriended Carol Morgan. Carol was the well-heeled wife of a doctor who volunteered at the homeless shelter three days a week. It just so happened that she needed a new cook on her household staff. She offered the position to Janie. The money was good, and Janie was soon able to get an apartment for her and her three children. She worked for Carol Morgan for nearly a year. That's when Elizabeth Pinera was introduced to her at a dinner party hosted by Carol Morgan. Elizabeth was impressed by Janie's cooking skills and offered her a new job as her cook.

Janie turned her down at first. She was happy working for the Morgans and grateful for the opportunity they had given her. But Elizabeth Pinera was not used to being turned down for anything. She was a woman that always got her way. A day later she phoned Carol Morgan and asked her to lunch. They met at a small café in downtown Prairie Village.

"I just had to meet with you, Carol," she said. "I've got some troubling news, and I just knew my conscience would be bothered until I told you."

"What is it, Elizabeth?"

"It's about your cook. Janie. Oh, I hate to tell you this. I really do. But I know if she worked for me, I would want someone to tell me."

"What is it, Elizabeth?"

"I saw her steal from you. I saw her take some silver and a bottle of whisky when I was at your dinner party last night. Carol, I am sick about this. I know how much you like her. I know how much she means to you. But after everything you have done for her, I think you deserve to know what she is doing behind your back."

Two hours later, Carol Morgan fired Janie. Two days later, Elizabeth Pinera hired her for less money than Carol Morgan was paying her.

Janie taught Elise how to cook. She was a fast learner—a natural, so to speak. Elise demonstrated her skills many times at the Glenn household. Between Susan Glenn's cooking skills and Elise's talent in the kitchen, dinner was the highlight of the day at the Glenn home. It was the only time that all four of the family members were together. Ron Glenn worked two jobs to make ends meet. He worked at Bendix during the day and at a local bar in the evenings. He was an old-fashioned man who believed his wife shouldn't work outside the home.

Susan Glenn and her daughter-in-law shared cooking duties. They worked well together and seemed to complement each other in the kitchen. Susan's biggest strength was cooking. She taste-tested everything and did not follow recipes. She added her unique flavors to everything she cooked and rarely cooked things she didn't like. Elise was the exact opposite. She followed recipes, carefully measuring everything. She rarely tasted her cooking before it was done, and she loved experimenting with new foods, even if they were foods she didn't care for. Every dinner was a wonderful adventure. Susan Glenn did much of the cooking and was in charge of the dinner. Elise did the baking and made a unique dessert almost every night. The two women drank wine and shared stories while they cooked. They laughed. They cried. They became good friends during those evenings in the kitchen.

Ron Glenn was much different than his wife. He was quiet. He smiled. He laughed. He enjoyed the company of his family but rarely monopolized a conversation. Dennis was much like his father. At dinner, the two women did most of the talking. The men listened, nodded, and smiled. They spoke when spoken to but rarely started the conversation. Still, the love in the Glenn household was evident. Ron Glenn was an old-fashioned man. He opened the door for his wife. He pulled out the chair for her at the dinner table. He told her he loved her every morning before leaving for work and every night when they went to bed. He never raised his voice to her and always told her how grateful he was to have her in his life. They had married when Ron was twenty and Susan was eighteen. They had met in high school and never dated anyone else.

Another thing that was different from Elise's family was that there were never any arguments in the Glenn household. Voices were never raised. Arguments never occurred. That's not to say that there weren't disagreements, because there were. But they never grew into arguments.

Elizabeth and Andrew Pinera often argued. Elise's father had a temper and a short fuse. Several of her parents' arguments turned into physical altercations. Yelling was normal. Fights were common. Love was one of the few four-letter words rarely used in the Pinera home. The family rarely came together for meals — her parents ate meals on their own, based on their schedules. Elise often sat at the dinner table by herself. People on the outside saw a totally different couple. The arguing, fighting, and coldness stayed on the inside of the Pinera house. Hers was a dysfunctional family.

Outside, her parents put on a different façade. In public, they acted like the perfect, loving couple. That was what was expected of them. They had to appear loving and caring for the sake of the business. Families they served in the funeral business expected that of them. So, they pretended that they loved each other when they were outside of the home. Elizabeth Pinera was the perfect funeral director's wife. She was attractive, well-mannered, and as fake as a clown's red nose. She wore her fake smile from the time she left the house until she returned, a forced smile. But the funeral home customers saw an authentic smile. To them, it was a soft, loving smile, a smile that showed she cared, that she understood their grief. They saw the empathy in her smile. She was a wonderful actor.

Elise was happy in the Glenn home. She could have stayed there for a long time. It was Dennis that insisted on moving. He wanted to begin his life with Elise and a home of their own. Not long after Dennis started working at the crematorium, he and Elise bought a small, two-bedroom, one bath, ranch-style home just three blocks away on the south side of Prairie Village. The house was small and old, built in the 1950s, but it had the two things both Elise and Dennis wanted — a large front porch and a fenced-in backyard. It was not the home that Elizabeth Pinera wanted for her daughter. It was on the wrong side of town, and it was small and old and depressing. It was not a house suitable for partying or suitable for the daughter of Andrew and Elizabeth

Pinera. Elise's father offered to pay the down payment for a more suitable home. He even offered to furnish the house. But Dennis and Elise turned him down. They did not want help. They wanted to do everything on their own. Besides, the Pinera money would come with strings. They didn't want to be obligated.

There was one other thing too. Elise didn't want the same things her parents did. They were happy on their side of Prairie Village. She was completely happy with the simpler side of life.

Elise shopped garage sales for most of her household furnishings. She could have afforded to shop at stores. She could have purchased new items for her home. The Pinera family paid her and Dennis very well. They could have spent more. They could have afforded a nicer house. But they were happy with what they had. Besides, Elise liked the idea of surrounding herself with furniture and household furnishing that had been loved by someone else. At garage sales, she talked to the owners. She listened to their stories. If she felt the owners were a loving family, she would buy items from their garage sale. She liked to think everything she purchased came from a loving home.

Once their house was furnished, the couple began visiting the local dog shelter. There would be no children in the Glenn household, but there would be two dogs, Hillary and Teddy. Both were only hours away from being euthanized. Instead, they found themselves in a loving home with two parents that treated them like the children they would never have. Hillary was a lab, old English sheepdog mix. Teddy was a cockapoo. Hillary grew to over eighty pounds. Teddy was tiny and low to the ground. Hillary ate like a horse, Teddy like a bird. But they got along great together. At night they both climbed up in bed with Elise. They kept her company while Dennis was at work. Hillary positioned herself at the foot of the bed, normally stretching out and taking up the full length of the king-size bed. Sometimes she ran in her sleep, causing the bed to rock with her leg movements. Teddy slept on the pillow next to Elise, sleeping in the same space Dennis would lay his head a few hours later. They slept there every night. In the morning, as soon as the sun crept over the horizon, Hillary crawled up the bed and licked Elise in the face. She was Elise's alarm clock. She rose, let the dogs outside, and made them breakfast, two slices of bacon and a bowl of dry dog food. Then she made a pot of coffee, took a shower, got dressed, and prepared breakfast for her husband. He would arrive home at seven-thirty. Elise would leave for work ten minutes later.

Elise's job at the funeral home placed her outside the offices where her mother and father worked. Although they were together all day, they rarely talked about anything outside of business. The funeral home was her parents' life. It wasn't Elise's. Her family was more important than her job. She was moving away from her parents. Their life was not her life. She worked at the family business because it was expected of her — it was expected of every Pinera family member. But she was a clock watcher. Her heart was not invested in the family business. She watched the clock for 5 p.m. to arrive, and when it did, she grabbed her purse and left.

Dennis felt differently about the crematorium. It was a job to him, but it was a job he enjoyed. Working alone suited him. Dennis welcomed the quiet solitude that came with working when everyone else was asleep. The dead bodies became his work friends. It was the one part of his life that he felt complete control over. Dennis loved his wife and his parents, but they always seemed to make decisions for him. Dennis was never in complete control at home. That was different in the crematorium. There he did as he wanted, and as long as he got his work done, nobody complained. Dennis was never uncomfortable around the dead that occupied the refrigeration room like he thought he would be when he first started mortuary school.

Before starting his job at the crematorium, he had only seen two dead bodies — his grandparents, killed in an automobile accident when he was ten. He remembered seeing their bodies laid out in their caskets at the funeral home. His mother held his hand and walked him up to the caskets. Dennis hesitated at first, but with his mother's encouragement, he walked up to the caskets side-by-side with his mother. She cried. He did not. His grandparents looked so life-like lying in their caskets. They seemed at peace, accepting of their fate. They looked so peaceful lying on the soft, white pillows on the bed in their casket. He reached down to touch his grandmother's face. Her skin was cold, rigid, and felt a little bit like a plastic doll. That's when it became apparent to him that his grandparents were dead. Still, it did not upset him. He believed they were together and believed that wherever they were, they were happy.

Dennis felt the same way about the bodies in the refrigeration room. He believed they were in a better place. But unlike his grandparents, the funeral director had not done his magic on these bodies. They were to be cremated. There would not be families visiting them, wanting to see their bodies preserved as they remembered them. No one cared what they looked like. Their bodies would be reduced to three to nine pounds of ashes before the night ended. The corpses in Dennis's refrigeration room lay on the metal tables in the same condition they died. Some were wrapped in plastic body bags. Some were not.

Plastic body bags were used for particularly gruesome deaths. Drowning victims, referred to as "floaters" by many funeral directors, were the only people that really bothered

Dennis, and they always came in body bags. He could normally smell them as soon as he opened the door to the refrigeration room. No one ever warned him when there was a "floater" in the room. His nose was his only warning. He hated the smell. It was something that lingered with him all night long. The stench clung to his clothes, and he wore the smell home with him. He would normally need to take two or three showers to get rid of the smell. The crematorium didn't get many "floaters," usually only three or four a year, but they were memorable, and they always were in body bags.

Floaters always made Dennis sick. There was no way to prepare for the smell when the body bag was opened. And if the smell didn't cause him to give back last night's dinner, the sight of a body that had spent long periods under the water was not something his stomach could tolerate. They were bloated, discolored. They had open wounds, and many times they had been a meal for many of the smaller creatures of the lake or river.

Body bags could not be burned in the cremation furnace — they emitted toxins under the extreme heat of the furnace. They also caused quite a mess inside. Unlike human flesh, they did not easily burn. The furnace was for humans, not for anything else. The body bags would be disposed of in the trash compactor behind the crematorium. The smell, particularly when the body of a "floater" had been inside the bag, was horrendous. Dennis would need to bury the bag in lime before throwing it in the trash compactor. Even then, the smell would travel, sometimes getting in the air of the neighborhood behind the crematorium. Sometimes the neighbors would complain. If they did, Dennis would be instructed to hold the used body bags in the back room of the crematorium until a rainy day. The rain had a way of disseminating the odor, so it was not noticeable by the neighbors.

Being located in a residential part of the city presented barriers to the operation of the crematorium for the Pinera family. In order to obtain the city council's approval to construct the crematorium, they had to agree to only operate the crematorium furnace between the hours of 11p.m. and 7 a.m. Those were the hours that most of their neighbors slept, and therefore, would not be exposed to the thick, dark smoke that poured from the top of the cremation furnace. They would also not be exposed to the various odors caused by burning flesh.

Dennis had gotten used to the smells, but he was cognizant that he carried those odors with him when he left work. The odors of decaying corpses and burning flesh soaked into his clothes. He rarely made a stop after work, afraid that people would be offended by the smell baked into his clothes. He almost always went directly home, took a shower, changed clothes, and threw the ones he had been wearing into the washing machine.

CHAPTER 4
A DYSFUNCTIONAL FAMILY

The Pinera Funeral Home was a family business that had been in the Pinera family for nearly a century. Every member of its staff was part of the family. Elizabeth and Andrew Pinera were the faces that most families saw at their time of grief. They ran the day-to-day operations of the funeral home. Lou Pinera paid the bills, negotiated contracts with vendors, and handled the accounting. He was not much of a people person, nor was he a hard worker. He kept his own hours and often worked out of his house. He had an office on the second floor of the funeral home but was rarely there. His two sons, Alvin and Tony, and his daughter Valerie also worked at the funeral home. Tony was the embalmer. Valerie was a funeral director and also did make-up and hair for the deceased. Alvin was the youngest of the children and worked the graveyard shift doing body pick-up and setting up for the next day's visitations and funeral services. Tony's wife, in addition to Rose and Valerie's husband, Richard, also worked as funeral directors at the Pinera Funeral Home. Elise and Dennis were the other family members on the staff.

The crematorium was a new addition to the funeral home, the idea of Lou. He'd purchased land across the street from the funeral home about six years earlier and made plans to build a crematorium. Unfortunately, zoning problems delayed the building. The Pinera Funeral Home was located in an upper-middle-class section of Prairie Village. Most of the residents had lived in that area for many years and were opposed to a crematorium being built in their neighborhood. There were several meetings between the Pinera family and the residents, none resulting in favorable progress for the Pinera family.

Lou met behind closed doors with the city council. He found a way to persuade five of the nine council members to vote in favor of the crematorium. The only condition was that the crematorium operated only at night when most area residents were asleep. It was a small concession, although the price tag for buying off five council members was much steeper. Tony Pinera operated the crematorium in its early days. Since he was the main embalmer, too, it meant working a double shift some days. He was happy to hand over the responsibility of the crematorium to Dennis.

No one ever asked Lou what it took to get approval for the crematorium. No one ever asked Lou about where or how he spent any of the funeral home money. He was the older brother. It was his business to run as he saw fit. As long as each member of the staff got paid every week, no one complained. Lou Pinera was generous with the salaries he paid the family members. And, if anyone needed extra, all they had to do was ask.

Dennis Glenn had just started working at the crematorium when Elizabeth Pinera announced the fall party at the Pinera house. Andrew and Elizabeth normally hosted two or three large parties at their home every year, but this was the first one that year. All family parties were held at their house. Lou never hosted a party. It was not something he enjoyed. However, he was the one that determined when a party would occur. The family parties were as much business as they were pleasure. When Lou determined he needed to entertain a business client, or in most cases, several business clients, he would ask Elizabeth and Andrew to set it up. They were great hosts, and Lou would pay whatever the costs were to throw an extravagant party. Like most in the past, this party would be held in the backyard of the Pinera home.

The dress for this party was business casual. "A nice polo shirt and slacks would work," Dennis said to himself.

Elise picked out a nice tan dress with spaghetti straps with a strand of imitation white pearls. The weather had not turned cool yet—it would be in the low to upper seventies for most of the evening—but she brought a sweater in case it was needed. They arrived thirty minutes early, as requested of all family members. Lou wanted the entire family to be present to welcome the guests as they arrived. Valets were positioned out front. Two lovely young ladies in long flowing white silk dresses were at the entrance to the house, passing out glasses of champagne to the guests as they arrived. Bouquets of red roses lined both sides of a red-carpeted walkway from the house entrance to the backyard. Two other young, attractive ladies in identical long flowing white silk dresses were at the rear exit of the house directing guests to the backyard, collecting empty champagne glasses and replacing them with fresh glasses of champagne.

One large white tent and one smaller tent were positioned in the backyard for guests to congregate out of the sun and heat. The larger tent was about fifty feet long by fifty feet deep. Inside were twelve large round tables covered in white linen, with ten place settings per table, each one with Waterford crystal wine glasses, Jardin D'Eden silverware, and gold plated fine china. The smaller tent was for private meetings. In one corner of the backyard was a band with a dance floor surrounded by tables and chairs. Rows and rows of hanging white lights encompassed the entire backyard to provide plenty of light when the sun went down.

Waiters dressed in black tuxedos and young, attractive women servers dressed in white silk gowns served hors d'oeuvres, champagne, and cocktails. A full bar with three bartenders poured libations of all types.

Even by Pinera family standards, this was a lavish party. Dennis and Elise were excited to see the guests that were invited. Lou invited the guests — the guest list had been kept secret. It was possible that even Elizabeth and Andrew didn't know who was invited.

Five minutes before the guests were scheduled to arrive, Lou and his latest girlfriend, Erika Bell, made an entrance from the small tent at the rear of the backyard. Lou Pinera had been dating Erika for about six months. Speculation was that they would announce wedding plans soon, maybe by Christmas. Erika was at least twenty-five years younger than Lou. She was knock-down gorgeous, tall with long, curly blonde hair that went down to her waist, piercing blue eyes, puffy, thick lips and large, perky breasts. Lou's latest arm candy had the body of a swimsuit model, and she clung to her boyfriend like honey to a beehive. Erika left no doubt that her biggest aspiration in life was to marry into money. In Lou, she had found her sugar daddy and was determined to hold on for the ride.

The elder Pinera brother paraded his new love through the

crowd of family members, shaking hands and giving hugs as the couple worked their way to the back door of the house. Elizabeth and Andrew followed a few steps behind. As the guests flowed out of the house and into the backyard, the Pinera brothers shook the men's hands and gave the women gentle kisses on the cheek. Elizabeth and Erika followed suit with hugs and kisses.

The rest of the Pinera family formed a line to welcome their guests. There was something odd about this particular group of guests. They weren't the usual guests that had attended previous Pinera family parties. Dennis was used to seeing members of the clergy, police department, city officials, and family friends. This group of guests was a rougher crowd, less versed in social etiquette, cruder, and significantly of Italian heritage.

"They look like they are members of the mob," Elise said to Dennis.

Most of the men wore suits. Their wives wore high heels and short dresses, more revealing and less conservative than the family wives, showing off their shapely legs, with jewelry that was abundant, large, and loud. The men smoked cigars and drank whiskey. The wives sipped champagne.

One by one, the male guests accompanied Lou into the small, private tent. Erika, Elizabeth, and Andrew were tasked with entertaining the rest of the guests. Liquor flowed, and the band started playing. At sunset, dinner was served in the large tent—lobster, steak with potatoes, assorted vegetables, and pasta. After dinner, tiramisu and gooey butter cake were served, followed by cognac and after-dinner liquors.

Music and dancing followed dinner. The bar kept busy. Guests got drunk. Deals were made in the small private tent in the back of the yard. The party lasted until the wee hours of the morning, but Lou never left the small, private tent. Drinks and food were carried in. Empty plates and glasses were carried out. Only Lou and the guests he invited into the tent knew what went on inside, but those secret meetings would have an immediate impact on the Pinera Family Funeral Home business.

Two days after the party, Dennis received a special order in the crematory, delivered by Alvin around 2 a.m. He provided Dennis with written instructions from Lou on the proper way to handle this and future special orders.

The body brought in by Alvin was different from others that Dennis had been used to. First, it had not been cleaned. Second, the head had a traumatic injury, a gaping hole where the face should be. Brain matter had spilled out to the neck and clothing. It looked like the face had been shot off by a sawed-off shotgun. It took a lot to make Dennis queasy, but the sight of that body made him sick.

Dennis heated up the cremation furnace to 1650 degrees and pushed the metal cart containing the body to the entrance to the furnace. Next, he raised the metal bed so the body could easily slide onto the conveyor belt that fed into the furnace, turned the conveyor on, and gently lifted the shoulders to push the body onto the conveyor belt. From there, the body moved into the cremation chamber and rested on a metal shelf.

The body was large, with a high percentage of fat. The flames ignited the body in a matter of seconds. Flames fueled by the body fat shot high into the furnace. Dennis closed the steel cremation door and waited. An hour and a half later, he opened the furnace door, and with his large metal mallet, he pounded what remained of the skull and large bone fragments down into the ashes. He waited another thirty minutes for the larger chunks to dissolve into a course gray gravel-like ash. When everything had burned down, he removed the ash and left it to cool on a metal table next to the cremation furnace. An hour later, the remains were put into a cardboard container, labeled as "John Doe," and put on the shelf to be picked up the next morning.

***

After that body, special orders became common in the crematorium—three or four a week, most weeks. Most of the bodies had some sort of trauma, enough to make Dennis suspicious. He first mentioned it to Elise. She mentioned it to her mother. Her mother mentioned it to her father. Andrew seemed surprised, completely unaware of the special orders coming into the crematorium. Elise was at her desk just outside her father's office when Elizabeth told her husband about the unusual bodies coming to the crematorium in the middle of the night.

"Andrew, do you know anything about special orders that are coming into the crematorium?"

"No. What are you talking about?"

"Elise says that Alvin is bringing in bodies to the crematory that are marked as special orders and that Dennis has received instructions about the disposition of the cremated remains for those special orders from Lou. He packages the remains and labels them all the same, John Doe."

"Liz, have you received any paperwork for those bodies?"

"No, I haven't. But I can tell you that we can't do any legal cremations without the proper paperwork signed by the family. I didn't know there had been deliveries of bodies to the crematory in the middle of the night. Andrew, don't you find that strange?"

Andrew motioned for his wife to leave the office and to close the door. Elise could see the light on the phone line light up, which indicated that her father was making a call. A few minutes later, she heard shouting but could not make out the conversation. The light on the phone line went dark, and a minute later, her father hurried out of his office and left the building. He didn't say where he was going or when he would be back. The look on Elizabeth's face showed concern. Elise knew that something troubling was going on, and she suspected it had to do with her uncle, Lou.

***

An hour later, the phone rang. Elise picked up.

"Hello, Elise. May I speak to your mother?"

"Yes, Dad. What is going on?"

"I'll tell you later. May I please speak to your mother?"

"Yes. I'll get her."

Elise knocked on her mother's door.

"Yes, come in."

"It's Dad on the phone for you, Mother."

"Thanks. Can you please give me some privacy and shut my door?"

Elizabeth picked up the phone as Elise exited the office and shut her door.

Elise sat at her desk and waited for the phone conversation to end. She hoped to get an explanation from her mother as soon as she got off the phone. But instead, when her parents finished talking, her mother opened the office door, told Elise she would be out the rest of the day, and then left the building. Her face showed concern as if she had been given bad news she did not expect. She looked puzzled and a little scared.

Elise phoned her husband at home. It was nearly two, and Dennis was sound asleep. The phone rang eight times before Dennis woke and picked up the receiver.

"Hello."

"I'm sorry, honey. I know you were asleep, but something has come up, and I'm worried."

"What is it?"

"I told my mother and father about the unusual bodies you are receiving late at night in the crematorium."

"Oh, Elise. I wish you hadn't done that. I don't want your family to think I am complaining or questioning my job."

"I know. But I thought my parents might have a simple explanation for them."

"Did they?"

"No. That's what concerns me. They didn't seem to know anything about those bodies. My mother didn't have any paperwork for them. There is no record of late-night pick-ups or any cremation agreements signed by the families to authorize the cremations."

"Don't worry, Elise. I'm sure there is an explanation. Have they talked to Lou?"

"I don't know. My father was on the phone with someone — it sounded like he was arguing with them — but I don't know who he was on the phone with. Then, he stormed out of his office and left the funeral home. He didn't give any explanation."

"Well, I'm sure your father will talk to Lou, and they will get everything straightened out. I just hate that I am caught in the middle. I get the feeling your family doesn't like me much as it is. I don't want them to think I am complaining about my job."

"I'm sure they won't. If anything, I think my parents were thankful I told them about it. See you when I get home."

"Love you, Elise."

Love you too, honey."

Elise tried calling her mother and father several times in the late afternoon and a few more times after dinner. There was no answer on either of their cell phones and no answer at the residence. Finally, about eight, she and Dennis drove over to their home. The lights were out. No one answered the door. Elise wrote a note and taped it to the front door.

> *Mom and Dad,*
> *Please call me as soon as you get home, no matter what time it is. I'm worried about you.*
> *Love,*
> *Elise*

That night when Dennis pulled into the parking lot of the crematorium, there were two other cars parked near the entrance. Both were new model Cadillacs, black with gold trim, top of the line. It was the first time anyone other than Alvin Pinera had visited the crematorium during the hours that Dennis worked.

The front door was unlocked. It had always been locked before. The lights were off. The crematorium was dark and quiet. Dennis flipped on the light switch at the entranceway, illuminating the long, narrow hallway that led from the front door to the cremation chamber. He followed the hallway to the cremation furnace, which was on and heated to 1650 degrees. The furnace had never been turned on before he arrived. The Pinera family did not like to waste energy. Besides, the agreement with the neighborhood and city council was that the furnace would only be run between 11p.m. and 7 a.m. It was 10:40 p.m.

Dennis walked past the cremation room into another long narrow hallway, which led to the refrigeration room. He flipped on the light switch at the beginning of the hallway. The light flickered but slowly turned on. Halfway down the hallway, he could see light jetting through the small openings in the door leading into the refrigeration room.

"Someone is in there," he said to himself.

His hand was trembling as he slowly opened the door. Four bodies were lying on metal tables lined up in the room, none wrapped in plastic. Dennis could see the red toe tags on each body. That was the color tag used for special orders. As he got closer to the bodies, he could see that each of the corpses had been shot in the head, from the back or side, with a high-powered gun. Each of the heads had been partially blown outward, with skin, tissue, and brain matter hanging loose from the rest of their face. He was looking at the corpses when he heard the sound.

He turned quickly to see the two men seated in the corner of the room. One was Lou Pinera. The other, a much larger, more intimidating figure, he did not recognize.

Lou pushed a chair in Dennis's direction. "Sit down, Dennis. We need to talk."

Dennis did as he was told. Lou had a stern look on his face. The other man looked angry.

"Dennis, you have disappointed me."

"How, Mr. Pinera?" Dennis said.

That's when the other man, a large man with dark eyes and greasy, short black hair, stood up, walked over to Dennis, and punched him in the stomach. Dennis fell out of his chair and rolled onto the concrete floor. The force of the blow left him gasping for air.

"Don't talk until Mr. Pinera asks you to talk," the man said to Dennis. Then he lifted him off the floor and sat him back in his chair. Dennis bent over, staring at the floor, trying to get his breath back. The force of the blow had hurt like hell, and it felt like one of his ribs had cracked.

Lou waited for a minute for Dennis to catch his breath. "As I was saying, you have disappointed me. I thought you were loyal. I didn't think you would talk about family business. I thought you would do as you were told and not cause any waves. Was I wrong about you, Dennis?"

"No, Mr. Pinera. You weren't wrong."

"Then why did you tell your wife about what was going on in the crematorium? It is none of her business. It's no one's business except mine. Do you understand?"

"Yes, Mr. Pinera, I understand. I told my wife because she is part of the family. I would never talk to anyone outside the family about the business."

Lou Pinera forced a small smile. "The problem is, Dennis, that even family members aren't aware of all the business arrangements I make. My brother and his wife run the funeral home operations. They do a good job of it, and I leave them alone. I run the financial end of the business. I am responsible for growing our business. I am responsible for generating the money that feeds and clothes our family and pays the bills. It is no one's business, not even my dear brother and sister-in-law's, how I generate the revenue that it takes to keep the business going. And frankly, no one cares as long as their lifestyle doesn't suffer. Do you understand?"

"Yes, Mr. Pinera."

"Good. From now on, I don't want you to discuss anything about the crematorium with anyone, not even your wife. Do you hear me?"

"Yes, Mr. Pinera."

"Your only communication will be with Alvin. You will follow his instructions and do exactly what he tells you. If you don't, or if you feel a need to talk to anyone else about the business, my friend that took your breath away tonight will pay you a visit, and I'm afraid he won't be in such a good mood. Now, take care of these bodies. You don't want to get behind.

I've got a feeling the crematorium business is about to pick up."

CHAPTER 5
AND THEN THERE WAS ONE

The blast at 3 a.m. woke people from a mile away. Shock waves caused windows to shatter and pictures to fall off walls. Fire lit up the sky like it was the middle of the day. People ran out of their homes, some wearing nothing but their underwear. The heat was intense. Siding buckled, grass ignited. Three cars were engulfed in flames.

The first fire truck arrived ten minutes after the blast. Three others soon followed. Police blocked off the street to let emergency vehicles through. Dogs barked, neighbors cried. Nothing like this had even happened on the north side of Prairie Village.

When the flames were put out, and the ashes had cooled, search dogs entered the ruins. Two bodies were found, together, side-by-side, burned beyond recognition.

Elise was sound asleep in her bed. The events the previous afternoon made it difficult for her to sleep. She took two Ambien and chased them down with a glass of red wine. That did the trick. Soon she was in a deep sleep and did not hear the explosion. She was awakened by the phone, which she thought was part of her dream. It rang and rang and rang. Finally, she started to wake up and picked up the phone.

"Hello," she answered in a groggy voice.

"Elise. It's me," Dennis said with his voice trembling. "There was an explosion at your parents' house. We need to get over there right away. I'll pick you up in ten minutes."

"No. That couldn't be. How are they? Are they hurt?"

"I don't know, Elise. I just heard about it. We need to get over there as soon as possible. I'm leaving right now."

Dennis hung up the phone. Elise fought back the tears and rushed to get dressed. Five minutes later, she was dressed and in the kitchen. She let Teddy and Hillary outside, then put food and water in their dog dishes, let them back in, and waited at the front door. Dennis pulled in the driveway a minute later. He honked the horn, and Elise ran to the car. When she got inside, Dennis hugged her. Then they drove to the Pinera home.

Police had blocked the entrance into the neighborhood. In the distance, a wall of flashing lights could be seen. Dennis honked his horn, and a policeman came to the car.

"We need to get through, Officer. My in-laws own the house that is on fire."

"What's your name?"

"I'm Dennis Glenn, and this is my wife, Elise. She is the daughter of the owners of the house."

"I'm sorry, sir. But you will need to wait here. I will have someone come to talk with you."

Dennis and Elise waited and watched. Smoke began to dissipate, although the smell of burning wood still filled the air. People began going back into their houses. Two ambulances left the neighborhood without their flashing lights. Two fire trucks left, one remained. The sun came up over the horizon. Finally, after nearly an hour of waiting, the policeman that had told them to wait moved the barrier blocking the entrance and motioned for Dennis and Elise to enter. He told them to drive down as far they could go and ask for Detective Jacks. They did as they were told.

A thin, muscular man with thinning hair and wearing a sports jacket approached the car. "I'm Detective Jacks," he said. "I understand you are members of the family that live at 411 Somerset."

Elise spoke up. "I am the daughter of Elizabeth and Andrew Pinera. They live at that address. What happened, Detective? Are my parents okay?"

"Ms. Pinera?"

"No, Mrs. Glenn. This is my husband, Dennis Glenn, Detective."

"Mrs. Glenn, I don't know any other way to tell you this. We found two bodies in the rubble. It will take time to identify them, but there is a strong probability that your parents were killed in the explosion and fire."

Elise began to scream, a loud, high-pitched scream that echoed down the street. She grabbed hold of her husband, and tears ran down her face. "No, no, no. It can't be!" she said. "You must be wrong."

Elise was inconsolable. She clung to her husband's shoulder, screaming and crying.

"Do you know what caused the explosion and fire, Detective?" Dennis asked.

"We suspect that it was a gas leak that ignited in the home. But we are still investigating. Again, I am so sorry for your loss."

Dennis drove back to their house as quickly as he could. He gave his wife two Ambien and helped her to bed. Then he called her doctor and got a stronger medication to help her sleep. He laid in bed with her and held her tight until she fell asleep. Then he called the funeral home and asked for Lou.

"Hello, Dennis. How are you doing?" Mr. Pinera asked.

"Sir, there was an accident at Elizabeth and Andrew Pinera's house this morning."

"I know, Dennis. I have talked to the police, and the news media has called me."

"They found two bodies in the house, and they think they might be Elizabeth and Andrew."

"I know, Dennis. I have already made arrangements to send their dental records to the coroner's office."

"Mr. Pinera, what can I do to help."

"Just take care of your wife, Dennis. She needs you now. I'll take care of everything else."

"Yes, sir."

"And Dennis, why don't you take a few days off of work so you can tend to your wife?"

"Yes, sir."

Dennis hung up the phone. There was something strange about that call, he thought to himself. Lou had been cool and businesslike in his tone. His voice did not show any emotion, as if he were talking to the family member of a deceased person he did not know, just another one of the funeral home's customers.

Elise slept the rest of the day and night and was still asleep at eight the next morning when the phone rang. Dennis answered.

"Hello."

"Hello, Dennis. This is Lou Pinera. I'm afraid the dental records confirmed that my brother and his wife were the two bodies they found in the home. The coroner's office will be releasing their bodies to me later this afternoon. I was wondering if you would like to handle their cremation. I'd like to have it done tonight. Can you make it into the crematorium around eleven?"

"Yes, I'll be there, sir."

"Good. As you can imagine, the bodies are unrecognizable. I would hate for Elise or any member of the family to see them in their present state. It will be best to cremate them as soon as possible, and we can have a memorial service this weekend."

"Yes, sir."

"Good, I trust you'll take care of everything tonight. I will leave you instructions, and I've selected two high-end urns that you can place the remains in."

Yes, sir."

With that, the phone conversation ended, and Dennis walked into the kitchen and made a pot of coffee. He did not relish telling his wife the news. She would be devastated. He sipped his coffee and thought about how he would break the news to her. There was no easy way. He would just come out and tell her. Still, Dennis couldn't help but wonder why Lou was so matter-of-fact about the loss of his brother and sister-in-law. Dennis had always thought he seemed self-centered and uncaring, but was he really so cold he couldn't express emotion for such a family tragedy?

Later that morning, when Elise woke up, Dennis gave her the news that her parents had died in the fire. She begged Dennis to call her uncle and tell him she wanted to see the bodies.

"Elise, you don't want to do that. You would not recognize them. It would only upset you more than you are now. Honey, it's best that you remember your parents the way you've always seen them. You don't want to have the image of them now as your last memory."

She was not happy about it, but Elise understood. She knew that Dennis was only looking out for her. He didn't want to see her hurt any more than she already was. She knew that he was right. It was best that she didn't see her parents' bodies.

Dennis gave his wife a pill to sedate her at about eight that evening. When she was sound asleep, he went to the crematorium. He arrived at about ten-thirty and found the lights were out. He'd thought maybe Lou would be there. He wasn't. Nobody was. He turned on the lights, heated up the cremation furnace, and went straight to the refrigeration room. Inside were two bodies on metal tables, both wrapped in plastic bags. When he got close, he could see that the remains were badly burned. No flesh remained on the bodies. Only the skull and charred bone fragments were in the bags. A note from Lou Pinera was lying on the desk.

Dennis,

Cremate my brother first. Then, cremate Elizabeth. Make sure the furnace is hot enough to sufficiently burn the bones. Use your mallet to break down the bone fragments and mix them in with the other ashes. Since the flesh is gone, the bone remnants will be the only ashes. Be sure to grind them down to give them the proper look of cremation ashes. I have placed their urns on the shelf next to the front door. Use the gold urn for Andrew and the bronze urn for Elizabeth. When you are finished, place the urns with their remains on that same shelf. I will collect them in the morning.

Yours,
Louis Pinera

The letter was to the point. Dennis followed the instructions. Four hours later, Elizabeth and Andrew had been reduced to ashes, and their urns sat on the shelf. Dennis turned off the cremation furnace, turned out the lights, and headed toward the front door.

That's when he stopped. The front door was open—he knew he had locked it. He always locked it. Then he saw the large figure standing next to the door. It was the same man that had been with Lou in the refrigeration room a few nights earlier. It was the same man that had threatened him and punched him in the stomach. He was alone, standing in the shadows of the hallway just inside the front door.

"What do you want?" Dennis asked with his voice cracking just a little.

"I have a message for you from Lou Pinera," he said.

"What is it?"

"He wants you to come back to work tomorrow night."

"He told me I should take the week off to take care of my wife."

The man, dressed in a black suit with a scar running down his left cheek, just stared at him. "Well, now he wants you back to work. There will be bodies coming in tomorrow night. Do you understand?"

Dennis was not about to argue with him. He knew how that would turn out. "Yes, I understand. I will be here."

With that, the stranger turned around and left. Dennis closed and locked the door, then sat down to collect his nerves. "How did he get in?" Dennis asked himself. "And, why didn't the bell on the door ring?"

Dennis looked up at the door. The bell was gone. Someone had removed it.

A cold chill ran through his bones. "That stranger must have had a key. Who was he?" Dennis didn't know who he was, but his intuition told him the stranger was trouble.

The next evening, Dennis explained to Elise that Lou needed him to come in that evening. "He has work he needs me to get done." He kissed his wife goodbye and promised to pick up some bagels and coffee for breakfast the next morning.

When he arrived at the crematorium, five bodies were laid out in the refrigeration room, all special orders. These bodies were different from all the previous ones. There were no gunshot wounds. They had not suffered traumatic deaths like the others. The bodies looked unharmed, like they had died peacefully, naturally maybe. The bodies were not wrapped in plastic. Each had a red toe tag. Two were women, three were men. There were no names listed on the red tags, only numbers — 11, 12, 13, 14, 15.

Dennis turned the cremation furnace on and prepared the first body, #11. It was a man, late twenties or early thirties, heavyset, naked except for his blue boxer shorts. His chest was covered in hair, as was his lower back. He had short, dark brown hair and a mustache. His brown eyes were open wide, both of them. It was the same with the other bodies. Each one had their eyes completely open. Dennis had seen his share of bodies before, and it was very unusual for the eyes to remain open after death. Usually, even if the eyes were open at the time of death, the eye muscles would relax after death, and the eyes would close. But not these five bodies. Their eyes were completely open, not just a little bit, but all the way, staring straight ahead. The pupils were large, the eyes glossy. They appeared to be damp, just a little watery.

Dennis remembered what one of his instructors had said. "The eyes are a window into the soul." He could see that as he looked into each of their eyes. It was as if they were telling a story. Each of their eyes had a sad look. They must have known they were dying before it actually happened. Their eyes looked frightened. They did not go into death easily.

The two women were young and attractive—they had their whole lives ahead of them. Both were dressed in evening dresses, long, flowing gowns. If they had jewelry, it had been removed. The older one, maybe in her early thirties, had a ring line on her left ring finger. She was tanned except for that part of her finger. "She was someone's wife," Dennis said to himself. The other woman, blonde, thin, and just over five feet tall, couldn't be more than twenty-five years old. She was gorgeous, with natural beauty that she covered over with a heavy coating of make-up.

Dennis moved his face to within inches of hers. There was something about her eyes. He looked deep inside them. They were trying to tell him something. "What is it?" he asked her. Her pupils were large, her eyes moist, glistening. "I know you want to tell me. What is it?" he asked her again. Then he noticed the spot of blood in the lower right corner of her eye. He hadn't noticed it before. It was barely visible. "What happened to you?" he asked her. He hadn't noticed the spot of blood in the eyes of other corpses. Maybe it had been there, and he just didn't notice it. He wouldn't have noticed it with this woman had he not gotten so close to her eye. He moved to the other side of her and looked closely into her other eye. "Yes, there it is," he said out loud. In the far left corner of her left eye was a small speck of blood. It was barely visible.

Did the other bodies have blood in their eyes that he hadn't noticed? Dennis moved to the married woman on the next metal table and leaned over to within inches of her right eye. In the far corner of her eye was a small spot of blood, almost like a tiny blood blister about the size of the head of a needle. He would never have noticed it if he hadn't been looking for it. Dennis walked over to his desk and reached up to the calendar above it. Then he removed the small pin holding the calendar in place and brought it over to the body.

The needle of the pin was sharp and thin. With it, he carefully penetrated the bubble of blood in the corner of her eye. The outer portion of the bubble had dried, forming a thick skin. He applied more force and penetrated the bubble. Blood began to trickle down the bottom lip of her eye onto her cheek. There was more blood than he expected. He put on a latex glove and wiped the blood with his index finger. Then he moved the finger up to his nose and smelled the blood. It had a bitter smell to it. With the tip of his tongue, he licked the blood. It was salty. It was sour. When he was younger, he had tasted his own blood on several occasions, when he would get a cut and the blood would get on his finger. Sometimes he would lick it off. He didn't know why. Maybe he was just curious what it tasted like. It was not salty, and it was not sour. It had a bit of a sweet taste to it, not unpleasant. The flavor of this corpse's blood was different.

Dennis was curious about the spot of blood, so he checked the eyes of the other three corpses. All five bodies had similar spots of blood in the corner of their eyes. With each, their eyes were wide open. With each, their pupils were enlarged. With each, their eyes appeared glossy, almost watery. And with each, there was a small spot of blood in the corner of their eyes. He wished they could tell him what had happened to them. Dennis could see them trying to tell him in their eyes.

When the cremation furnace had heated to 1650 degrees, Dennis began the cremation process, just as he was instructed. It took most of the night to complete. When he finished, he lined the cremation container containing their ashes on the shelf near the front door, #11 thru #15 lined up in order. He wondered who would pick the containers up. They always picked them up after he left for home. He never saw the person.

Dennis turned off the cremation furnace, turned out the lights, locked the door, and headed home. It was nearly eight. He had worked longer than normal. It took more time to cremate five bodies. There had never been that many corpses in the refrigeration room at the same time. The drive from the crematorium to his house took thirty minutes. He was caught in the traffic of people going to work. When he got back home, there was a note taped to the front door.

We need you to come back to work tonight. We have a busy week. Lou

"That was odd," he told himself. "Why didn't he call or write that in the instructions he left on my desk last night? Why would he drive all the way out here to pin a note on the door?"

There was something else that was odd, too. The front door was unlocked. Dennis was positive that he locked it when he left the house the night before. "Maybe Elise is up. Maybe she went out to get the newspaper." He looked on the driveway. The paper was gone. *That must be it*, he thought. *She woke up and went out to get the newspaper and forgot to lock the door when she came in.*

Dennis walked into the house. It was quiet, and no lights were on. He walked to the bedroom and opened the closed door. It was dark and quiet inside. "Elise, are you awake?" he asked quietly. There was no answer. Hillary and Teddy were barking in the backyard, so he turned the light on, went to the back door, and let them inside. That's when he saw the pot of coffee, still hot. *She must be awake*, he thought. He went back down the hall into the master bedroom. She was not in bed, but the covers were pulled back, and the sheets were wrinkled. The bedspread was in disarray. Dennis hollered her name. There was no response.

Dennis rushed to the kitchen. On the breakfast table was the newspaper, opened to the obituary notices. One had been circled—the obituary for Elizabeth and Andrew. Next to the newspaper was a partial cup of coffee, warm to the touch. "She must be here," he said to himself. He went to the back hallway. That's when he saw the light coming out of the small opening at the bottom of the bathroom door.

He called her name one more time. There was no response. Dennis slowly turned the knob of the door and opened it. The shower curtain was closed, and someone was in the tub—he could hear movement. "Elise, are you in the tub?" he hollered. There was no answer. His heart was pounding, his hands shaking as he reached for the edge of the shower curtain and opened it.

Inside the tub, with her head partially underwater, was his wife. Frantically, he grabbed her arms and pulled her out of the tub onto the tile floor. In desperation, he yelled her name and shook her face. There was no movement. He felt for a pulse. There was one, but it was light. In a final effort to save his wife, Dennis performed CPR, pushing in on her chest and blowing into her mouth. Six, seven, eight pushes on her chest, each with more force, each with more panic. He breathed strong long, deep breaths into her mouth.

After the eighth compression on her chest, a small trickle of water came out of her mouth. That was followed by coughing and a gasp for breath. When she began to come to, he phoned 911. An ambulance arrived fifteen minutes later and took her to the hospital.

CHAPTER 6
A CLOSE CALL

Dennis rode with his wife in the ambulance to the hospital, where they put her on oxygen and monitored her vital signs. She was in the emergency room for several hours. The doctor said she was lucky — there didn't appear to be any damage to her heart or brain or any of her other vital organs. She had nearly drowned. Dennis reached her just in time.

When she was out of danger, Dennis called his parents and told them what had happened. Susan was distraught. He could hear her crying on the other end of the phone. Elise was like a daughter to her. His parents rushed to the hospital and waited.

In the small room where she lie in a bed, hooked up to an IV and with oxygen running into her nostrils, Dennis held her hand and stared into her face. *She is so beautiful*, he thought. He loved her so much, and he had nearly lost her.

"Honey, what happened?" he asked.

"I guess I fell asleep," she said.

"Why were you in the bathtub?"

"I woke up, and you weren't there. I was worried, so I walked through the house looking for you. When I didn't find you, I assumed you had run an errand. So I took a bath and waited for you. I don't remember falling asleep, but I guess I must have. That's all I remember until I woke up with you pressing down on my chest. Damn, my chest still hurts."

"Sorry, I was worried about you. You scared me to death. Elise, why did you close the shower curtain?"

"What are you talking about? I didn't close the curtain. I never close the curtain when I'm taking a bath."

"Well, it was closed when I entered the bathroom."

"That's strange," she said

"Honey, did you go outside to get the newspaper after you woke up?"

"No, I didn't. All I did was look for you in the house. Then I started the bath."

"Do you remember making a pot of coffee and pouring a cup?"

"No."

"So, you didn't sit at the breakfast table to drink a cup of coffee and read the newspaper?"

"No. What are you talking about, Dennis? You are talking as if you need this bed more than I do."

An hour later, Elise was released from the hospital. Dennis's parents drove them home. Susan asked Elise what had happened, and she told her the same story she had told Dennis an hour earlier.

"Elise, I insist that you and Dennis come stay with us for a few days. I'll take care of you."

"I appreciate the offer, Susan, but I think I'll be more

comfortable at home. Besides, someone needs to be home to take care of Hillary and Teddy."

"Well then, I insist that I stay at your house for a few days. You need someone to look after you while you rest. You've been through a lot the last few days, too much for anyone to have to bear. I'll make the meals and keep the house in order while you rest. Now, please don't argue. God knows my son can't cook. A few meals from him, and you're likely to end up in the hospital again."

"Okay, Susan. But only until after the memorial service. I should be fine after that."

"It's a deal. Ron, drop me off at the house. I'll pack a bag and come right over."

As soon as they arrived home, Dennis took Elise to the bedroom. After he gave her a glass of water and an Ambien, she got undressed, got into bed, and was sound asleep thirty minutes later. Dennis stayed with her until she was in a deep sleep, then walked into the kitchen. He was curious about the newspaper and cup of coffee. Either his wife was too groggy to remember getting the paper and making a pot of coffee, or someone else had been in the house.

When he walked into the kitchen, his mother was washing dishes. The pot of coffee was gone, and so was the cup of coffee and newspaper.

"Did you pick up the pot of coffee that was on the counter and the newspaper and cup that were on the breakfast table, Mom?"

"No, I didn't see them. There was nothing on the breakfast table, and the coffee pot was empty. There were dinner dishes in the sink, though. I cleaned them."

Chills ran down Dennis's back. Someone had been in the

house. Ten minutes later, he was on the phone with a locksmith. Two hours later, he had new locks on all the doors and a deadbolt lock added to the front door.

Dennis didn't want to leave his wife that night, but he knew he needed to go to work. Lou would suspect something if he didn't. Then he sat down with his mother and told her about the coffee and the newspaper and about the shower curtain.

"That is why I had a locksmith change all the locks in the house."

His mother started to cry. "You need to call the police. You need to tell them what you have told me."

"I can't. They wouldn't believe me. There is no proof that anyone else was in the house. And even if they did believe me, there is nothing they could do. Nothing was stolen. Nothing was damaged. Mom, I would feel better if you called Dad and had him spend the night, too."

"You're not going into work tonight?" she said in a motherly tone that was more of a demand than a question.

"Yes, I've got to. There are things going on at work that I need to take care of."

Susan called her husband, who packed a bag and rushed over. He arrived just before Dennis left for work.

"Thanks for coming, Dad," Dennis said. "It's probably nothing, but I feel better knowing you are here."

"What's going on, Dennis?"

"Probably nothing. Mom will tell you about it. I need to leave for work."

Dennis walked into the bedroom, gave his wife a gentle kiss on the cheek, and walked out of the house. Elise was sound asleep.

There were three bodies in the refrigeration room that

night, all in body bags, none special orders. They were city contracted pick-ups—the paperwork indicated that. It was the first of the new business that Lou had contracted with the city. He won the business by providing the lowest bid among four funeral homes. Many of the bodies the city sent to Pinera Family Funeral Home were thought to be homeless people that died on the streets of Kansas City. Others were unclaimed bodies, "John Does," or people without families to take responsibility for their burial. The crematorium would benefit by the majority of that business. Burial spaces came at a premium cost. Cremation was inexpensive, and disposal was simple.

From the looks of the bodies laying on the metal tables, the three corpses were likely homeless people. They looked ungroomed, dirty, with torn clothing. *Three homeless bodies in one night seems strange*, Dennis thought. It hadn't been particularly cold out the last few nights. The bodies showed no signs of dying from exposure. They looked peaceful like they had died while asleep.

Dennis left the refrigeration room to check the temperature of the cremation furnace. It was thirteen hundred degrees—another twenty minutes, and it would be ready. He returned to the room to complete the city paperwork. The small desk in the refrigeration room was where he spent most of his time when a body wasn't in the furnace. That was his private space where he ate lunch, read, and took naps on particularly slow nights. It had been a while since he had taken a nap there, though. Business in the crematorium was busier than ever.

The temperature in the refrigeration room was set at forty degrees. When he first started working, the cold bothered Dennis. But now, he was used to it. Most nights, he didn't even wear a jacket when he was in the room. He wasn't wearing one that night either. The rest of the crematorium, outside of the cremation chamber, was cool also. It had been built underground to keep cooling and heating costs down. The temperature usually ran around sixty degrees, but inside the cremation chamber, when the furnace was being used — when a body was inside it — the temperature around the furnace could easily reach a hundred degrees. The hottest part of the job was when he needed to open the heavy metal door to the cremation furnace. Inside, the temperature would be between 1400 and 1650-degrees. That's what the protective clothing that hung on the wall next to the furnace was for. He put the protective suit, goggles, and protective gloves on before opening the cremation furnace. If he didn't, the intense heat from the furnace would cause heat blisters on his skin in a matter of a few seconds. Goggles protected his face from the intense heat. Long metal tools were used to move deep within the furnace so as not to expose his hands and arms to the intense heat. Still, when he opened the furnace door, the blast of heat would nearly knock him off his feet. It was so incredibly hot. It was suffocating — it took his breath away. During busy nights, Dennis was constantly going between the cremation furnace with its intense heat, the cremation room, which could be as warm as seventy or eighty degrees depending on how close he was to the furnace, and the refrigeration room, which stayed at a constant forty degrees. Maybe that was why the cool temperatures in the refrigeration room didn't seem to bother him. The refrigeration room seemed pleasant to him after being exposed to the intense heat of the cremation furnace.

Dennis sat at his desk and grabbed the paperwork the city required from his inbox. That's when he noticed the note that was also in the inbox.

Dennis,
There will be an important staff meeting in the funeral home
parlor this morning at 7:30 a.m. Everyone is required to attend.
Louis Pinera

"That is odd," Dennis said to himself. He had never been required to attend any staff meeting before. They had only included the funeral home staff in previous meetings. The crematorium was always treated as a separate entity, kind of like a bastard child of the funeral home.

Dennis finished his work that night, then called home to let Elise know he would be late. She was still asleep, so his mother answered the phone. Dennis explained that he needed to attend a staff meeting and would come home after it ended.

"Mom, how is Elise doing?" he asked.

"She slept soundly all night. In fact, she is still sleeping. She needed the rest."

"Good. I'll be home as soon as I can. Love you."

"We love you too, Dennis."

Dennis carried the three cardboard containers with the cremation remains to the outgoing shelf near the front door. Then he turned out the lights and left. He decided to walk across the street to the funeral home rather than drive his car. It seemed silly to drive less than a block. Besides, the cool, crisp fall morning felt good. The air was fresh. The leaves of the trees were turning. Fall was Dennis's favorite time of the year. He loved the smells and the vibrant colors of the leaves on the tall oak trees just before they would fall to the ground for their winter nap.

It was a cloudy day. The sun was fighting to show itself from behind a wall of dark clouds. It would storm that day in more ways than one.

There were a dozen cars in the parking lot of the Pinera Family Funeral Home. Dennis recognized many of them—he had seen them at family gatherings before. But there were several cars that Dennis didn't recognize. They were expensive cars—two BMWs and a Mercedes. Lou and Andrew Pinera would never allow family members to drive foreign cars. Kansas City was a strong union market with conservative ideals. There were local Ford and General Motors manufacturing plants. The Pinera family members were expected to reflect the same ideals. They were expected to support the local union employees by driving either Fords or Chevys.

He entered the funeral home and walked into the parlor. A refreshment table was set up in the back with donuts, coffee, and juice. Chairs were lined up in two rows toward the front of the room. People seemed to be gathered into two separate groups, talking and laughing. Dennis recognized one group. They were family members, but he was not friendly with any of them. He never socialized with them, but he remembered them from family gatherings. The second group of people, seven of them, he did not recognize. They were dressed in well-tailored expensive suits and wore expensive gold watches and rings. They looked to be of Italian heritage, although that didn't seem significant since the entire Pinera family was of Italian heritage. Within the circle of men was one familiar face—Lou Pinera.

Ten minutes later, Lou walked to the front of the room and requested that everyone sit down. Once everyone was seated, he began to talk.

"I have some exciting news for the Pinera Family Funeral Home. After the untimely death of my dear brother and his wife, I needed to make some challenging decisions about the future of Pinera Family Funeral Home. I know that each one of you cares deeply about our family business and wants it to grow and prosper for many years to come. The loss of my brother and sister-in-law has left a big hole in our business, as well as our hearts. I was approached recently with an opportunity that will insure the growth and prosperity of our family business for many years to come. With the future of each and every one of you at the center of my heart, I made a decision to take on a partner. Mr. Joseph Cuneo offered us an opportunity that will double, maybe triple, our business. With his help, we were able to obtain the city contract for indigent burials and cremations. He has connections with many of the local unions, which will benefit our future business, and he has connections with the Catholic diocese, which has promised their endorsement with their parishes. With Mr. Cuneo's help, we think the Pinera Family Funeral Home will become the largest and most successful funeral home in Kansas City. Now please, give a warm welcome to my partner, Mr. Joseph Cuneo."

Everyone stood up and clapped loudly, and Cuneo made his way to the podium at the front of the parlor. He stood at the podium, took a sip of water, and spoke.

"I am grateful to have the opportunity to work with such a fine individual as Mr. Pinera. As he explained, we have gained several new business sources that will insure the prosperity of the funeral home and all of you for many years into the future. The added business will require some changes. We will add several members to our existing funeral home staff. Those new employees are in this room today. All new employees that have been assigned to the funeral home, please stand up."

Six men stood. Dennis recognized them. They were the other people that were talking with Lou before the meeting started.

"These individuals will be assigned positions within the funeral home. They will assist the existing staff to insure quality service to the additional families that we expect to serve. Lou will integrate them into the funeral home staff as he sees fit.

"The major change to our operations will take place in our crematorium. Over the next few months, we will add two more cremation furnaces and four employees. We anticipate a 200-300% increase in our cremation business. So as not to disrupt our cremation business while we grow, Lou and I have plans to build a new crematorium on the grounds of the existing crematorium. This will allow our existing cremation business to go on, uninterrupted through the construction process. The new crematorium will house two cremation chambers. Even after construction is finished, we will continue to operate the existing crematorium. That will provide us three cremation chambers and three furnaces, which will effectively triple our output. Unfortunately, we are still constrained by the city ordinance that requires all of our cremations to take place between 11p.m. and 7 a.m. To maximize our cremation output, we will operate the furnaces seven days a week."

After the meeting, Dennis started to leave. Just before he got to the front door, Lou stopped him.

"Dennis, I would like to meet with you in my office for just a few minutes before you leave."

"Yes, sir," he said.

Five minutes later, he walked into Lou's office. Sitting there was Joseph Cuneo and a younger gentleman. They stood up when Dennis walked in. Cuneo extended his hand, and Dennis shook it. His grip was strong, forceful. Cuneo was an older gentleman in his fifties, with a touch of gray in his hair and a thick, rough-looking face with pitted skin. His dark brown eyes and a scar that ran down part of his right cheek made him look intimidating. His hair was straight, thin, and greased back with no part. The older gentleman was immaculately dressed with a tailored, dark pinstriped suit and a light blue monogrammed shirt with the initials JMC. He had gold cufflinks with the same initials and was smoking a cigar. Cuneo had the look of a man that had aged beyond his years. Cuneo resembled a man that drank heavily and had been in his share of fights. Dennis thought that if he saw him walking down the street, he would likely cross to the other side of the street to avoid him. One thing was certain, he certainly didn't look like any funeral director Dennis had seen before.

"Hello, Mr. Glenn. I'm Joseph Cuneo, and this is my eldest son, Michael Cuneo."

Dennis shook Michael's hand. "Good to see you, Michael. It's good to know both of you. Where is Mr. Pinera? He asked me to meet him in his office."

"I'm afraid Lou had something he needed to take care of. You'll be meeting with me and my son."

"What is it that I can do for you, Mr. Cuneo?"

"Dennis, we plan some big changes for the crematorium. Lou told us that you handled all the crematorium business. He said you know everything about the operation of the crematorium."

"Yes, that is correct, I suppose."

"Outstanding. Then we are meeting with the right person. Dennis…may I call you Dennis?" Cuneo asked.

"Yes, you may."

"Good. Dennis, as we explained in the meeting, we have big plans for the crematorium. We will be expanding that business very shortly. We hope to begin construction on the new crematorium within the next few weeks. We estimate that we should be ready to open the new building sometime next spring. When open, we will be able to handle three times the volume of cremations that we can currently do. You have a great opportunity here, Dennis. But you will need to adjust to some changes in our business."

"What sort of changes are you talking about, Mr. Cuneo?"

"Well, for one thing, we are going to have a much larger staff working in the crematorium. You will no longer work alone. That's why I asked my son, Michael, to join us for this meeting. Michael is going to start working with you beginning next week. He knows nothing about the cremation business. You will need to teach him everything."

"Okay. I'll be happy to teach him the business."

"Good. Lou said you would be cooperative."

"Have you filed the paperwork with the funeral director's association so Michael can start working next week?"

"Well, no. That's where we need your help, Dennis. Michael isn't a licensed funeral director. We need you to be the face of the crematorium. Michael will work with you, but off the books, so to speak. Do you understand?"

"Mr. Cuneo, I can't do that. If the board ever found out that an unlicensed person was working in the crematorium, I would lose my license and could even go to jail. I just can't do that. He'll need to get a funeral director's license."

The smile on Cuneo's face disappeared and was replaced with an angry look. His face began to turn red, and his dark eyes stared directly into Dennis's face. The look sent chills through Dennis's body. Cuneo sat there silently, staring at Dennis for what seemed like several minutes. Then he stood up and moved to within a few inches of Dennis. He put his right hand on Dennis's shoulder and talked directly into his face.

"Dennis, I know we just met. But trust me, I am not a person you want to say no to, and I am not the type of person you want to disappoint. I am not asking you to teach my son the cremation business. I am telling you to do it. Do you understand?"

Dennis hesitated for just a second. *Was he threatening me? It sounded like he was threatening me*, Dennis thought. Cuneo's hand had a tight grip on Dennis's shoulder. It was beginning to hurt.

Unsatisfied with the slow response to his question, Cuneo said, "Look at my face and tell me you understand."

"Yes, I understand, Mr. Cuneo."

When the meeting ended, Dennis rushed out of the funeral home, walked across the block to his car, got in, and started home. It had begun to rain. The clouds were dark and thick.

"Jesus Christ," he said out loud as he turned out of the crematorium parking lot. "What the hell is going on? Who are those people that Lou brought into the business? They sure as hell weren't funeral directors."

He thought about what Joseph Cuneo had told him to do. If he did what he wanted and he got caught, he would likely go to jail. What he was asking was illegal. Dennis had never so much as shoplifted a candy bar before. He had never even gotten a speeding ticket. Now he was being told to commit a felony. To allow unlicensed people to work in the crematorium, he would need to forge paperwork. He would need to lie to the state board. He would be completely liable for everything the unlicensed people did. There was no way he could do that. Michael Cuneo would start working in the crematorium in four days. Dennis would need to come up with a plan before that.

The rain was beating down on the car. Lightning was illuminating the sky. It was a miserable day. Dennis couldn't help but wonder if the storm was a sign of things to come.

When he got home, Elise was seated at the breakfast table with his father, enjoying a cup of coffee together. His mother was making breakfast in the kitchen, scrambled eggs and bacon to go with the English muffins with some of her homemade preserves. The smell of sizzling bacon reminded Dennis of simpler times when he was young, and his mother made a hot breakfast for him every morning. Right now, he wished he could go back to those times. He wasn't looking forward to the next few days. In his near future was the memorial service for Elise's parents. He needed to remain strong for his wife. She needed him more than ever right now. He would wait until after the memorial service to tell Elise about the meeting. She, hopefully, would be stronger then. She could help him decide what he should do. One thing was certain, he wasn't going to do anything that was illegal or would jeopardize his family.

He greeted his wife with a kiss on the cheek. "Hi, honey. How are you doing this morning?"

"Feeling better and hungry as a horse," she said.

"Breakfast is served," his mother said as she brought the food to the breakfast table.

"It smells great, honey," his father said.

"Yes, it does, Mom," Dennis said as he got up to get a coffee mug and the pot of coffee. He brought both over to the table and sat down.

"How was the meeting?" his father asked.

"Fine, just a silly meeting. Nothing important. How'd the evening go?" Dennis asked his parents.

"Fine. It was quiet except for that damn thunder," his father said. "By the way, son, you need to replace the porch lights. They wouldn't turn on last night."

Dennis nearly dropped his fork. He'd just checked those

lights the night before after it appeared someone had been in the house. There were three lights on the front porch, and all of them were working fine two nights ago. It was understandable that one could burn out, but not all three.

His gut began to bother him. His gut told him that trouble was coming. His gut was almost always right.

CHAPTER 7
THE MEMORIAL SERVICE

The memorial service for Elizabeth and Andrew Pinera was held two days later and was conducted in the main visitation room at the Pinera Family Funeral Home. There was no member of the clergy present. Elise's parents had lost interest in the church many years earlier, although, as far as Elise knew, they both believed in God. Their urns were placed on a large, oak table at one end of the room. Surrounding the urns were bouquets of white and red roses—her mother's favorite flowers. Every birthday and every anniversary, her father would bring them home to his wife. Even during the last few years, when her parents seemed to argue constantly when their marriage seemed to be in trouble, her father would still bring roses home.

Standing on a separate table off to the side were several picture boards with pictures of Elise's parents taken by relatives. Elizabeth had a large collection of family photos. She loved taking pictures. But all those photos were destroyed in the fire. The picture boards were made up of memories that other family members had of Elizabeth and Andrew. No one had asked Elise to contribute to the picture board, and she was disappointed about that. She had a family album with quite a few pictures of her parents. They would have certainly added to the picture boards displayed in the main parlor.

Rows of folding chairs lined both sides of the room, with an aisle running between them. After entering and receiving condolences from the family members in attendance, Elise walked up the aisle to the two urns sitting on the table. She gave both urns a gentle kiss, then went down on her knees, gave a sign of the cross, and said a prayer. Elise was raised Catholic, although she had not been to mass in several years. Her parents had been raised Catholic, too, although the last time she remembered them attending mass was when she was a young girl. She remembered going every Sunday when she was young. Her parents would sit beside her, always in a pew near the front of the church. She sat silently until the homily, then she would leave the pew to go with the other children to Bible study. Her parents would pick her up after mass, and they would go to breakfast.

She had fond memories of church. The last time she could remember attending church was on her confirmation day. She'd worn a beautiful white gown. Her parents and her grandparents from her father's side of the family were present for the ceremony. Elise never knew her mother's parents. They had died in a car accident before Elise was born. The irony was that her father's parents died in a head-on collision the next day on their way to mass. The confirmation ceremony and dinner that followed were the last time that Elise would see her grandparents. "Two separate car accidents that claimed both sets of my grandparents. What were the odds of that happening?" Elise would say to herself. Her parents must have thought the odds were pretty slim, too.

They blamed God and the church and never attended another mass.

Elise never asked to go to mass after the accident. She, too, blamed God for taking her grandparents. She had been baptized in that same church. She had attended mass every Sunday since she could remember. But at the age of twelve, she stopped going to mass. She could have told her parents she wanted to go back, and they probably would have taken her. But she never did. It was just easier not to go.

There were only about two dozen people at the memorial service, all family members. Susan and Ron were there, although they hadn't been invited by Lou. They insisted on coming out of respect for Elizabeth and Andrew and to show support for their son and daughter-in-law. Susan hugged her daughter-in-law as soon as she entered the parlor. They cried together, and they prayed together. Dennis couldn't help but notice that they were the only people that were expressing much emotion. The other family members seemed cold and distant, focusing their attention on Lou, and paid little attention to Elise. When she first walked in, it had been different. Each family member lined up to hug her. They said their condolences and then went away. It was as if they did only what was expected of them and nothing more. Elise didn't notice. She was too busy grieving for her parents. But Dennis noticed. There was something odd, something cold about the way the Pinera family members treated Elise. It was as if she were a stranger that they were simply trying to express their condolences to. They showed no real emotion, no tears, no empathy in their voices. It was as if they were going through the motions. The family had known Elise's parents all their lives. They had attended parties at their home on a regular basis, had exchanged Christmas presents and birthday presents. But today, they weren't showing the emotion or the empathy that Dennis expected. In a way, he was glad his wife was so distraught that she didn't notice. Her heart would tear even more if she felt her family was not grieving with her.

With Elise still on her knees in front of her parents' urns, eyes closed and deep in prayer, Dennis walked up beside her, got down on his knees, and prayed, too. It was the first time he had prayed in years. He was only slightly less apathetic to the church than his wife. Raised a Lutheran and attending church nearly every Sunday before he married Elise, he had drifted away from the church. During most services, he would daydream. He tried to focus on the sermon, but it just didn't seem relative to his life. Despite getting little out of the church service, he always felt good after attending the Sunday service, but he never understood why. When he left the service, he felt like he was in God's good graces for another week.

When Elise finished her prayer and gave a sign of the cross, Dennis reached for her hand. He pulled her up, gave her a tissue to wipe her eyes, and walked her to a seat at the front of the parlor. Susan and Ron sat down beside them.

When the other family members had taken their seats, Lou stood up and walked to the podium. The talking ended, and the room became silent.

"What happened to my brother and his wife is a tragedy. They died at such a young age. However, we can take comfort knowing they did not suffer during the last moments of their lives. They were good people, and they will be missed by all of us. Our hearts go out to their daughter, Elise, and their son-in-law, Dennis. I, too, am suffering. I've lost my only brother. We've spent the last twenty-three years together building this business. It's been a wonderful journey, and without my brother's help,

I am certain we would not be as successful as we are today. He put his heart and soul into the business, and just recently, we had turned a pivotal corner with our business. I had just spoken with Andrew about the new business opportunity the night before he died. He was excited and optimistic for the future. He gave me his blessings for the new direction we were taking. It's a shame he won't be here to enjoy our future prosperity. We'll miss him and his dear wife."

Elise turned to Dennis, her mouth open. She was shaking her head. "What the hell is going on, Dennis? What kind of eulogy was that?" she whispered.

Dennis reached over and hugged her. Then he stood up. "I'd like to say something," he said and walked up to the podium. Dennis had always been socially awkward. He never cared much for polite conversation and never talked to a crowd of people. But he felt he needed to say something.

"Mr. and Mrs. Pinera were good people. They weren't exactly happy when Elise and I ran off to get married, but they accepted it and welcomed me into their home. Mr. Pinera put me through mortuary school. When I graduated, he gave me a job. He and Mrs. Pinera treated me kindly and with respect. They loved Elise very much, and she loved them. They helped build a great business that they put their hearts and souls into. They were good, caring, honest people that I was proud to call my family. They are loved, and they will be missed."

Dennis wiped a tear from his eye and walked back to his chair. Elise was crying. The room was silent. A few moments later, Lou stood up and announced that drinks and refreshments would be served in the lounge. Family members moved out of the parlor and headed for the lounge.

Before she could leave, Lou stopped Elise. "Could you and

Dennis meet me in my office in a few minutes? I have something I need to discuss with both of you."

"Okay," Elise said.

They said their goodbyes to Susan and Ron and headed to Lou's office. "We'll be home if you need to talk," Susan said to Elise.

Dennis took her hand, and they walked to the other end of the funeral home, where the offices were located. They expected to go up the stairs to the loft area above the offices. That was where Lou's office was located. But instead, they noticed that he had moved into Andrew Pinera's office. A large plaque on the door read "Louis Pinera, CEO." Her father's furniture, pictures, portrait, and personal items were all gone. Her uncle had cleared everything out and moved his furniture and personal items in.

Elise and Dennis sat in the chairs across from her uncle's large oak desk and waited silently. A few minutes later, Lou walked in carrying the two urns that held the remains of Elise's parents. He set them down on the desk in front of her.

"I'm so sorry for your loss, Elise. I'm sure you have a special place you would like to spread your parents' ashes. Now, here's what I want to talk to both of you about. I realize the timing is not good for this news, but I assumed you would want to know right away. Your mother and father's wills left everything to the business. The fact of the matter was that your parents really didn't have any assets of their own. Everything was owned by the funeral home. Even their cars and house were purchased by the funeral home and leased back to them. The insurance policy that covered their house and the furnishings within it was owned by the funeral home. There was some investment money and money in their bank account, but I'm afraid your parents had a rather large loan from the funeral home that will need to be paid back from those proceeds. In short, there isn't anything in their estate. If you were expecting an inheritance, there won't be any. However, I want both of you to know that your positions at the funeral home are secure and that your salaries will not be altered in any way. My brother was very generous with the salaries he paid. We may need to adjust those salaries for some members of the staff, but you have my word that we will honor the salaries your father gave both of you if you should decide to continue your employment with us."

Elise looked dumbfounded. Dennis sensed anger building up inside her. She didn't speak. She simply stood up, took one of the urns, handed the other to Dennis, and walked out of the office without saying a word. Dennis stood and shook Lou's hand and said, "Thank you, Mr. Pinera. We both plan to continue working here. My wife is distraught over the loss of her parents. I would appreciate it if you could give her a few more days off. I'm sure she'll be fine and ready to come back to work after a little rest."

"Absolutely, Dennis. Why don't you have Elise take a week off? She can start back to work a week from tomorrow," Lou said with a forced smile on his face. "But Dennis, the week off applies only to your wife. I need you back to work tomorrow night."

"Yes, sir. I understand."

Dennis left the office and followed Elise down the hallway toward the parking lot. He found her standing just outside the lounge, a few steps from the front door.

He could hear laughing. Liquor was flowing in the lounge. Food was abundant. People were socializing like it was a party. Elise looked disgusted at what she saw inside. It was like a celebration, certainly not the way she expected her family members to act after the memorial service for her parents. Elise shook her head and walked on, out the door to the car, Dennis following. Inside the car, with only Dennis to witness her, she lost control. She screamed. She cried. She pounded the dashboard with her fist. She was inconsolable.

When she had settled down, Dennis drove them home. Elise withdrew from life for several days. She was depressed. She slept. She cried. She didn't eat. Dennis didn't leave her side, except when he had to go to work. On those nights, his mother stayed at the house to keep an eye on her daughter-in-law. Her doctor prescribed antidepressants for her, but she refused to take them. Dennis even asked the local parish priest to stop by to talk to her. He did, but it didn't seem to help.

What finally pulled her out of depression were the two pieces of news that came a few days later. The fire marshal ruled that the explosion and fire that erupted at the Pinera residence was caused by a gas leak that ignited in the kitchen. Later that same day, the coroner's office ruled the cause of her parents' deaths as "undetermined." That was odd since it seemed obvious that they had died in the explosion and fire. Elise's depression was replaced with anger. She was convinced her parents had been murdered. She was convinced that her uncle was involved.

"The only gas appliance in the kitchen was the stove, and my parents never used it. Janie did all the cooking, and she wasn't home that night. There is something bad going on at the funeral home. My parents must have found out about it and confronted Lou. They probably threatened to go to the police or expose what was going on. They must have been murdered because of that. You need to find out what is going on, Dennis. You just have to."

Even as crazy as she sounded, there was logic in what she was saying. Dennis knew that. He hadn't told his wife about the recent special orders or the visits from Lou and the stranger. He hadn't told his wife about the sudden increase in the cremation business since her parents had died. He didn't want to worry her. But he couldn't help but think that his in-law's deaths and the strange occurrences at the crematorium had something in common.

Dennis took Elise in his arms, hugged her tightly, and said, "Promise me that you won't tell anyone you suspect your parents were murdered. I will do my best to find out what is going on in the funeral home, but I need to know you won't say anything to anybody. If your parents were murdered or if something illegal is going on at the funeral home, you could be in danger if they discover you suspect something. So promise me that you won't say a word."

"I promise, Dennis."

"Elise, there are some things I need to discuss with you."

"What is it, Dennis?" she asked with a concerned look on her face.

"I've put off telling you about some things going on at work because you've been dealing with so much lately. I didn't want to add any more stress to what you are already dealing with."

"Just tell me, Dennis. After today, I think I need to hear whatever you have to say."

"There have been some strange things going on in the crematorium. Our business is picking up, but not in a normal way. Most of the increase in business is from Lou's contract with the city and from special orders. You remember me telling you about the special orders, right?"

"Yes, I remember. But you didn't think there was anything terribly unusual about them before."

"Yes, but that was when we only received them every so

often. Lately, they have been in the refrigeration room almost every night, sometimes two or three a night. But that's not the strangest thing. The strangest thing is the condition the bodies are in when they arrive. They show obvious signs of trauma. Some have bullet holes. They are not cleaned or prepped like required for a lawful cremation. Honey, I think most of the corpses we receive as special orders have been murdered."

"Oh, God, Dennis. You've got to go to the police."

"Elise, I wish that I could. But I think that would put both of us in danger. I need to tell you everything."

Elise began to tear up. "I think I'd better sit down. Can I have a glass of wine?"

Dennis poured her a glass of wine, then poured himself one and sat down beside her. After taking a couple of sips, he opened up to her about everything.

"At Lou's staff meeting the other day, he introduced a new partner. His name is Joseph Cuneo. I googled him. His business is importing and exporting. He has never been in the funeral business before. There is something scary about him. He looks like he could be a paid assassin or a member of the mob. The look he gave me sent chills down my back. Something's not right about that partnership. I don't know what he is bringing to the table that is going to benefit the funeral home, but I'm willing to bet that whatever it is, it's illegal. Elise, Lou called me into his office after the staff meeting, but he wasn't there. The only people in the room were Joseph Cuneo and his son Michael. Cuneo told me that they had plans to build a second crematorium with two additional cremation furnaces, enough to handle twelve bodies in an eight-hour shift. Elise, I doubt that many cremations are done in all of Kansas City in one average day. Then he told me he wants me to train his son, Michael, to do the entire cremation process. The thing is, he admitted that Michael doesn't have a funeral director's license. Therefore, it is illegal for him to be doing cremations. That means I would need to sign all the paperwork. It also means that if he gets caught, I could go to jail."

"No, you can't do that. You need to go to the police, or you need to quit," Elise said with a tone of desperation in her voice. "We'll both quit. We've got a little money in savings. We can find other jobs."

"Elise, slow down. It's not that easy. Whoever your uncle has gotten mixed up with are the type of people that wouldn't think twice about hurting us if we got in their way. Honey, remember when you nearly drowned in the bathtub? It was probably an accident. But what I didn't tell you is that someone was in the house before I got home that morning. Someone took the time to circle your parents' obituary notice in the paper and make a cup of coffee in our breakfast room."

"Oh, God," Elise yelled with tears rolling down her face.

"I don't know what is going on, but I'm not about to put you in any danger."

"What are you going to do, Dennis?"

"I'm not going to do anything right now. I want the new partner to think I'm a loyal employee. I'm going to do exactly what he asks of me until I can come up with a safe way for both of us to get out. They want me to train an unlicensed person. I will do what they want. I should be fine, legally, as long as I do all the work and he just observes. That will buy us some time."

"Okay. What do you want me to do?"

"Take a week off work. Your uncle said that was okay. Hopefully, I'll have a solution by then. Just please, don't say anything about what I've told you to anybody, even my parents. Anybody you tell could be in danger, too."

"Okay. Dennis, I'm scared. I don't know if I can stay in this house after what you told me."

"Elise, I think it would be a good idea for you to stay with my parents. They will look after you."

"Aren't you coming with me, Dennis?"

"No. I think that I need to stay here and keep an eye on the house. Besides, Hillary and Teddy will need to be taken care of. I'll have dinner with you every night, though, and we can talk whenever you want. Hopefully, this will only last for a week or so."

Elise protested, but she finally admitted Dennis was right. She packed her bags, and an hour later, Dennis drove her to his parents' house. He told them he would feel more comfortable if she stayed with them for a few days while he got some work done at the crematorium. They were happy to help.

On the way back to his car to get his wife's luggage, his father followed him.

"What's going on, son? I don't buy that you feel your wife would be more comfortable here. Tell me what is going on."

"I can't, Dad. Please trust me. I've got everything under control. I'll just feel better if you and Mom keep an eye on Elise for a few days."

"Okay. But know that you can talk to me about anything. If you or Elise are in trouble, I know I can help."

"Thanks, Dad. I appreciate that."

That evening they ate dinner as a family. Afterward, Dennis kissed Elise goodbye and headed back to their house. There were a few things that he needed to take care of before he went to work—feed Hillary and Teddy, replace the lights on the front porch, check the locks and deadbolts on the doors. Then he placed a video recorder on a bookshelf in the living room. He pointed it toward the front door, turned it on, and concealed it between two large books on the top shelf of the bookcase. Before leaving the house, he checked the windows to make sure they were locked and checked to make sure the screens were on all the windows. When he was satisfied that the house was secured, he closed the bedroom and bathroom doors and placed the dog beds in the living room. There was one thing that had bothered him about the day Elise had almost drowned. Someone had been in the house that morning. He was sure of it. But the dogs didn't bark. Or if they did, Elise didn't remember hearing them. That seemed odd to Dennis. Hillary and Teddy barked at every sound. They would normally go crazy barking when the doorbell rang, or a stranger came into the yard.

Why didn't they bark? Dennis thought to himself. He couldn't remember. Where were the dogs when he entered the house that morning? They always greeted him when he arrived home. He was so concerned about Elise that he couldn't remember if he'd seen the dogs that morning.

Dennis rubbed Hillary and Teddy's bellies. Both dogs loved that. They usually slept in the bedroom with Elise when Dennis was at work. She would not be home tonight, and the dogs would be by themselves. Dennis wanted them to stay in the living room that night. If anyone came to the door, they would start barking, and hopefully, the stranger would leave. He brought the dog's food dish and water dish into the living room next to their beds, petted them one more time, and then left the house, locking it behind him.

He got into his car, backed out of the driveway, and headed to work. A hundred yards down the block, a chill ran through his body. There was a car, a large, newer model black car, parked a few houses down the road. Inside was a man, a large man, who lowered his head as Dennis drove past. Dennis watched the car in his rearview mirror until the car was out of sight.

   It's probably nothing, he thought. But his gut was telling him otherwise.

CHAPTER 8
GROWTH PAINS IN THE CREMATORIUM

When Dennis arrived at the crematorium that night, two cars were in the parking lot, and the lights were on. He walked in and heard laughter coming from the cremation room. Sitting on two chairs were Joseph Cuneo and his son, Michael.

"Dennis, it's about time you showed up," Mr. Cuneo said when he saw him enter the room. "What time do you normally come to work?"

"My shift doesn't start until eleven. So I normally get here about fifteen minutes early."

Cuneo was wearing a three-piece, black pin-striped suit with a gold silk tie. He looked like he'd just come from a party, and from the smell of his breath and the loud tone of his voice, Dennis figured he must have been celebrating for several hours.

"Well," he said to Dennis. "You've got five bodies to cremate tonight, and that's going to be a slow night from now on. You better start coming in a couple of hours earlier."

"It won't do any good, Mr. Cuneo. The city ordinance

only allows us to operate the crematorium from 11 p.m. thru 7 a.m. It doesn't matter how early I come to work. We can't start cremating until eleven."

Dennis watched Joseph Cuneo's face turn a deep shade of red. His anger moved from his neck to his hairline in a matter of seconds. "We'll see about that. No damn city ordinance is going to slow our business. Until we get more cremation furnaces built, we're going to have a lot of bodies to burn in the one cremation furnace we have. Dennis, I don't give a damn how you do it, but you are going to cremate every body we put in your refrigeration room. Do you understand?"

"Yes, sir. I understand."

Dennis wanted to tell him there was just no way to completely cremate more than four or five bodies in the eight hours a night that the city ordinance allowed the cremation furnace to operate. He wanted to tell him, but he didn't. Joseph Cuneo was drunk, and he was angry. There was no way to have a rational conversation with him. Dennis had the feeling that not too many people had ever dared to tell him "no." He was used to getting his way and damn any law or obstacle that stood between him and what he wanted.

After getting an assurance that Dennis would do what he wanted, Cuneo's face softened. The red in his face began to disappear. "Dennis, I want you to teach Michael everything about this business. He'll be supervising a new crew to assist you when the additional cremation furnaces are operational."

Dennis nodded in agreement. Michael was thinner and a good six inches taller than his father. He was less intimidating too and dressed more befitting of an employee working the night shift at a crematorium in blue jeans and a sweatshirt.

"I look forward to working with you, Dennis," he said

with a broad smile.

Dennis returned the smile. "Me too."

The smiles were not contagious. Cuneo still looked pissed. "Good, now get to work. You've got five bodies you need to take care of by morning, and I've got a party to get back to."

This was the first time that Dennis ever had someone else working with him in the crematorium. He walked into the refrigeration room and began his work, explaining every step of the process as he did it. Michael seemed bored, disinterested. Maybe it was the hours of work. The graveyard shift was difficult to get used to. Dennis remembered how challenging it was for him to stay awake and stay focused in the middle of the night when all his body wanted to do was sleep. He chalked Michael's inattentiveness up to his body trying to adjust to the unusual working hours.

Around three, Michael took his lunch break, fell asleep, and stayed asleep until Dennis woke him up at eight to go home. Dennis had cremated the five bodies but had to keep the furnace going until seven-thirty to complete his work. Even with that, he kept the cremation furnace at a higher temperature than he usually would and had to take a few shortcuts to complete his night's work on time. Five bodies was pushing the envelope of what he could cremate in an eight-hour time frame. He was thankful that Michael had fallen asleep. He was able to work faster without having someone standing over his shoulder that he had to explain every step to. Besides, he had taken shortcuts to finish his work that night that he would rather Michael not know about.

His drive home that morning provided him some time to think. The training of an unlicensed person in the crematorium was illegal. Building two additional cremation furnaces without the proper permits and staffing them with unlicensed workers was illegal. Granted, that hadn't happened yet, but that appeared to be Joseph Cuneo's plan. And, if Cuneo forced the cremation furnaces to run beyond or before the 11 p.m. thru 7 a.m. timeframe mandated by the city council, that would be illegal too.

Dennis had to do something. He was hopeful that Lou Pinera was not aware of what his new partner was doing and that Lou would set his partner straight. He needed to talk to Mr. Pinera. When he arrived home, nothing appeared to be out of order, he thought. The doors were locked. The dogs were in the living room where he had left them the night before. The windows all appeared closed and locked. The car with the man inside that he'd seen parked down the block as he left for work the night before must have had an innocent explanation. He hadn't checked the video camera he hid on the bookshelf at one end of the living room, which would record any activity at or near the front door. He would check it when he got back home. But he felt secure that no one was in the house while he was at work. Dennis fed the dogs, let them outside, and then phoned the funeral home. Lou had not arrived yet, but they expected him to arrive within the next hour.

Dennis hung up the phone, left the house, and drove to his parents' house, hoping to have breakfast with them and check on his wife. When he arrived, his wife and mother were in the kitchen, sipping coffee and talking.

Elise greeted him with a big smile and a kiss. "Hi, honey. How was work?"

"Fine, thanks. You seem happy."

"That's what a good night's sleep will do for you."

"Dennis, can I make you anything to eat?" his mother said, reaching in for a hug and kiss.

"No, I'm fine, Mom. Maybe just a cup of coffee? Where's Dad?"

"It's nearly nine. He left for work over an hour ago," she said.

"I guess I lost track of time. I had to stay at work a little longer than usual."

"Is everything okay?" Elise asked.

"Yes, fine. Just a busy night. I would like to talk to both of you, though. Do you have a few minutes?"

"Of course we do," said his mother.

They both sat at the breakfast table. Elise reached for his hand and held it gently. She knew something was wrong. Sometimes she seemed to know Dennis better than he knew himself.

"There are some things going on at the crematory that concerns me."

He then explained about Michael Cuneo and his father's plans to expand. "Much of what he has plans to do is illegal and could come back on me as well as the funeral home."

"What do you think you should do?" Elise said.

Before he could answer, his mother said, "I think you need to quit. You need to get out of there before you're forced to do something that could get you in trouble."

"Believe me, that is what I want to do. But I can't. This new partner of Lou's scares the hell out of me. I'm afraid of what he might do to me or Elise if I tried to leave."

"Then go to the police," his mother said.

"I've considered that. But he hasn't actually done anything illegal yet, nothing I can prove anyway. The police wouldn't be able to do anything, and if they talked to him, and they probably would, he would know I spoke to them. If he is as dangerous as I think he is, he might come after us."

"What about my uncle, Dennis? Can you go to him? Do you think he is aware of what his partner is up to?"

"I don't know, honey. I suspect he knows some of Cuneo's plans. But I don't know if he is aware of the laws he intends to break. Your uncle was never very involved with the operations of the funeral home. Your parents used to handle all of that. So I guess it is possible he has turned a lot of the operational decisions over to his partner and is oblivious to what Cuneo is doing."

"Maybe you should talk to him, honey," his wife said.

"I agree. I've already tried to call him this morning, but he wasn't in the office yet. I thought I would try again before I leave. Mom, is it okay if I use your phone?"

"Absolutely."

Dennis excused himself and called the funeral home. Erika Bell, Lou's girlfriend, answered the phone. "Pinera Family Funeral Home, Erika speaking. How may I help you?"

"Hello, Erika. This is Dennis Glenn. May I please speak to Lou?"

"Yes, just a second, Dennis. I'll get him for you."

"Thanks."

A few seconds later, Lou picked up the phone. "Hello, Dennis, how are you doing?"

"Just fine, sir."

"Great, and how's Elise?"

"She's doing much better, sir."

"Good. What can I do for you, Dennis?"

"I was wondering if you might have a few minutes to meet with me privately."

"Yes, of course. What's bothering you, son?"

"It's just some crematorium business that I need to talk to

you about, sir."

"Well, if it's crematorium business, you really need to talk to Joseph. I've given him control of the crematorium operations."

"This is something I can't talk to Mr. Cuneo about. I really need to speak to you."

"Okay, I'll be in the office the rest of the morning. Why don't you come over as soon as you can?"

"Thank you, sir. I'll be there in about twenty minutes."

Dennis kissed his wife and his mother goodbye, left the house, and entered the funeral home twenty-three minutes later. When he walked in, he noticed there were no visitations or funeral services scheduled that day. The funeral home had always posted a list of their services on a board at the entrance of the funeral home. It helped direct families to the correct parlor if an attendant wasn't available to assist them. There was nothing posted on the board.

He walked into the main reception area and down the hallway past the break room. There were six male employees sitting, talking, and drinking coffee. Dennis didn't recognize any of them—they weren't Pinera family members. He was sure of that. *They must be new employees brought in by Joseph Cuneo*, he thought. As he stopped and looked into the break room, one of the men noticed him. *Damn. I hope they don't know me*, he said to himself. He sure as hell didn't need someone telling Cuneo that he was in the funeral home. In hindsight, Dennis wished he had asked Lou to meet him outside the funeral home. Now there was a chance that Cuneo could find out about their meeting.

As he passed through the main portion of the funeral home, he saw Erika sitting at the reception desk outside of Lou's office, working a jigsaw puzzle and drinking a cup of coffee. She was more conservatively dressed than he remembered her from the last party at the Pinera house. *Lou must have talked to her about the proper attire for a funeral home*, Dennis thought to himself. Still, even conservatively dressed, she was gorgeous. In her mid-twenties, she looked like a model — thin, with long shapely legs and thick, firm breasts that stretched her silky white blouse, taxing the workload of the buttons that kept the blouse together. Dennis noticed another thing too. On her ring finger was a huge diamond ring — an engagement ring, Dennis assumed. No one had told him that Lou and Erika were engaged.

"Hello, Dennis. How are you?"

"Fine, Erika. Thanks for asking. I guess congratulations are in order," Dennis said.

"What for?" Erika asked.

"The engagement ring on your finger," Dennis said. "I assume that is from Mr. Pinera."

"Yes, he finally popped the question," she said gushingly. "We're flying to Vegas next month to get married."

"That's great. I'm so happy for both of you."

"Thanks, Dennis. You can go right into Lou's office. He is waiting for you."

Lou's door was open. He stood up to shake his hand when Dennis walked in. "Hello, Dennis. It's good to see you. How is Elise doing?"

"She fine, thanks. Congratulations on your engagement."

"Thanks, Dennis. Not too many people know about it yet. But the way she flashes that engagement ring around, everyone will know soon enough. What can I do for you, Dennis?"

"There is something I wanted to talk with you about. I'm afraid it is rather sensitive. Do you mind if I close the door?"

"No, go ahead."

Dennis turned and closed the office door, then turned

back to Lou. The smile that had been on Lou's face when he first walked in had disappeared, replaced with a more serious look. Dennis sat down in the chair across from Lou, who sat down too. He crossed his arms and sat back in the chair. Dennis leaned forward and put his hands on the desk.

"Mr. Pinera, there are some things going on in the crematorium that I think you need to know about."

"I'm listening, Dennis. What is it?"

"I'm not sure that Mr. Cuneo fully understands the crematorium business or the laws that regulate it."

"Dennis, you are probably right. He hasn't been in the funeral business before. He's excited about the growth potential and has big plans for expansion. If he doesn't fully understand the business, it's your job to educate him. Dennis, I don't understand the purpose of this meeting. If you have issues with the plans that Joseph wants to implement in the crematorium, you need to discuss them with him. I already told you that he has operational control of that end of the business."

"Yes, sir, I know. But quite frankly, Mr. Cuneo doesn't seem to be very receptive to what I have to say."

"Damn it, Dennis. That's your problem, not mine," Lou said, showing his impatience with the direction the conversation was going.

"Sir, with all respect, it may become your problem. Some of his directives are moving toward breaking the law, and if he does, the funeral home and you and I are going to pay the price. I'm only trying to look out for our best interest and that of the family business."

"Okay, tell me what is going on that concerns you so much." Pinera's tone seemed to soften just a bit.

"Well, for one thing, he wants me to train his son, Michael, to do cremations."

"What's wrong with that? It seems like a reasonable request."

"Michael doesn't have a funeral director's license. If he gets caught working in the crematorium, I'll lose my license, and the funeral home will get fined."

"I see. But tell me, Dennis—when was the last time the board inspected the crematorium during the graveyard shift?"

"Not since I've been here, sir. The annual inspections have always been scheduled during the regular business hours so far. But sir, all it takes is one time. If the board gets a complaint or if someone tells them about an unlicensed employee, they could easily make a surprise visit."

Lou crossed his arms again and sat back in his chair. He had a stern look on his face when he spoke. "Who is going to call the board, Dennis? Only you, I, Joseph Cuneo, and his son know that he is unlicensed and working there. Are you threatening to tell the board, Dennis?"

"No, sir. I would never do that. Besides, I would be liable, too, since I'm the one training him."

"All right, what else is it that concerns you, Dennis?"

"The city ordinance states that we can only operate the cremation furnaces from 11 p.m. to 7 a.m. But Mr. Cuneo wants me to extend the operation of those furnaces outside of that eight-hour period."

"What's the matter, Dennis? Can't you get your work done in eight hours?"

"I could, and I can if we have no more than four bodies to cremate during that eight hours. But last night, there were five, and Mr. Cuneo expects that to increase."

Lou stood up. Dennis could almost see the steam of anger

shooting off his face. "Goddammit, Dennis. Do you want me to tell him to send some of the bodies back? The man is doing exactly what I hoped. He is bringing us additional business. I'm not going to tell him to stop or to slow down because you can't keep up with the workload. I don't give a fuck what you need to do, but get the work done and stop bothering me about these petty things. Next time, work it out with Mr. Cuneo. Now get the fuck out of my office!"

Dennis stood up and walked out in shock. He hadn't expected that kind of reaction from Mr. Pinera. *This is his business. He should be concerned if someone is doing something that could jeopardize it*, he thought.

Dennis got in the car and drove away but didn't go home. Instead, he went to a bar. Dennis needed to settle his nerves. In all his years, he had never been screamed at like that before. Dennis needed to think. His first inclination was to write a resignation letter. That's what he wanted to do. He could find another job. Elise could find another job, too. That wasn't the problem. The problem was Joseph Cuneo. Dennis was afraid of what he might do if he tried to leave the business. Dennis was afraid of him. His hands were shaking as he lifted the first frosty mug of beer to his lips. Dennis wasn't much of a drinker and could not remember being drunk—maybe a little tipsy, but never drunk. Three drinks in one evening was the most he had ever had, and that was a New Year's Eve party when he consumed the drinks over a five-hour time frame.

The beer came. It was a draft beer served in a frosted mug and went down smooth, so he ordered a second. He grabbed a pen from his shirt pocket, reached for his bar napkin, and began writing down his options.

Quit.

Go to the police

Keep working until I can find a safe way out of the business.

Then, beside the options, he wrote down the possible consequences of each action:

Quit. Joseph Cuneo would be upset. He might decide to hurt me or Elise.

Or worse than that.

2. Go to the police. I have no evidence. They might not believe me. They would contact Lou Pinera and Joseph Cuneo. Mine and Elise's lives might be in danger.

3.Keep working. The safe choice. Joseph Cuneo needs me. He wouldn't hurt me unless he thinks I am going to cause trouble.

Dennis finished the second beer and ordered a third one. He was starting to relax.

The third option made the most sense. As long as he did what he was told, didn't cause any waves, and acted like he was on board with whatever Mr. Cuneo wanted, he figured he and Elise would be safe. The third option would protect his family now and would buy him time to find a way out.

Dennis reached for his beer. Three beers were his limit. After this one, he'd go home. Maybe the beer would relax him and help him sleep. He took his first sip from the third beer when a fresh beer was placed in front of him. Dennis lifted his head to see who put the beer down. It was Joseph Cuneo.

CHAPTER 9
SECRETS

Cuneo took the seat next to Dennis at the bar. He didn't say a word. Dennis moved his hand to hide the bar napkin with his notes, but Cuneo took it first. He sat there silently, reading Dennis's notes on the napkin. Fear ran through Dennis's bones. He forced himself to watch Cuneo's face. *He wouldn't dare do anything to me while I am in the bar. There are a dozen witnesses."*

Then he saw a small smile come over Cuneo's face. He shook his head slightly. Dennis waited for a look of anger to come over his face, but it never arrived. He just sat there, smiling and reading and re-reading Dennis's notes for several minutes. Then he took the napkin, folded it, and tucked it in his coat pocket.

"Dennis, which option did you pick?" he asked with a smile still on his face.

Dennis hesitated.

"It's a simple question, Dennis. But think carefully about how you answer. Your decision could have consequences that you would rather not face." The smile had disappeared from

Cuneo's face.

"I'll keep working and do exactly what you tell me."

"I thought you would, Dennis. It's really the only option that won't result in a lot of pain for you and your family. So finish your beer, Dennis. Let's take a ride together. There's something I want to show you."

Dennis didn't want to go, but he didn't have much of a choice. "Okay," he said. "But, my wife is expecting me home anytime now. She'll be worried if I'm not home by lunchtime."

"Oh, I think she'll be fine. I believe she is grocery shopping with your mother right now. How does she like staying with your parents?"

"You've been watching her?" Dennis asked nervously.

"That shouldn't surprise you, Dennis. Now, let's go for a ride."

They left the bar together, got into a large, black Mercedes, and drove away. Cuneo didn't say a word as he drove down the street, past the funeral home and into the downtown section of Prairie Village. Dennis sat still and didn't say a word either. He was scared. His body was shaking. Cuneo was crazy. The old man's eyes were dark and cold. Dennis thought of his wife, Elise, and his mom and dad and wondered if he'd see them again. Damn, if he'd just not written his thoughts down on that bar napkin.

The Mercedes turned onto several neighborhood streets. Dennis thought he knew where Cuneo was taking him. A few minutes later, the car pulled up in front of the burned-down Pinera Mansion. Outside the home, trucks were hauling away debris while tractors were leveling the landscape. As he parked, looking at the lot where a grand home once stood, Cuneo finally spoke.

"It's amazing to think that after such a tragedy, life goes on. Soon a new home will be built, and no one will remember the fire that destroyed the last home and claimed the lives of the people that lived in it. Don't you find that amazing, Dennis? It's the circle of life. People die. Homes get destroyed. But other people always take their place. New homes get built. When you stop and think about it, our lives are inconsequential. We must always be cognizant that our lives can end anytime. We must take care of what is most important to us now because we don't know what is going to happen tomorrow. Do you understand, Dennis?"

"I think so, sir."

"You love your family, don't you, Dennis?"

"Yes, very much."

"Would you say they are the most important part of your life?"

"Yes."

"And you would probably do whatever it takes to protect them, to keep them safe?"

"Yes, I would."

"Good. Now, let's get you back to your car. You'll want to get home right away. I'm afraid something has happened to your dogs, Hillary and Teddy. After you tend to them, you will probably want to call your wife to tell her that you love her. A wife likes to hear that, especially when you have bad news to tell her."

Cuneo dropped Dennis off next to his car and sped away. Dennis got in his car and hurried home. Tears were rolling down his cheeks, thinking about Hillary and Teddy. They were like children to him and Elise, members of the family. They were loved. He thought about how they would run and greet him when he arrived home. He thought about how they would lay next to him in his chair as he read the morning paper. He thought about how they loved to ride in the car with him or Elise when they ran errands. Both would lay at the foot of the bed with him when he slept. They did the same for Elise. They were like children, totally dependent on him and Elise, but so loving, so gentle. He pulled into the driveway, ran up the stairs onto the porch, unlocked the door, and tried to prepare himself for what was on the other side.

The lights were off. Hillary and Teddy were not in the living room. Their beds were there, their food and water bowls were there. He looked in the bedroom. They were not there. He looked in the bathroom. They were not there, either. Finally, he walked into the breakfast room. There was a mostly empty cup of coffee on the breakfast table. Next to it was a note. His body was shaking as he made his way to the breakfast table. He lifted the note and began to read it.

Dennis,
Your mom and I picked up Hillary and Teddy and took them to the park. We thought we would keep them today so you can get some rest. Surprised that you weren't home. Give me a call when you get in.
Love,
Elise

Dennis picked up the phone and called his mother's house. His mother picked up the phone. "Hello, Mom."

"Where have you been? Your wife is worried, and I was too."

"Sorry, Mom. I'll explain later. May I speak to Elise?"

"Yes, she is standing right here. Is everything okay?"

"Yes, it's fine, Mom. I'll talk to you at dinner."

"Okay, here's Elise."

"Honey, I'm sorry. I've got a lot to tell you. But first, are Hillary and Teddy okay?"

"Yes, of course, didn't you get my note? I left it on the breakfast table."

"Yes, I got it. I was just worried when I got home, and they were gone."

"They are fine. But where have you been? Did the meeting with Lou last all morning?"

"No, the meeting was short. But I had an encounter with Joseph Cuneo that we need to talk about."

"Really? Are you okay? Do you still have a job?"

"Yes, I'm fine. I'll tell you about everything tonight, after dinner. Right now, I just need to get a little sleep. I'll see you tonight. I love you."

"I love you too. Get some rest."

Dennis hung up and walked into the living room. It had been a day since he'd checked the video recording. He pulled the video camera off the bookshelf. The recorder had stopped. The memory card had run out of space. Dennis figured it recorded for about twelve hours, so it would have run out of memory around 10 a.m. When he removed the memory card and put a new memory card in, he didn't turn the video recorder on. It only had about twelve hours of recording time, and he would turn it on before he left for work that night.

Dennis thought about playing the video but he was exhausted, so he went to bed instead, deciding to play the recording when he got back from dinner. A quick shower, a couple of aspirin for the headache he had, and Dennis fell into bed. He slept soundly for the next three hours until the alarm woke him up at five-thirty.

Rubbing the sleep from his eyes, he dressed and then drove to his parents' house, arriving at a few minutes past six. Hillary and Teddy greeted him at the door. That brought a smile to his face. Elise was right behind the dogs. She greeted him at the door with a hug and kiss. "What's going on, Dennis?"

"Is Dad home?"

"Yes, he's at the dinner table."

"Good, I need to talk to all of you."

Dennis walked to the dinner table, gave his mother a hug and kiss, and asked everyone to sit down.

"I'm afraid I have some bad news," he said. "I don't want to scare anybody, but the fact is that we may all be in danger."

"What's happened, son?" his father asked.

"I was threatened—we were threatened by Lou Pinera's partner, Joseph Cuneo. He is a dangerous man, maybe even a psychopath. He or someone associated with him has been watching us. He knew that Mom and Elise picked up the dogs today. He knew that you took them to the dog park. He knew when you went to the grocery store, and he knew when you came home. He knows that I suspect him of doing something illegal. He knows that I was considering going to the police."

"Oh God, Dennis. What does he want?"

"He wants me to do exactly as he says. He wants me to be the frontman for illegal activities going on in the crematorium."

"Dennis, did you talk to my uncle? Did you tell him about what was going on?" Elise asked.

"Yes, I met with him this morning. I tried to tell him what was going on, but he didn't want to hear it. He told me to get out of his office. Elise, I think Lou knows exactly what is going on. I think he is involved in the illegal activities. There is something else, too. I don't think your parents' deaths were accidental."

"No. God, no!" Elise shouted, with tears beginning to roll down her face.

"I'm sorry, honey. But you need to know. Joseph Cuneo drove me to their house. He hinted to me that they were murdered. By the tone in his voice, by the look in his eyes, I knew he had murdered them."

"Why? What did they do or know that got them murdered?" his mother asked.

"I don't know. But I think it may have had something to do with the conversation you had with your parents about the unusual activities in the crematorium that I told you about. You said that your parents acted surprised, didn't you?

"Yes."

"You also told me your father rushed out of his office, presumably to talk to your uncle, right?"

"Yes, right."

"Elise, I think your parents were unaware of what was going on in the crematorium. I think your father confronted your uncle, and whatever conversation they had was what got your parents killed."

"No, that couldn't be. You weren't even sure that anything illegal was going on in the crematorium. You were only questioning the unusual state of some of the corpses and the special orders you were getting. That's all I told my parents about."

"But Elise, I wondered several times why Lou was giving instructions about operations in the crematorium. Your parents handled the funeral home operations. Your uncle never got involved in operations. He seemed only interested in managing the books. Do you think your father knew his brother was as involved as he was in the crematorium?"

Dennis didn't wait for his wife to answer. He had more that he wanted to say. "I think your parents were good, honest people. I think they were doing an admirable job running the funeral home. I don't think they ever did anything that would jeopardize their business or risk their reputation. Your conversation made your father realize that maybe his brother was doing something illegal. I think he confronted him, maybe even threatened to go to the police. I think your uncle, or maybe Joseph Cuneo, decided they needed to be murdered to keep them silent. Let me ask you this, Elise. Do you remember signing any authorization to cremate your parents' remains?"

"No. I didn't know I was supposed to sign anything. Everything happened so fast. My uncle just said my parents' remains were in no condition for viewing and that they needed to be cremated."

"Yes, I understand. But still, you were your parents' next of kin. So barring your parents designating their funeral wishes ahead of time, you were the one that should have made that decision. Did your parents have a funeral prearrangement contract?

"Not as far as I know. If they did, they never told me about it."

"If they did, your uncle should have told you that a cremation was your parents' wishes. Then he would have produced the signed contract. Without a signed pre-arrangement contract, the funeral home would have required a signed authorization from you to do the cremation."

"Dennis, why would he cremate my parents without my authorization?"

"I don't know. Maybe he was concerned you would want to have your parents buried. If they had been buried, there would be remains that could be dug up and re-examined. If your parents died of something other than the fire, he wouldn't want to chance remains being available for a future autopsy."

"Oh God, Dennis. If they killed my parents, then we could be next. We've got to go to the police."

"No, Elise. They are watching us. We don't even know who 'they' are. I'm certain your uncle is involved, and so is Joseph Cuneo, but there are probably others. There have to be others considering how extensively they are watching us."

Dennis put a hand on Elise's shoulder and looked at both his parents. "Besides, I think we are safe now, for a little while, anyway, as long as we don't go to the police. They need me right now. I am the only one that can operate the crematorium. I think I am being set up to take the fall if anything happens. They need me as long as they think they can trust me. As long as I do exactly what Cuneo tells me to do, they need to keep me around."

Ron Glenn stood up, an angry look on his face. "No, I'm not going to stand by and see my family threatened. I'm not going to sit still waiting for someone to come after us. I intend to do something. They are not going to intimidate us."

"Dad, no. I understand how you feel — I feel the same way. But you don't know how dangerous Cuneo is. We don't know what he is capable of, but if they did murder Elise's parents, just imagine. They won't just come after you or me. They will come after our entire family. So we need to fully understand what we are up against. I need time to find out what they are doing and what they intend to do. I need time to find out who is involved and who we can trust."

Ron Glenn sat back down. "I've got to do something. I can't just wait for someone to come after us. I've got a friend at Bendix whose son is in the security business. I'm going to talk to him about a security system for both our homes, and I'm going to buy a gun."

"No, Ron. You know how I feel about guns," Susan said.

"Honey, don't worry. I was in the army for six years. I know how to handle a gun. Dennis, you should get one too."

"No, Dad. But I would like to talk to your security expert. Mom and Dad, could you keep Elise and the dogs here for a few days? I'd feel safer with them here."

"Sure, son," said his mother.

It was nearly nine when they finished dinner. Dennis excused himself, gave his wife a hug and kiss, and headed back to the house. He wanted to check the tapes from last night's video recording before he had to leave for work.

When he arrived home, the lights were off on the porch and inside the house. It was light out when he left for his parent's house, and he'd forgotten to turn them on. There were no street lights near the house, and with the cloudy sky, the moon was not visible. It was completely dark. The headlights of Dennis's car provided the only light.

When he turned the car engine off, it was pitch black outside. He walked to the front door and got his house key out of his pocket. It was difficult to put the key in the lock without any light. He tried several times before finally unlocking the door. As he reached for the light switch, he saw a small dot of light coming from the other side of the living room. He couldn't make it out. It was about the size of the barrel of a pencil, pointing toward him. Dennis flipped on the light switch. What he saw sent shivers down his back. Sitting twelve feet in front of him on the couch was Joseph Cuneo. The light that Dennis had seen in the dark was the end of a lit cigar that he held in his right hand.

"Come in, Dennis. We need to talk."

Dennis walked into the house and shut the front door behind him. That's when he noticed the video camera sitting next to Cuneo on the couch — the same camera that Dennis had hidden on the bookshelf. After taking two steps into the room, a large, heavyset man caring a gun stepped out from the breakfast room. He had been hiding in the shadows. Dennis did not see him until he stepped forward.

"Sit down, Dennis," Cuneo ordered as he motioned to the chair sitting next to the couch. "We've got several things to talk about."

Dennis took a seat. The large man with the gun stood a few feet away, the gun pointed downward. Dennis hoped he didn't intend to use it.

Cuneo picked up the video recorder. "Where are the other memory cards?"

"There is only one," Dennis said. "It's in the top drawer of my desk in the bedroom. I haven't even looked."

"Max, go check the desk," he ordered the man with the gun.

Cuneo sat and silently waited for his associate to come back. A few minutes later, he walked back into the room and handed Cuneo the memory card. Then he put his gun away and took a position near the front door. He was an intimidating figure, well over six-foot tall and weighing around three hundred pounds, most of it muscle.

"I will assume the use of the video recorder was an error in judgement that you will not make again," he said, staring directly into Dennis's face. "Now, let's talk about the conversation you had with your wife and your parents a little earlier this evening."

"Okay, what do you want to know?"

"Did you tell them about our meeting today?"

"No. I wouldn't do that."

"Are you sure, Dennis? Max is kind of a human lie detector. He can read when someone is lying and when they are—well, let's just say Max gets a little angry."

"They asked me how my meeting with Lou went this morning. I told them he was not receptive. I told them he told me to work out any crematorium issues with you."

"Max, what do you think? Is the kid telling the truth?"

Max walked over to Dennis, looked him in the face, and then hit him in the gut. The force of the blow caused Dennis to double over and fall to the floor in pain. He gasped for breath. The blow knocked all the air out of him.

"Look at Max, Dennis. He needs to read your face."

Dennis coughed up a little blood on the carpet in front of him. Then, he turned his head and looked up at Max. "I'm not lying. That is all I told them."

Max looked at Dennis and then turned to Joseph Cuneo and nodded his head.

"Well, good news, Dennis. Max believes you are telling the truth. Max, set Dennis in his chair. I need to talk to him. Dennis, we've got a lot to discuss. But first, after finding your hidden video recorder, I feel the need to make a few suggestions. I know you are probably in a bit of pain now and will find it difficult to talk for a little while, so just nod, so I know you are in agreement with my suggestions. First, I would suggest that you do not try to videotape or record anything again. Do you agree?"

Dennis nodded his head.

"Second, I would suggest that you don't talk about me, the crematorium, or the Pinera family business to anyone, including, but not limited to your wife, your parents, your friends, or the police. Do you agree?"

Dennis nodded his head.

"Third, I suggest that you have your wife and your dogs come home. This is where they belong. Do you agree?"

Dennis nodded again.

"Fourth, I suggest that you don't try to run. By now, you should know that we have eyes on you and your family. Running would be a mistake. Do you agree?"

Dennis nodded.

"Good. Now that we are in full agreement let me tell you what I need from you. The contract we have with the city is going to require a considerable increase in the number of cremations we do. I don't need to tell you what a large homeless population we have in the city. The mayor wants to reduce that considerably. We are helping him with that effort. Of course, in an effort to move the homeless into shelters, we are discovering some that are too sickly to move. A considerable amount of those individuals will succumb to the harsh winter elements. The city council would prefer that we bury those individuals in unmarked graves, but you can imagine the cost of doing so. Cremation is much more profitable for us. Soon, I believe you will see a considerable increase in the number of bodies in your refrigeration room. Those bodies will need to be cremated. You will find the workload to be challenging. I have faith that you will find creative ways to get your work done and not create problems with our neighbors. Can I count on you to take care of things?"

"Yes, sir," Dennis answered.

"I knew I could. You'll have the help of Michael, of course. And we hope to have the other cremation furnaces operational by spring."

"Yes, sir."

"Also, the paperwork from the city for those bodies will

indicate a burial. I want you to sign the paperwork and do not mention anything about cremation on the disposition forms you sign. Do you understand?"

"Yes, sir."

"One last thing. Occasionally, you will receive bodies with a special red toe tag marked special order. Those bodies are to be done first, before any of your other work. They should be cremated based on the instructions you have been given before. Dennis, those bodies are to be done 'off the books.' There will be no paperwork with them. You are not to tell anyone about them. Their cremation remains are to be given to Michael. He will know what to do with them. Do you understand?"

"Yes, sir."

"Good. Well, Max. I think we should go so Dennis can get ready for work. Have a good night, Dennis. I believe it's going to be a busy evening for you."

After they left, Dennis pushed himself out of the chair. Moving was painful. He could not stand all the way up. It felt like his ribs were damaged from that blow to the stomach. He moved slowly to the front door and locked it. *How did they get into the house?*

The back door leading to the yard was locked. All the windows were closed, and the screens were on them. Dennis had no idea how they got into the house. It didn't matter. Obviously, if they wanted in, they would find a way. He went into the bathroom, took his shirt off, and examined his stomach. There was a large red mark where he had been hit. His ribs were sore but didn't appear to be broken. He took a couple of pain pills, changed clothes, and headed to work.

Michael was already there when Dennis arrived at the crematorium. There were seven bodies in the refrigeration room, all city contracted pick-ups. Just as Cuneo had said, the paperwork for each of the seven bodies indicated that the bodies would be buried. Dennis knew when he signed the paperwork, he would be verifying that all the bodies were buried. He would be breaking the law. But he did not have any choice.

His bosses would pocket a nice profit by cremating the bodies rather than burying them. No doubt, the city was paying for a casket, preparation, and burial. Dennis figured the funeral home was making several hundred, maybe even a thousand dollars for everybody cremated instead of burying. Still, Dennis was curious why there were so many bodies. There couldn't possibly be that many unclaimed bodies in Kansas City. Something else was going on, something worth killing to protect. Then, there was the question of the special order bodies that showed up from time to time in the crematorium. Evidence of murder was easily destroyed in the cremation process. Dennis had seen those bodies. Many had died from traumatic injuries. Dennis was certain that foul play was involved. He was also certain that Lou and Cuneo were benefiting financially from those bodies. The relationship between the two partners was tight. Dennis sensed that Cuneo was calling the shots, and Lou was following his lead.

Dennis speculated that maybe Lou had gotten in over his head. He liked to spend money. He liked to gamble. He liked to party. Maybe he'd spent beyond his means and used funeral home money to pay for his lifestyle. The funeral home's business had been level for some time, yet the spending of its owners seemed to increase. Lou kept the books for the funeral home. Dennis doubted if the funeral home was in trouble that anyone other than Lou would be aware of it.

He speculated that Elise's parents were murdered because they discovered something that Lou was doing. The relationship between him and Cuneo was an odd one. Neither Cuneo nor any member of his family had any funeral home experience. None of their family members even had a funeral director's license. So there had to be some other reason for the partnership. Dennis guessed that reason was money. But the money they made from the city contract wouldn't be enough to justify the partnership. Dennis was sure the special order cremations must be another reason for the odd partnership. But how were they making money off of them? Was it possible those bodies were contract killings? There was speculation that Cuneo was involved in the mob. Maybe he was profiting from the disposal of bodies that the mob was bringing him. Cremation was the perfect way to dispose of evidence. But the ideas that ran through Dennis's mind were purely speculation. He had no proof.

One thing was certain. Dennis and his family were in danger—not today, not tomorrow, but in the near future. It would end at some point, and it would end badly. He just didn't know when. He had to find a way to turn it around to protect his family. He just didn't know how.

Right now, he had seven bodies to cremate and less than eight hours to get the work done. "One problem at a time," he said to himself. Michael Cuneo was sound asleep at the desk when Dennis walked in. He woke him up, and they began the work.

"Mike, why don't you just watch me tonight while I get the cremations started? We have a lot of work to do in a short amount of time tonight."

"Sounds good to me, boss," he said, still yawning from his nap.

Every one of the bodies was wrapped in a plastic body bag. Dennis unzipped each one and pulled the bodies out—four males, three females, varying in age. Dennis noticed that every one of the bodies had both their eyes wide open. He had seen that before with Gloria Jean Booker and a few of the special orders. It was rare. One of his instructors in mortuary school had told him once that when a corpse's eyes were open, it was a sign that they had died suddenly, from a traumatic cause. It was unusual to get any bodies that had both eyes fully opened – it was nearly statistically impossible to get seven bodies with open eyes in one night. Dennis moved to within a few inches of a corpse's face. She was a young lady, not more than thirty, wearing raggedy clothes. She had emerald colored eyes. Her pupils were large and looked dilated. The eyes almost glowed and appeared watery. Dennis took his index finger and gently touched her eye. It was dry, not moist like it appeared. He stared directly into it. It was as if she were trying to tell him something. "What are you trying to say?" Dennis asked softly. After a minute or so, Dennis moved back to the desk. He needed to get started. Seven bodies to cremate in eight hours. It was an impossible task if he cremated them properly.

There was only one way that Dennis could think of to cremate seven bodies in eight hours. He would need to cremate multiple bodies at one time. That would mean their ashes would be mixed, but since nobody was claiming the remains anyway, it wouldn't matter. Weight could be an issue. Dennis was careful to separate the bodies into two groups, with both groups weighing about the same. To expedite the cremation process, Dennis instructed Michael to cut the arms and legs off from the torsos of the four bodies in the second group. That would help the bodies burn faster. It would take Michael at least an hour to cut up the remains, so Dennis moved the three bodies he had separated into the first group into the cremation chamber. He would cremate their whole bodies. Their combined weight was nearly five hundred pounds, too heavy for Dennis to lift into the cremation furnace by himself, so he got Michael to help. Once they were inside the furnace, he closed the steel door and waited. He would need to mash bones down several times during the process to dissolve everything into ashes.

Meanwhile, Michael put on protective clothing and began to saw the bodies into more manageable pieces. Dennis could hear him gagging from the other room. "This will be a night that Mike will not forget," he told himself.

It took nearly three hours for the first group of bodies to fully cremate. During that time, Dennis mashed larger bones into smaller pieces with his steel mallet, then mixed the bones in with the ashes. His arms ached from the work, and he had soaked his clothes from the sweat that resulted from the intense heat of the furnace. Even with his protective gear on, the constant opening of the furnace door to mash bones caused the heat to penetrate his suit, resulting in constant sweating.

Dennis and Mike loaded the second group of body parts into the furnace. Then it was time to separate the ashes from the first group into three separate cardboard containers. Dennis thought it seemed unnecessary to do that since the bodies were unclaimed anyway, but those were the instructions his boss had given him—one cardboard container for each body.

The second group of corpses burned quicker than the first. Cutting up the bodies seemed to expedite the process. That would be one of Michael's jobs for future cremations. He didn't know it yet, but Dennis had decided it would become Michael's responsibility to prep the bodies for the cremation furnace. He would also clean the inside walls of the cremation furnace and wash down the floor in the refrigeration room after. Those were jobs that Dennis didn't have any desire to do. Delegating those jobs to Michael was the best benefit of being the boss. It might be the only benefit, considering what he had done that night was illegal. He was sick about it. He had committed at least two felonies. He knew he'd had no choice, but that didn't make what he had done that night any easier to swallow.

Dennis was traveling down a dead-end street at a high rate of speed. Death was the only way out if he continued down this road. He had to find a way to turn around before everything came crashing down.

CHAPTER 10
DAMNED IF YOU DO.
DAMNED IF YOU DON'T

Dennis drove home, watching the rearview mirror for any signs that he might be followed. He didn't notice anyone behind him. Three blocks from home, he stopped at a Quick Trip. He filled up with gas, got a breakfast sandwich and a cup of coffee, and walked to the payphone on the side of the building. Before dialing, he scanned the area around him for anyone that might be watching.

"Mom, hi, it's Dennis. I don't have much time. May I speak to Elise."

She turned the phone over to her. "Honey, what's the matter?"

"Elise, I need you and the dogs to come home tonight. I can't talk right now, so please don't ask any questions. Just pack your bags and come back home tonight. Okay?"

"All right, Dennis."

"I love you, honey."

"I love you too, Dennis."

He hung up, got in his car, and drove home. Dennis was exhausted. He'd barely gotten any sleep the night before. Stress from his busy night and from Joseph Cuneo's visit had his stomach in knots. He took several antacid tablets and sat down at the breakfast table to enjoy his breakfast sandwich and cup of coffee. He opened the newspaper to do some light reading while he ate. That's when an article on the front page of the Kansas City Star caught his attention.

Mayor forms task force to reduce homeless population

One of the members of that task force named in the article was Joseph Cuneo. Dennis felt a pain in his gut. *Is it possible that Joseph Cuneo is using the crematorium to reduce the homeless population in the city? Is it possible that he, or someone else, is ridding the city of their homeless by murdering them, a few at a time? And, if so, are both the mayor and Joseph Cuneo involved? That would explain the large increase in the number of bodies in the crematorium at night. But, if they are being murdered, how is it being done?* he thought. Dennis had not noticed any visible signs on the corpses. *Poison is the likely way they would have killed them. But what kind of poison?*

Then he remembered the bodies from the night before. Every one of the corpses had died with their eyes open. That was extremely unusual. Most people closed their eyes just before death. If the eyes remained open, it was usually after a traumatic, sudden death, one that was unexpected, one that the mind did not have time to prepare for. Last night's corpses had similarities to Gloria Jean Booker's death. There were no obvious signs of what caused their deaths. That was the same with Gloria's body. But, the biggest similarity was in their eyes. Just like Gloria Jean

Booker, the eyes of the bodies last night were all open. But, it wasn't just the fact that they were open. Their eyes were bright, shiny, almost glowing. They looked like they were trying to tell Dennis something. Perhaps they were trying to tell him how they died. "What did those eyes see in the last few seconds of their life?" Dennis said to himself. "Why did what they saw frighten them so much that they refused to close their eyes and accept their fate?"

Dennis thought he knew part of the answer. He was convinced those bodies were murdered. But he didn't know how and wasn't sure he knew why. He couldn't help but think that the city contract and the task force dedicated to eliminating the homeless population had something to do with it. He couldn't help but suspect that Cuneo and Pinera were involved in more than profiting from the contract.

Lou was a pawn. Dennis was convinced of that. He had been manipulated by Cuneo, maybe willingly, maybe not. Dennis wasn't sure. Maybe Lou got in over his head. Maybe, in an effort to save the family business, he enlisted the help of Cuneo. Dennis wasn't sure. But he did know that he and Elise and his parents were caught in the middle of whatever was going on. Pinera and Cuneo had Dennis by the balls. He was damned if he did and damned if he didn't. But, for now, he would do as he was told until he could find some way out.

Dennis was exhausted. He had barely slept in two days. He unplugged the telephone, pulled the shades down in the bedroom, and got into bed. He slept until the dogs jumped up in bed and woke him up a little after five. Elise was home. Hillary and Teddy were home. The dogs greeted him first with several licks in the face, a welcoming bark, and a flop on his belly. Elise came in after and gave him a big hug and kiss.

"Hi, honey. I hope you slept well," she said.

"I did. I'm glad you are home."

"You told me to come. What's up, Dennis?"

"Elise, I don't want to frighten you, but I think we are being watched, and I think someone is listening to our phone conversations. I think they are watching and listening to my parents, also."

"Dennis, we have to do something."

"Yes, I know. But right now, I don't know what we can do. Cuneo made it clear that he wants you and the dogs at home. I think he wants you here, so it's easier to keep an eye on you. We need to make him think we are going to do whatever he tells us. I think we are safe as long as he doesn't think we are trying to escape or contacting the police. We just need to try to live as normal a life as we can without bringing attention to us."

"What about your parents, Dennis? Your dad bought a gun today. He talked to a security company. They are coming out later this week to talk about setting up surveillance cameras and an alarm system."

"I think that would be a good idea for my parents. They should be safe as long as you and I cooperate. But I don't think a gun and added security will do us any good. We need to find a different solution."

That night Elise made lasagna with cheese garlic bread, and five olive salad. They drank glasses of Chianti. That was Dennis's favorite meal. They ate by candlelight and talked about better times. Both were trying to get their minds off today. The wine dulled the memories. It allowed them to think only of the love they had for each other. When the bottle was empty, Dennis took his wife's hand and walked her into the bedroom. He held her tight, kissed her softly, and they made love. It was slow. It was passionate. It was like their very first time. They watched each other's eyes as if this would be the last time. They saw each other's passion intensify with every movement of their bodies. They had made love many times before, but not like this. It was natural. It was genuine. It was intense and more pleasurable than any time before. They watched each other's eyes widen and roll back as they reached a climax at exactly the same time. Their love for each other had never been greater. They laid together still in the embrace of passion, unable to move and completely exhausted. Neither wanted that moment to end.

They were still laying on the bed, naked, holding each other, ten minutes later when the sound of the doorbell forced Dennis off his wife. He dressed quickly as the bell rang a second, then a third time. He rushed out of the room, closing the door behind him so Elise could finish getting dressed. Before he opened the door, Dennis glanced out the window to see who was ringing the doorbell. Standing on the porch were two men dressed in sports jackets. Dennis didn't recognize either of them.

He opened the door.

"Dennis Glenn?" one of the men asked.

"Yes"

"I'm Detective Jacks. This is Detective Gregory," he said, flashing a badge. "May we come in?"

"Yes, of course. What can I do for you, Detective?"

"Is your wife home, Mr. Glenn?" Detective Jacks asked.

"Yes, she is in the other room. Do you need to speak to her?"

"Yes, we need to speak to both of you."

"Okay, I'll get her. Would you gentlemen like to take a seat?"

Dennis walked to the bedroom. Opening the closed door,

he saw Elise standing just a few feet away, now dressed. From the look on her face, Dennis could tell that she had been listening to the conversation.

"Elise, two detectives are in our living room. Can you come out?"

"Yes, of course."

Elise walked into the living room with Dennis a few steps behind her. "Hello, I'm Elise Glenn," she said, holding out her hand to shake.

"I'm Detective Jacks," he said, "and this is Detective Gregory. We only need a few minutes of your time."

"Well, what can we do for you, Detectives?" Dennis asked.

"It's about the death of your parents, Mrs. Glenn. We have a few questions," Detective Jacks said.

"Okay, what can I help you with?" Elise asked.

"Mrs. Glenn, what I'm going to ask you might seem a little insensitive, but I need to ask."

"Go ahead, Detective."

"Do you know if either of your parents were depressed to the point that they may have considered suicide?" Detective Jacks asked.

Dennis put his arms around his wife. That was not a question either of them had expected to be asked.

"No, Detective. Neither of my parents was depressed, and neither would have considered suicide. That didn't happen. What a crazy thing to ask. They died from a gas explosion."

"Yes, Mrs. Glenn. That is right, but the strange thing is that the gas company did not discover any gas leaks. It appears that the gas stove in your parents' house was left on and ignited somehow. We are trying to determine if one of your parents did that by mistake or on purpose."

"Detective Jacks, there is a third explanation," Elise said, with her face seething with anger. "They could have been murdered."

Dennis grabbed his wife's hand with a tight hold in an attempt to get her to not say anything more.

"Yes, murder would be another explanation. But we have no evidence of that. Do you know something we don't, Mrs. Glenn?"

"Forgive my wife, Detectives. She has been through a lot. If you don't have any other questions for us tonight, I need to get ready for work and my wife needs to get some rest."

Detective Jacks smiled. "I understand. But I do need your wife to answer my question. Mrs. Glenn, do you know any reason someone would want to murder your parents?""

"No, I'm sorry, Detective. I guess I just got a little upset at your question."

"That's okay. Here's my card. If you think of anything, please give me a call." Both detectives stood and began to walk away when Detective Jacks stopped and turned to both of them. "I do have one more question for you. Were you aware that your uncle took out a two-million-dollar life insurance policy on both of your parents just two weeks before their deaths?"

"No, why would he do that?" Elise asked.

"Well, according to him, it was a business policy that would enable the funeral home to continue operation in the event of your parents' deaths. The odd thing is that the sole beneficiary of the death benefit was Lou Pinera."

Elise wanted to scream. She wanted to tell the detectives that she was convinced her uncle had murdered her parents. But she couldn't. The police could not protect her or her husband or her in-laws. She could only lower her head to shield her tears from the detective's eyes.

Elise and Dennis watched as the detectives walked to their car, got inside, and drove away. They were still standing at the front door when a stranger's car drove slowly down the street, stopping briefly in front of their house. It was dark outside and impossible to determine who was in the car, but when the driver rolled down the window and looked directly at them, Dennis recognized the person in the car. It was Max, the man that was in his house with Cuneo the night before, the man that beat him up and threatened him. He wanted Dennis to see him. He wanted Dennis to know that he was watching him.

***

Erika Bell left the funeral home at nine that evening carrying a briefcase, which contained evidence of criminal activity at the funeral home, taken from Lou Pinera's office. One week earlier, she'd found out about Lou's newest affair. She had suspected he was cheating on her for some time. He had asked her to marry him the last time she confronted him about an affair and promised to marry her in Las Vegas a week later. But that didn't happen. He postponed the trip because of business. The business turned out to be another lover. He began working later and later, coming home during the wee hours of the morning smelling like a brewery. He also smelled like another woman. One night after he fell asleep, she checked his phone. One number popped up a lot. She called the number, and a woman answered. That was all the evidence she needed.

Erika was a vengeful woman. She was also smart enough to know that her lover was involved in illegal activities and exactly where to find the evidence locked away in his safe—and she knew the combination. He gave it to her to unlock the safe when he needed some extra cash. Inside the safe were burial contracts from the city, the originals and the fake ones that Lou had forged to overcharge the city. Also inside the safe was a second set of books, which showed funeral home revenues that far exceeded actual business revenue.

That evening the funeral home did not have any visitations. Everyone left early, except the embalmer. But he was downstairs, far away from Pinera's office. About seven, when she was sure everyone was gone, Erika walked into Pinera's office and opened the safe. She carefully copied every bit of evidence, put the copies in her briefcase, put the originals back in the safe, turned out the lights, and left.

Three days before, Detective Jacks had paid her a visit at the funeral home. He wanted to talk to Lou, but he wasn't in. He left her his business card. She'd called him the night before and told him that she had evidence of criminal activity that involved her boyfriend. She promised to bring the evidence to the Prairie Village police department that night. Detective Jacks was waiting for her.

Erika Bell never showed up.

She made it as far as her car in the parking lot of the Pinera Family Funeral Home. A stranger was waiting for her. He grabbed her from behind and put a cloth soaked in chloroform over her mouth. She struggled for a few seconds before he pushed a needle into a vein in her neck. That ended her struggle, and she fell into his arms.

Her car was driven into a crime-infested area in the city. It was delivered to a "chop" shop, where parts were removed from it and what was left was destroyed at a local salvage yard.

***

Dennis entered the crematorium at ten-fifty that night. Mike Cuneo's car was in the parking lot, but the building was dark. *That's strange*, he thought. *Mike would need the lights on to do his preparation work.* Dennis turned on the lights to the entrance, walked to the cremation chamber, and flipped on those lights. The cremation furnace was not on. "Damn it," he said out loud. "Mike should have turned the furnace on already." Dennis turned it on and set the temperature at 1650 degrees. It would take at least thirty minutes to reach that temperature.

He walked toward the refrigeration room, turning the lights on as he went. Something seemed wrong. Dennis could sense it. The crematorium was cold, colder than normal. Cold chills ran down his body as he walked farther down the hallway. Dennis had the feeling he wasn't alone. He was afraid that Cuneo and his henchman, Max, might be waiting for him like they were the night before. Ten feet from the refrigeration room, Dennis could see that the door was partially open. "That's why it was so cold in the hallway," he said to himself. The lights were off in the refrigeration room, but the door was partially opened. Someone was either in there or had been in there recently.

"Mike, are you in there?" he yelled. There was no response. Dennis stopped just outside the door, listening for any movement, any noise coming from the room. He heard heavy breathing and a rocking sound coming from inside. "Mike, are you in there?" he yelled again. There was no response. He stepped inside just far enough to turn on the light, keeping his body weight on his back foot in case he needed to run.

When he flipped on the light switch, he saw Mike naked from the waist down on top of a corpse on the metal table at the back of the room. Dennis screamed, "Get off that body, you sick son-of-a-bitch." Mike did not move. Dennis ran up to him and pulled him by his shirt collar off the corpse. He fell backwards and landed face-up on the floor. His penis was erect, his love juice spilling down his leg. Dennis had pulled him off the body just as he climaxed.

"What the hell did you do that for?" he screamed at Dennis. "I should kick your fucking ass. Don't you ever disturb me when I'm in the middle of fucking somebody."

Dennis was pissed. "Don't ever fuck a corpse again. If I catch you doing it again, I'm going to cut your pecker off, you fucking pervert."

Mike jumped to his feet and pushed Dennis back against the wall. Then he punched him, twice in the stomach and once in the face. Dennis bent over in pain and fell to the floor.

"Let me tell you something, boss," Mike yelled back at Dennis while he stood over him. "You don't call the shots around here. My father does. You're damn lucky he even lets you live, considering some of the shit you've pulled. If you want to continue to live, I suggest you go along with whatever I want and whatever my father wants. You have no idea who you are messing with. So, next time I decide to relieve some stress on one of your corpses. I suggest you just walk away until I'm finished."

With that, Mike walked out of the refrigeration room and into the restroom to clean himself up and put on his pants.

Dennis stood up, wiped off his face and walked over to the only body in the refrigeration room that night. He knew her—it was Erika Bell. Dennis covered his mouth and ran a few feet to a mop bucket sitting in the corner of the room. He lifted it and vomited several times. Lou Pinera's girlfriend was laying completed naked, on her back with her legs spread. Her eyes were wide open, staring toward the ceiling. She had a red toe tag on her left foot. She was a special order.

Dennis walked out of the room for a few minutes to let his stomach settle. Mike was leaning over Erika's body when Dennis walked back into the refrigeration room.

"She was a good fuck," Mike said when he saw Dennis enter the room. "She's my first corpse fuck, you know. You've probably fucked several during your time in here," he said, looking directly at Dennis.

"You're disgusting," Dennis said.

"Come on, you can tell your buddy, Mike. How many cold bodies have you fucked?"

"None. I would never do something that twisted."

Mike smiled. "Well, I've got to tell you, buddy. Fucking a corpse is pretty fucking awesome. Especially when they look as good as Erika. Look at her, Dennis. She's gorgeous. Big, thick boobs with hard nipples, long, skinny legs, a face of an angel— and look at her cunt. It's shaved. It made my dick slide in so good. And you know what, boss? Her pussy was tight. I always wondered if death caused the pussy walls to contract, and you know what? I think it does. Look at her face, boss. Her make-up is on. It looks fresh. Her hair looks freshly brushed and styled. Her lips are coated in bright red lipstick. It's a little smudged now. I used her mouth before I put my dick in her pussy—damn near shot my load in her mouth. You know, Dennis, she looks like she was going out on a date just before she died. Do you think she was cheating on Lou?"

Before Dennis could respond, Mike answered his own question.

"No, I don't think she was cheating on Lou. I think she was going to cause trouble for the funeral home. I think she was going to meet with someone tonight and rat on Lou. I think she got exactly what she deserved."

Dennis didn't say anything. He knew Mike was threatening him. His dad probably found out that two detectives were at his house earlier that evening. What Mike had done that night was probably ordered by Joseph Cuneo. He wanted Dennis to be scared, to do exactly what he was told. Dennis also knew that if Cuneo wanted him dead, he would have killed him. He wouldn't have gone to the trouble of having his son put on this show. This was a warning, nothing more.

"Dennis, do you see how her eyes are wide open? Her pupils are large. The eyeballs appear to glow. They look wet. It looks like she is trying to tell me something, don't you think? Do you think she is trying to tell me how much she enjoyed fucking me? I think she wants more. It's a shame you didn't let me finish earlier. I think I left her unfulfilled. Why don't you get the fuck out of the room so I can finish what I started? I'll call you when I'm done."

Dennis wanted to kill him. He had never hated anyone as much as he hated Mike Cuneo at that moment. But there was nothing he could do. "Please, don't," he said. But it was no use. Dennis walked out of the refrigeration room, closing the door behind him.

Thirty minutes later, Mike walked out of the refrigeration room, fully dressed. He looked directly at Dennis. "I've had an exhausting night. I think I'll take off early. You don't mind taking care of our special order and cleaning up afterward, do you, Dennis?"

"No, I'll take care of everything."

"Good. And Dennis, if you want to have sloppy seconds with her, I'm sure she won't mind."

Dennis wheeled Erika into the cremation chamber. He opened the furnace door, lifted her body onto the steel shelf, and rolled her into the furnace. The flames exploded as they consumed her body. Dennis moved back to protect himself from the extreme heat. That's when he heard it. It sounded like a distant scream, a painful yell, so soft he could barely hear it. He looked down into the furnace. It seemed like the sound was coming from inside, but he saw nothing but flames. He heard nothing but the popping sound of flesh bubbling from the intense heat.

CHAPTER 11
CONFRONTING HIS DESTINY

Lou Pinera was awakened in the middle of the night by the doorbell and pounding on his door. He had been out partying until two and had just fallen asleep, still dressed. As soon as he arrived home, he just fell into his bed. His suit smelled like cigars and whiskey, which didn't help his pounding head. He staggered to his feet and stumbled to the front door. When he opened it, Joseph Cuneo and Max were standing there.

"Let's us in, Lou. I'm afraid I have some bad news for you," Cuneo said. "Damn, you smell like a distillery. How much whiskey did you put away last night?"

"I don't know. I lost count."

"Buddy, you need to get your act together. Be respectable. You're the owner of the most successful funeral home in Kansas City. People expect you to take care of them. What would they think if they knew you can't even take care of yourself? Max, go make Lou some coffee. He needs to sober up. Lou, sit down. Are you sober enough to understand what I'm about to tell you?"

"Yes."

"Good. I'm afraid your girlfriend, Erika, has had an unfortunate accident. You're going to need to forget about her. She won't be coming home."

"What? What happened to her?"

"Let's just say she was about to turn on you, Lou. She was about to cause a whole lot of trouble for you and me. She had to be dealt with."

"Fuck, you killed her?"

"Now, Lou, be careful what you say. Our partnership is important to me, but if I need to, I can always find another partner. You know, Lou, if you are going to involve your girlfriends in the business, you really shouldn't let them find out that you are fucking around on them. Women tend to get pissed about that. You were stupid, Lou. You gave her too much access to the business. I don't need a stupid partner. From now on, keep your dick in your pants and don't involve anyone else in our business. Do you understand?"

"Yes, but you didn't need to kill her."

Cuneo signaled to Max. He walked directly in front of Lou and hit him twice in the stomach. The blows sent Lou crashing to the floor, doubled over in pain.

"Don't ever tell me what to do. Don't ever question my actions. I pulled your ass out of the situation you were in. I paid off your gambling debts. I kept you from losing your business, and this is the thanks I get? You pathetic drunk. If you ever question me again, I'll kill you." Cuneo turned to Max. "Go get this asshole a cup of coffee. He needs to sober up."

Lou Pinera was a man of many vices. He had always counted on his brother, Anthony, to keep him grounded. But now, his vices had resulted in the deaths of his brother and sister-in-law. Lou never wanted to run the family business. Dealing with grieving families wasn't something he enjoyed. His brother had the empathetic qualities that suited him best for that job. Managing the books and purchasing merchandise was what he enjoyed. Still, he never viewed the funeral home as anything more than a job, as a place to go when he had no place better to be. It provided him an air of respectability. Lou had always considered himself the black sheep of the family, and as no one expected too much of him, he liked it that way. Lou didn't like the responsibility he shouldered now that his brother was dead. He hated himself for getting in this situation. His weaknesses were destroying his family. There was no one to turn to. There was no one that could get him out of the jam he had put himself in.

Damn, he wished he could turn back the clock. He would make different choices. But that was impossible. He would need to live with the consequences of his actions. But maybe, just maybe, he could correct some things in his life. He felt that he was at a fork in the road. If he went one way, it would be safe, but he would always be under Joseph Cuneo's control. But if he chose the other way, there would be risk, but he could still make something of his life. He decided that night to take the direction that provided him the chance to make something out of his life.

Lou didn't go back to sleep that night. Instead, he drank a pot of strong, black coffee. He showered and shaved and dressed in his favorite gray suit and took several aspirins for his headache and antacid for his stomach. He was in the funeral home at eight. He felt motivated for the first time since his brother died. He felt good, except for the hangover and the pain of his ribs where Max had hit him. Still, he was sober now and ready to take control of his funeral home.

But that wasn't going to happen. That became apparent

when he walked into his office. The safe had been removed. His accounting books were no longer there. Software pertaining to the company financial records had been removed. His computer was missing files. Then, he noticed the video cameras. There were two in his office, hanging from the wall in opposite corners. He was being watched. Just then, the door to his office opened, and an older, attractive brown-haired woman that he guessed was in her early forties was standing in the doorway.

"Hello, Mr. Pinera. Mr. Cuneo said you would be in this morning, but we didn't expect you so early. I'm Linda Collins, your new secretary. I understand your last secretary left rather abruptly. You won't have that problem with me. I've worked for Mr. Cuneo for almost ten years. I know how he likes things done. I'll help you get acclimated to the operation. Mr. Cuneo requested that I send you up to his office as soon as you came in. Can I get you any coffee?"

"No, I'm fine. Thanks."

Lou walked out of his office and up the steps to the second floor. That was where Cuneo's office was. On the ceiling leading up the stairs was another video camera. From it, whoever was watching would know whenever someone came up those stairs. The cameras were new. Lou was certain he would have noticed them before. At the top of the stairs was a door, also new. The second floor had always been open. The door was locked, so Lou knocked. A few seconds later, the door opened. Max was standing there.

"Hello, Mr. Pinera. Mr. Cuneo is expecting you. Please come in."

The entire second floor had been renovated. Before, the upstairs consisted of a large open room used mainly for receptions. There was one small office at the other end of the room. That had been Lou's office when his brother managed the funeral home. Now offices were lining both sides of the room. A hallway ran between them. There were security cameras at both ends of the hallway. Max led him down the hallway to the third door on the left. There was no sign on the door, no indication of who occupied the office. He knocked on the door.

"Yes, who is it?"

"It's Mr. Pinera, sir."

"Send him in."

Max opened the door, and Lou walked in. Seated at a large redwood desk was Joseph Cuneo.

"Sit down, Lou," he said. "Can Max get you a cup of coffee, or maybe a bottle of scotch?" Joseph Cuneo said with a bit of a sarcastic laugh. Getting no reaction from Lou, he said, "Just kidding, Lou. You really need to loosen up. Listen, I called you in here because I don't want you to misunderstand our conversation last night. I can be a little rough sometimes, particularly when someone upsets me, and you certainly did that last night. You were fucking wasted. I understand. You probably said some things that if you were sober, you wouldn't have said. I just want to clear the air. Understand?"

"Yes, I understand."

"What happened to your girlfriend was done to protect you. She had broken into your safe. She took some material that would have hurt you if it had fallen into the wrong hands. We took care of the problem for you. We did it because we need you, Lou. We are partners. We need each other. You need to trust me, Lou. Do you trust me?"

"Yes, I trust you."

"Good, because trust is everything in our business. If you can't trust someone, they become your enemy, and if they are your enemy, you do whatever is necessary to destroy them. Understand?"

"Yes."

"You're a man of few words, Lou. That's good. Always choose your words carefully, and only speak when it is absolutely necessary. That's what my father used to say anyway. Lou, there are going to be a few changes around here, a division of managerial responsibilities, so to speak. You've probably noticed that your safe is gone, and the financial records are missing from your office. Don't worry. Everything is safe. I have them. I am taking control of the financial end of the business. I will see that you and your family members get paid just as you have before. However, you will need to learn to live within your salary without the added piggy bank of the company credit cards. The fact is, Lou, and you would have to admit this yourself, you had been fucking the company for a long, long time. Oh, I don't blame you. Your brother had to know, and he let you do it. You're a weak person, Lou. You've got many vices, and you've used the family business to pay for your vices. That won't happen anymore. Do you understand?"

"Yes."

"That's what I like to hear, Lou. If you just keep saying yes to me, we'll get along fine. Now, Lou. You are probably asking yourself what your responsibility in this partnership is going to be. Well, that's the beauty of our new business arrangement. All I need from you is to take care of the families that come into the funeral home. Nothing more. It's really very simple. We need to give the appearance that we are a fully functioning funeral home. You have a funeral director's license. Your family members are licensed. All you need to do is keep the doors open, receive families, and conduct funerals. You can use your family members to assist you any way you want. Attend your Rotary Club meetings, the Chamber of Conference meetings, and whatever other community programs you're involved in. Enjoy life, Lou. Spend as little or as much time as you want here, just as long as the funeral home continues to operate as normal. Do you understand?"

"Yes."

"Good. And, a few other things, Lou. I don't want you or any member of your family to ever come upstairs again unless I call for you. This is my private area. You will not ask about what takes place up here. You will not tell anyone about it. You will pretend the upstairs does not exist. Understand?"

"Yes."

"Another thing, Lou. I want Elise Glenn to work in the funeral home every day. Give her some job, maybe receptionist or something. I don't care, anything except working as your secretary. That will be Linda's job. She's going to keep an eye on you, just to make sure you behave. One last thing, Lou. You are not to go to the crematorium. I will manage it. Don't step foot in it, and that goes for any member of your family. Do you understand?"

"Yes."

"Good. Now go downstairs."

Lou stood up and walked out of the office. Max was waiting for him. He followed him to the door leading downstairs, watched Lou start down, and then shut and locked the door behind him. Lou felt like he had just been de-balled. He was angry, but the anger was tempered by fear. Cuneo was a psychopath. He was sure of it. Lou's life depended on doing exactly as he was told. At that moment, Lou knew he had taken the wrong path when confronted with the fork in his road. He had taken the road that led to a dead end. He was traveling down that road at a high rate of speed with absolutely no control of the steering wheel. He knew how his path would end, but he was powerless to stop it.

On the main floor, Lou headed for the breakroom. His head was pounding. He poured a cup of strong, black coffee and headed back to his office.

Linda Collins was seated at her desk just in front of his office door. She looked up as he approached.

"I see you decided you needed that cup of coffee, after all, Mr. Pinera. Next time, just tell me, and I'll get it for you."

"Thanks. Linda, can you hold my calls? I'm feeling a little under the weather. I'd like to rest my eyes for a few minutes."

"Sure. Do you need me to get you anything?"

"No thanks. I just need a few minutes of rest and quiet."

Lou walked into his office and closed the door behind him. He wanted privacy. He needed privacy. But he knew the cameras planted on his office walls were recording everything he did. He sat at his desk and removed a bottle of aspirin from his top drawer. Opening it, he removed four aspirin, put them in his mouth, and chased them down with his coffee. Then he reached down to his bottom drawer, opened it, and pulled out a half-empty pint of Old Crow. He drank the coffee down to about a quarter of a cup and poured the remaining Old Crow into the cup. They were watching him. He knew it. It didn't matter. He was a drunk, after all. They expected him to drink. He raised the cup to his mouth and drank the mixture of coffee and Old Crow down in one, large gulp.

"A hair of the dog that bit me," he said to himself. Then he laid his head down on the desk and closed his eyes.

The knock on his door woke him from a sound sleep thirty minutes later. "Come in," he said loudly, trying not to sound like he had just woken up from a heavy sleep.

Linda opened the door. "Sorry to disturb you, Mr. Pinera, but two detectives are here to see you."

Oh shit, Lou thought. He was in no condition to talk to the police. He had a slight buzz from the half-pint of Old Crow he had chugged. He reached in his desk drawer and pulled out a container of breath mints. He put three in his mouth and said, "Go ahead and send them in."

Detective Jacks and Detective Gregory walked into the office. Mr. Pinera, we're investigating the disappearance of your girlfriend, Erika Bell."

"What?" Lou said, trying to act surprised. "She's disappeared? That can't be. I just talked to her yesterday. She was working here, just outside my door. You must be mistaken."

"Have you heard from her, Mr. Pinera?" Detective Jacks asked.

"No, not since she left work yesterday afternoon."

"Don't you find that odd, Mr. Pinera, considering that she and you live together?"

"How'd you know that?"

"Her residence is listed as your residence. You do live together, don't you?"

"Yes."

"And you didn't find it odd that she didn't come home last night?"

"No, not really. We've had some difficulties we've been trying to work out. The fact is that she hasn't been living with me for several days."

"Where has she been living?"

"I don't know. She didn't tell me, and I didn't ask. How do you know she is missing, Detective?"

"I was supposed to meet her last night. She didn't show up. She called me yesterday to say she had some information about illegal activities you were involved in. She wanted to talk to me about them. Do you know what she was referring to, Mr. Pinera?"

"No. I have no idea. I'm not involved in anything illegal. Trust me, Detective. You've got to understand, Erika. She is a wonderful woman, but she has a temper. I fear that she wanted to get back at me. She found some texts on my phone from another woman. The texts were completely innocent, I assure you, and strictly business-related. But she imagined something otherwise. She lost her temper, stormed out of the house, and hasn't been back since."

"That must have made her working here very difficult, Mr. Pinera," Detective Gregory said.

"Yes, it was difficult. The fact is that I was about to let her go. I had worked out a nice severance package for her and was about to type up a reference letter. But when she didn't show up for work today and did not call, I assumed she had decided to leave on her own."

"Mr. Pinera, what about her possessions, her clothes — are they still at your house?"

"I believe so, Detective. I haven't noticed anything being gone."

"Don't you find that odd, Mr. Pinera? Wouldn't you think that most women would pack their clothes if they were going to be gone for a while?"

"I guess. She was pretty mad when she stormed out of the house. I guess she didn't think about it."

"But didn't you say that she had been gone for several days?"

"Yes, that's right."

"Did she have a key to your house?"

"Yes, of course."

"And during those several days, she didn't come back and get some of her things? Even if she didn't want to see you, she had a key, so she could come back and gather her things when you weren't around."

"Yes, that's right. You know, Detective, now that you mention it, it is possible she came back to the house and gathered some of her things. I wouldn't have known because her clothes are in a separate closet than mine. Come to think of it, I don't think I have been in her closet since she left."

"Then why did you say her clothes were still there?"

"I guess I just assumed they were. She never said anything about picking them up. If she did, I didn't know she had."

"Mr. Pinera, do you mind if we check? You can come with us, let us in, and we can see if she has removed anything."

"Well, I don't know. I'm quite busy. I don't think I can leave the funeral home right now."

"Fine. What is a good time for you? How about lunchtime? You surely take some time for lunch."

"Okay. We can do that."

"Twelve-thirty? How does that sound? We can meet you at your home then."

"Okay."

"One last question, Mr. Pinera. Did you know that Erika was working late at the funeral home last night?"

"No. She left about four as I remember, and I thought she was gone for the evening."

"Yes, well, she was here. The call she placed to me last night came from your office."

The detectives didn't wait for a response. They stood up and walked out of the office. When they left, Linda walked in with another cup of coffee. "Thought you could use this, Mr. Pinera. That Old Crow does nasty stuff to a person's stomach. You should really stock your desk drawers with a better quality whiskey."

Lou had lied to the detectives. Erika had not left several days earlier. She was in his bed just two nights ago. She was upset at him after she checked his cell phone and found the messages. They argued, but she didn't leave. Lou slept on the couch that night, but the next morning, they talked. Things seemed like they were returning to normal. She kissed him goodbye in the morning and was fine all day at work. *What happened?* he thought. He was surprised when she didn't come home last night, but she had done that before. They had a turbulent relationship, mostly because Lou cheated on her. She had stayed out all night before to cool off. He always gave her space. Besides, she always came back home.

Lou was certain that Erika's clothes were in her closet and that she had not packed any of her items. When the detectives saw them, he would be their number one suspect. She was dead. Joseph Cuneo had said as much. When she didn't turn up, he would be the prime suspect in her disappearance. Damn, he wished he had another bottle of whiskey in his desk drawer.

A little after noon, Lou left the office and drove to his house. Detective Jacks and Gregory were waiting in his driveway when he pulled in. He walked up the sidewalk, unlocked the door, and opened it for the two detectives to walk in.

"Can I get you gentlemen anything to drink? I have scotch, bourbon, beer, and I think there is some soda in the refrigerator."

"No thanks," Detective Jacks said. "It's a little early

for drinking. Besides, we're on duty. Let's just head up to the bedroom."

"Okay, but it's been a rough day for me. Do you mind if I made a drink to settle my nerves?"

"What do you have to be nervous about, Mr. Pinera?" Detective Gregory asked.

"Nothing. I'm not nervous, just upset about Erika. Do you know anything new?"

"No, nothing we can share," Detective Gregory said.

"I understand. Do you mind if I make a drink?

"No, it's your house, Mr. Pinera. Do what you want."

Lou walked to his den, pulled down a bottle of Jack Daniels from a liquor cabinet behind his desk, and poured a double with one ice cube. He took a long, slow drink and then another until his glass was empty. Then, he filled it a second time.

"Okay, Detectives. I'm ready to take you upstairs now."

Lou carried his drink with him up to the bedroom on the second floor. He took another large drink of courage just before he opened the bedroom door. He needed the drink. In a few seconds, the detectives would open the closet, see Erika's clothes, and then he would be their prime suspect in her disappearance. He let the detectives in the room and pointed toward the large walk-in closet. Her clothes would be hanging inside, and her personal items would be in a dresser at the back of the closet. Lou finished off his drink, waiting for the detectives to come back out of the closet.

Five minutes later, they existed. "Well, Mr. Pinera," Detective Jacks said, looking directly into his face. "It looks like your girlfriend has packed and left you. All of her clothes and personal items are gone. Thanks for allowing us to look. If we have more questions, we'll let you know."

Detective Jacks handed Lou his card and told him to call if he heard from Erika. Then they left.

Lou needed another drink. Someone had been in his house and removed his girlfriend's clothes. He knew that because he had seen her clothes hanging in the closet that morning. Erika was dead, so it couldn't have been her. It had to be someone associated with Cuneo. They must have been listening to his conversation with the detectives in his office. They were watching him. They had broken into his house. He checked the door and the windows, but there was no sign of a break-in. The only person with a key to his house was Erika.

"Did they take the house key from her after she was murdered?" he asked himself.

Lou walked into his den and poured another drink. Then he picked up the phone.

"Linda, I'm not feeling well. I'm going to take the rest of the day off."

Then he picked up the phone again and called a locksmith. He needed to change the locks on his doors.

CHAPTER 12
THE MAYOR

Ky Cole had only been mayor of Kansas City for three years and had lived up to his campaign promises. He had won the election based on his promise to clean up the streets of Kansas City. When he took office, Kansas City's murder rate was one of the highest in the country. Gangs and the mob had infiltrated the inner city and brought drugs, prostitution, and fear to the city. Businesses had abandoned the city for the suburbs or other cities with less crime. The unemployment rate had doubled, and the homeless population was larger than it had ever been. Kansas City was on a downslide. Something needed to change.

Ky Cole would make that change. He was the cousin of Joseph Cuneo, and it was Cuneo that suggested he run for office. It was Cuneo that financed his campaign. Ky Cole was not the sharpest knife in the drawer, but he could talk like he was. He was a born salesman. He could sell snowballs to an Eskimo. But when it came to delivering those snowballs, he had no clue. That's where Cuneo came in. He made the plans and implemented them.

Between the two of them, they had followed through on those campaign promises. Cole had become a very popular mayor. Crime was down over 80%. The homeless population was a small fraction of what it used to be. He took the credit, but it was Cuneo that got the results. All that he asked in return from his cousin was to be awarded the city contract for the burials and some help in getting approval for two additional cremation furnaces to be built. It was a small price for Cole to pay. Getting the city contract was easy. The mayor was able to get his hands on the bids for the contract before the decision was made. He altered the bids and make sure that Pinera Family Funeral Home's bid was the lowest.

Getting approval to build two more cremation furnaces proved more difficult. The funeral home was located in Prairie Village, which was its own municipality. Cole had no influence over their city council. What he did have was a city contract for trash removal. When trash service became less dependable, particularly in the neighborhoods where city council members lived, the council opened up discussions for the additional cremation furnaces.

The final vote was held during a closed-door session of the council. It would not be a popular decision with the residents of Prairie Village. The council voted unanimously to allow construction, with some conditions. The furnaces were to only operate from midnight to 6 a.m. to minimize the amount of smog their residents would be exposed to. To compensate for the reduction in time that the furnaces were allowed to operate, the council approved the construction of three furnaces instead of the two requested. One additional change was made, superseding the rules outlined by the funeral directors' association. The change allowed for unlicensed individuals to work in the crematorium as long as they were supervised by a licensed funeral director.

Cole had done Cuneo a huge favor, although he didn't realize it at the time. Construction on the crematorium addition began immediately. Neither Cole nor the city council of Prairie Village had any idea why the Pinera Family Funeral Home needed to grow their cremation business. To their knowledge, there were few cremations done in Prairie Village. But they were wrong. The cremation business was about to take off.

Cole never asked how Cuneo was lowering the homeless population in Kansas City. He didn't care. He was too busy taking credit for it. He also didn't ask how Cuneo was lowering the crime rate. Gangs were disappearing. The mob was less active. The crime statistics had never looked better. That was all he cared about.

Ky Cole was the perfect mayor for Joseph Cuneo. He sold his agenda. He didn't ask questions, and he would be the fall guy if anything went wrong.

Cuneo ran what was now the largest mob in Kansas City. With the blessing of his cousin, he was systematically ridding the streets of gangs, the homeless, and his rivals. And the beauty of it was that nobody seemed to notice. Bodies were not piling up on the streets. Cuneo had seen to that. The crematorium was the perfect place to dispose of his victims. Now, with the additional cremation furnaces, he could finish his work and completely eliminate his competition. He could take complete control of the city, becoming a very wealthy and powerful person.

Cole had no idea he was being used. The mayor had a fine home, a beautiful wife, and two adoring children and was extremely popular. He also had a rather large ego, an ego that made him feel that he was destined for bigger things than being mayor of Kansas City. Cole had larger political aspirations—

he had set his sights on being Governor. He hadn't discussed his intentions to run with Cuneo yet. Ky knew Cuneo would be disappointed, but it was his life, after all, and his decision. Besides, he figured he had done Cuneo enough favors and didn't feel he owed him anymore.

***

The construction of the addition to the crematorium moved rapidly with the city council's approval. Cuneo had crews working on the addition seven days a week. From sun-up to sundown, they worked on the outside construction. During the evening and morning hours, they worked on the inside. In less than four weeks, construction was completed.

Six additional workers were hired to assist Dennis in the crematorium. None had funeral director's licenses, and none were the type of employees that Dennis would have hired. They were all Cuneo family associates, and, as such, they took their orders from Michael Cuneo. Dennis was no more than a means to an end. He was necessary because he was a licensed funeral director. By law, he was required to be present whenever the crematorium was operated. But he had absolutely no control over what was going on. Mike Cuneo made the decisions. Dennis signed the paperwork.

With the completion of the additional cremation furnaces, the body count in the refrigeration room increased drastically, so much so that bodies lay on gurneys in the hallway waiting for space to open up in the refrigeration room. On any given night, there could be fifteen or more bodies waiting to be cremated. Many would arrive in the middle of the night, but they weren't being delivered by Alvin Pinera. He had been assigned to exclusively pick-up bodies that were designated to go to the funeral home. No Pinera family member was involved in the crematorium business anymore. Most of the bodies were delivered by unmarked trucks or vans, with drivers that Dennis didn't recognize. The bodies were wrapped in plastic. Many had traumatic injuries — gunshot wounds, knife wounds, body parts blown off, strangulation.

Dennis knew they had been murdered and was certain the Cuneo family was involved. Newspaper articles tied Cuneo to the Kansas City mob. From the looks of many of the bodies coming into the crematorium, Dennis figured the deaths were mob-related. There was a mob war going on, Dennis was certain, but evidence of it was not staying on the streets. The bodies were being destroyed. The evidence of the crimes was burning up in the cremation furnaces. Some bodies appeared to be homeless people. Some appeared to be gang members. Some appeared to be mobsters.

The streets of Kansas City were being rid of criminals and the homeless. Crime statistics had not looked better in many years. People felt safe. They were returning to the city. Businesses were starting to come back. Construction was on the increase.

Dennis was certain he knew what was happening. The mayor and Joseph Cuneo had an arrangement. Cuneo's associates were killing the criminals and the homeless. Ky Cole knew about it. But it just seemed like too many bodies were coming into the crematorium for someone not to notice. What about the family members of the victims? Why weren't they speaking out? And then there was the sheer number of bodies coming into the crematorium, averaging fifteen or more a night. *They can't all be coming from the streets of Kansas City*, Dennis thought. *Something else has to be going on.*

He knew he had to do something. With the added cremation furnaces built and operational and with the workers in place to cremate the bodies, there would be little need for Dennis's services after a while. He was an outsider, a liability, and so were his wife and parents. They were all in danger. He would need to take a chance soon. He would need to trust somebody. He had to protect himself and his family.

Elise was working in the funeral home again as a receptionist. Dennis was sure she had been given the job so Cuneo could keep an eye on her. There was another reason she was working there, too. Her uncle had become less reliable. His drinking had taken control of him, and he was often not in a condition to meet with families. Elise was a licensed funeral director. She was also a member of the Pinera family, the most polished and presentable family member. She began taking over more and more of the responsibilities of making funeral arrangements and conducting funerals. She was good with families, and she kept the operations running. Cuneo needed her.

Pinera's drinking was making him less needed and more of a liability. Cuneo sent Max to have a talk with him. It was a little after two in the morning. Lou Pinera was in his den, drunk as usual, with a half-empty bottle of bourbon in his right hand. Max used a spare key that had been provided by a locksmith that worked for the Cuneo family and also happened to have changed the locks on Pinera's doors a few months earlier. Max slowly and quietly walked to the den. Pinera's back was facing the door. He was slumped over, nearly passed out. Max pulled a needle from his pocket and jabbed it into Pinera's neck. Lou swung his right hand around, the hand that was holding the bottle of bourbon. The force of the bottle hitting Max's arm knocked the needle out of his hand. Lou swung the bottle wildly at Max, knocking him backwards.

Lou seemed to sober up instantly. He lunged at Max. They wrestled for an instant, and then Lou fell to the floor as the substance from the needle took hold and slowly became paralyzed. Lou was awake, but he could not move. Max carried him to his car in the garage and sat him in the driver's seat. Lou saw him place the half-empty bottle of bourbon on the passenger seat next to him. He saw him reach into his pocket and pull out the car key, and turned the ignition. The garage door was closed. The house door leading to the garage was closed. Lou had a full tank of gas. He watched as Max walked out of the garage. Lou was powerless to move, and he knew what was going to happen, but there was nothing he could do about it.

Lou fought for his life as he tried desperately to move his fingers, his feet, anything. Smoke was accumulating around him. He was getting tired. It would have been so easy to succumb to his fate and fall asleep, but he refused to. If he was going to die, he was going to put up a fight first.

Lou focused his eyes on his right hand and felt a tingle in his index finger. Then he saw movement—not much at first, but then more. More of his fingers began to move. Lou felt the same tingle in his toes, followed by small movements. Whatever poison was put into his bloodstream was starting to wear off. Finally, he was able to move his right arm a few inches. He was getting so drowsy and fought to stay awake as he used all of his willpower to reach his right hand to the car key and turned it slowly. Finally, the engine shut off. He waited for a few minutes for his body to regain some movement, then opened the door and moved slowly to the garage door opener. Lou was coughing, gagging, and barely cognizant of what was going on, but he managed to get back inside the house.

Lou locked the doors and sat in his kitchen, gasping for air. Joseph Cuneo wanted him dead and had sent Max to do the job. They wanted to make it look like suicide. That type of death would be easily believed based on Lou's frame of mind recently. He had to do something. When they discovered he was alive, they would finish the job.

He reached for the phone. Lou thought about calling the police, then thought again. Cuneo had police on his payroll. He wasn't sure who or how many, but he didn't know who to trust and who not to trust. Erika had called the police, and later that night, she was dead. Lou couldn't risk calling them. Besides, he was involved in the murder of his brother and sister-in-law and in cooking the books at the funeral home for the mob. A call to the police would either get him killed or get him arrested.

He decided that his best, and maybe only, option was to run. He packed a bag, drove to an ATM, and got as much cash as he could. It was only enough to last for a few days—he needed more. There was cash in his office, several thousand dollars, that he had hidden away for play money. It was in a small safe that he had placed in his office closet. But there was no way he could go to the funeral home. So instead, Lou drove to Dennis Glenn's house. He parked the car a few blocks away and walked. *They might still be watching him*, he thought. *Best if I park somewhere else and walk.*

It was nearly seven as Lou walked to the street directly behind the Glenn house. He jumped a fence and walked to the back door, from where he could see Elise cooking in the kitchen. He went to the window and knocked on it.

The sight of him knocking on her window startled her. She yelled for Dennis. He came running. "What's the matter, Elise?"

"Look," she said, pointing to the figure in the window.

Lou tried to smile, tried to set their minds at ease.

Dennis opened the back door. "What do you need, Mr. Pinera?"

"Please, let me come in. I need to talk to you both for just a few minutes."

Dennis opened the door all the way and motioned for him to come in. "What's up? You really startled my wife."

"Sorry about that, but I couldn't take a chance of coming to your front door. They might be watching you."

"Who might be watching us? Do you mean Joseph Cuneo and his associates?"

"Yes, that's right. Please sit down. I don't have much time."

Elise turned the stove off and came into the dining room to join Dennis at the table.

"Please don't say anything. I need to tell you some things."

"Okay."

"Joseph Cuneo tried to murder me this afternoon. He sent one of his henchmen to do the job. I'm sure he thinks I am dead, but soon they will find out otherwise and come looking for me. I need to disappear, but I need money. I have some hidden in a wall safe in my office closet. But for obvious reasons, I can't go get it. I need your help. Elise, you go in that office a lot. No one would suspect that you were up to something if you went in it tonight."

"Wait a second, Lou," Dennis said. "My wife is not going to take a chance like that. If they suspected her of doing something to help you, they wouldn't think twice about killing both of us."

"Yes, I know. If I could think of any other way, I wouldn't be here. You've got to believe me. I need that money to get by for a while until I can figure something else out. Joseph Cuneo and his associates are psychopaths. They'll kill me, you, and anyone else that gets in their way."

"Why don't you go to the police?" Dennis asked.

"Because they have the police on their payroll. Erika was killed just after contacting the police. Someone on the force must have told the Cuneo family that she called. That had to be why she was murdered."

"I thought she ran off," Elise said with a puzzled look.

"No, believe me, she was murdered. I can't trust the police, and you can't either, at least the local police. If I could, I would go to the FBI—not the local office, but maybe another one, perhaps on the East or West Coast. I don't think the Cuneo influence stretches outside of the Midwest."

"Then why don't you do that? Drive to the East or West Coast and contact the FBI there?" Dennis asked.

"I can't. I have done some bad things, things that would land me in prison if they were to get out, and the Cuneo family would make sure they got out if I dared go to the FBI. That's how they tie innocent people to them. They force you into committing criminal acts, and then they hold the evidence in a safe place. They can expose you at any time. They use that evidence to keep you doing their dirty work and to prevent you from going to the police."

"I'm sorry, Lou, but I won't put my wife in a situation that could get her killed," Dennis said.

"You already have, Dennis. The day you started doing what Joseph Cuneo told you to do in that crematorium, you put yourself, your wife, and your family in danger. You know what that crematorium is being used for, don't you?"

"No, not for sure," Dennis said. "What is it being used for?"

"Joseph Cuneo is the head of the Kansas City mob. He's using the crematorium to destroy the evidence of mob murders. They are eliminating their competition. They are cleaning the streets so the Cuneo family can take complete control of narcotics, prostitution, gambling, and other vices in the Kansas City market. Once their competition is gone, they will control everything. Kansas City is only the beginning. The Cuneo family is already moving into other markets — St. Louis and Chicago, I believe. Dennis, you are smack in the middle of his operation. You are doing his dirty work by destroying evidence of his murders. Haven't you wondered why he needs three more cremation furnaces? Haven't you wondered why there are so many bodies?"

Dennis bent over and put his head in his hands. "I had no idea. Are you absolutely sure?"

"Yes, I am. Dennis, you are a dead man walking. It's not a question of if. It's a matter of when. When the Cuneo family no longer needs your services, they will eliminate you, your wife, and anyone else that stands in their way. Whether you want to admit it or not, you and I are in the same boat. The only difference is that my time is up. I can help you, Dennis, but I need your help first. Get me the money I need to run. In exchange, I'll help you save yourself and your family."

"How are you going to do that, Lou?"

"I have evidence that Joseph Cuneo is using the funeral home to launder money. I have a second set of books, which I removed from the funeral home before Erika was murdered. Those books show money flowing into the funeral home from other mob sources. The books show exaggerated expenses, exorbitant costs, and completely fake expenses that allow the mob to wash their money. The books I have could break the Cuneo family mob. You could run with your family. You could take the evidence to the FBI in exchange for protection. They can put you and your family in witness protection. You would be safe."

"You're telling me that my family and I need to run. We

would have to hide out the rest of our lives. That doesn't sound like a very good option," Dennis said.

"It beats the alternative. Dennis, you have no choice. At some point, the Cuneo family is going to decide that you are a liability. When that happens, you are dead, and so are your wife and your parents."

"Where are the books?" Dennis asked.

"They are in the basement of my house, locked in a small vault behind a false wall in the medicine cabinet in the bathroom in the finished part of the basement. Here is the combination to the safe." Lou handed Dennis a small piece of paper with a series of three numbers written on it. "Turn the lock clockwise once, counter-clockwise twice, and clockwise once."

"What about Max? Won't he or another one of the Cuneo goons be there?" Elise asked.

Lou looked directly into Elise's eyes. "I don't know, but I don't think so. That's why Dennis needs to go into the basement tonight. Max thinks I'm dead. By morning, he will know otherwise. If you wait, they will probably be in the house or watching it. You've got to go tonight."

"Okay. I don't like it, but I think you are right. Those books give us the best option. I just don't know how I am going to convince my parents that they need to run with us."

"You don't have any choice, Dennis. If you run, they must run also. Joseph Cuneo won't think twice about killing them once he discovers you have run," Lou said.

"If I'm going into your house, then you're going too," Dennis said to Lou.

"I'll make you a deal, Dennis. I'll come if your wife goes into my office tonight and gets the money I have in the safe. I need it tonight," Lou said.

"Okay, I'll get it," Elise said. "There is a family visitation tonight. I can use that as an excuse for being in the funeral home. There are cameras on both sides of your office. I'll need to get into your safe without anyone noticing."

"There are supplies in that closet too. Grab some supplies from the closet when you open the safe. The supplies can conceal the money too. Anybody that is watching will just think you are getting some supplies," Lou said. "Make sure that you spend some time with the family at the visitation so no one will be suspicious. There is one other thing, Dennis. Do you have a gun?"

"No. Why?"

"We're not going into my house without a gun. If Max or someone else is there, we need something to protect ourselves," Lou said. "Without a gun, it is too dangerous."

Dennis thought for a second. "I know where we can get a gun."

Fifteen minutes later, Elise left for the funeral home. She would spend twenty or thirty minutes with the family, then go to Lou's office to get a little work done. Sometime after, she would go to the closet, open the safe, remove the money, and grab some supplies. She would hide the money in the middle of the supplies she grabbed and go back to the desk. At some point, she would drop the money into her purse, continue working until a few minutes before the visitation ended, wait for the family to leave, turn out the lights, and leave.

Dennis walked out to the car in his garage. Lou followed him and got in the back seat, and laid down on the floorboard so no one could see him. Dennis opened up the garage and drove away. He drove several blocks, looking in the rearview mirror for anyone that might be following him. When he was certain he didn't have a tail, Dennis drove to his parents' house. Lou remained in the car while Dennis went into the house.

His mother greeted him at the front door.

"Is Dad home, Mom?"

"Yes, he's in the kitchen. What's wrong?"

Mothers have a sixth sense about things. She seemed to know that something serious had happened just by looking into Dennis's face.

"I need to talk to him."

Dennis hurried into the breakfast room with his mother right behind him. His father was reading a book. He often did that at the breakfast table after dinner. "This room has the best light for reading," he would say.

"Dad, I need your gun."

Those five words got his father's attention. He dropped his book and looked up at Dennis.

It also brought out a cry of protest from his mother. "No," she yelled.

"Dad, I don't have much time to explain. I will later, but right now, I need to borrow your gun."

"Dennis, there is no damn way I am giving you my gun. You've never even used one before. That's crazy."

"Listen, Dad. Lou Pinera was nearly murdered tonight. The people that tried to kill him will be coming after me soon. There is something in Lou's basement that will protect me and Elise. I need to go into that house tonight and get it. I don't think anyone will be watching, but just in case, I need the gun to protect myself."

"Dennis, look me and your mother in our face and tell me there is no other solution to your problem. Tell me this is the only way for you to protect you and Elise."

Dennis looked both his parents in the eyes. He didn't

need to say anything. His mother could tell from his face that he needed to do this. But his father needed Dennis to tell him so.

"Mom and Dad, this is the only way I can protect myself and Elise. Retrieving the evidence in that basement is our only chance. And it's not just for me and Elise. That evidence will keep you and Mom safe too. The Cuneo family will not stop at hurting Elise and I. They will go after my family. I have no choice. I'm running out of time, and I need that gun."

Ron stared cold-faced at his son. He knew he was telling the truth. He knew his son needed protection.

"I'm not giving you the gun, Dennis."

"Dad, I've got to have it."

"I know, son. But you don't know how to use a gun. It would be more dangerous in your hands than if you didn't have one at all. Instead, I am going to come with you."

"No, Dad. I don't want you involved."

"I'm afraid you have no choice, Dennis. If you want the gun, I am coming along to carry it. If it needs to be used, it's better if I do the shooting."

Dennis didn't argue. His father was trained to fire a gun. He was not. Besides, he felt safer going into that house with his father beside him.

Five minutes later, they were getting into Dennis's car. Ron saw the figure hiding in the back seat and nearly shot him.

"Sorry, Dad. I forgot to tell you that Lou is coming with us."

"Give me a little warning next time. I nearly splattered blood all over your back seat."

CHAPTER 13
THE BASEMENT

Dennis drove around Lou's neighborhood several times, looking for any suspicious cars. He didn't see any. So they parked a couple of blocks away and walked behind the house, and entered through the back door. It was dark and quiet inside. Lou grabbed a flashlight from a kitchen drawer and turned it on. The trio followed the light to the basement door. Lou opened the door, flipped on a light, and then closed the door behind them. Lou took off his shirt and stuck it underneath the door opening so the light from the basement would not be visible from inside the house.

The stairway leading down to the basement was carpeted. Their footsteps made no noise going down the thirteen steps to the finished part of the basement. At the bottom of the stairs was a large open room with a fully stocked bar and a big-screen television. Four large, cushy, leather recliners sat in front of the television, and the bar was directly behind them. Lou stopped at the bar to pour a tall Old Crow.

"Damn it, Lou. Can't you wait for a drink?" Ron said.

"I have waited," he said back.

Drink in hand, Lou led the group to the bathroom on the other side of the room. Inside, directly behind the sink, was a medicine cabinet. He opened it, removed the contents, and placed them in the sink. Then he removed a back panel—a fake wall. Inside was a safe. He turned the lock—thirty-six left, nineteen right, twenty-three left. The safe opened. Inside were two ledgers and a wad of twenty-dollar bills.

"Hell, I forgot I had any money in here," Lou said with a smile on his face, taking another sip of his drink. Lou handed the ledgers to Dennis. "Here you go, Dennis. Take these to the FBI, preferably an office far away from here, and they'll keep you safe."

"Dennis, what's he talking about?" his father asked. "Are you planning on running?"

"Yes, it's the only way we can be safe."

"What the hell are you mixed up in, son?"

"The mob. I didn't want to tell you back at the house in front of Mom, but the mob controls the funeral home and the crematorium. They are using them to launder money and destroy evidence of their crimes. They have threatened me, and because of that, we need to run."

"What do you mean by 'we'?" his father asked.

"I mean, we need to run—me, Elise, you, and Mom."

"No fucking way. I have never run from a fight, and I won't now."

"Dad, you have no idea what these people can do. Once I run, they will come after you and Mom. They won't think twice about killing both of you."

Ron had a defiant look on his face. "Let them try. I'll be

waiting for them."

There was no arguing with his father, not right now, anyway. They needed to get out of the house.

Lou put the empty safe back in its place. He placed the fake wall in front of it and replaced the contents of the medicine cabinet, and they walked out of the bathroom.

As he approached the bar, he took one last sip from his glass to finish it off. Then he stopped and poured another tall one, this one just a little taller than the last.

"Damn it, Lou. You're a fucking drunk," Ron said.

"Yes, I am, and damn proud of it," he said, taking the first sip from his fresh drink. "Let's go, boys."

With that, the group of three moved toward the steps leading upstairs. That's when they heard someone walking around on the floor above them. They stopped in their tracks and listened. There were voices coming from upstairs—two, maybe three of them. The footsteps would stop, then they would resume. The strangers were moving from room to room. One set of footsteps could be heard going up the stairs to the second floor. The footsteps were loud and quick, perhaps running.

Lou could make out that someone was in his den. He heard desk drawers being opened and closed. He heard the movement of liquor bottles from his bar. One fell, shattering on the hardwood floor. It made a loud noise as it hit the floor just above them.

"What happened, Max?" they could hear the stranger on the second floor yell down the stairs.

"Nothing, damn it. I just knocked over a bottle."

"Did you find anything upstairs?"

"No, not yet."

"Come on down. Let's check out the garage."

The heavy footsteps could be heard coming down rapidly from the second floor. Then, footsteps could be heard walking toward the garage.

"There are just two people upstairs," Ron Glenn whispered. "If we are going to get out of here, we need to do it while they are in the garage. Everyone, remove your shoes, so we eliminate as much noise as possible. When I signal, let's quietly walk up the stairs and get out the front door."

Dennis wished he had a better plan, but he didn't. Max and the other stranger would surely check out the basement when they discovered Lou's car was gone.

When they heard the door leading into the garage open, the trio moved quickly to the top of the basement stairs. Lou turned out the basement lights and grabbed his shirt from underneath the door. He opened the door slowly, quietly.

"What the fuck? The car's gone. He's gone. Shit, we need to check every bit of the house. Check the basement, now."

It was Max's voice. Lou recognized it. Dennis did too. They needed to run. The footsteps were coming rapidly across the kitchen floor and toward the basement door. Lou dropped his drink and ran. He was the first one out of the basement. Dennis and his father were right behind him. Lou reached the front door and opened it.

Dennis and his father heard the shots, three in rapid succession, and saw Lou Pinera fall to the ground. Standing just outside the door on the front porch was a third stranger. Smoke was coming from the barrel of a gun he was holding in his right hand. Lou never had time to react. He lay on the floor, a pool of blood gathering underneath his lifeless body.

Dennis and his father turned and ran back down the steps, shutting the door behind them. The stranger at the door got a brief glimpse of them as they ran down the basement stairs.

"There are two more of them. They are in the basement," they could hear the stranger at the front door say.

Dennis and his dad ran down the stairs into the finished part of the basement. There was no place to hide. Ron opened a door at the back of the room, which opened into the unfinished part of the basement. He flipped on the light and looked for any place to hide or to escape. They were sitting ducks. In a few seconds, the three strangers would be in the basement. They had guns. Ron had one too, but three against one was not the type of odds he liked.

Dennis saw a smallish window at the far end of the basement. He might be able to fit through it, but it would be a tight squeeze for his dad. Then he saw the electrical box. Ron ran to it, opened the box, and turned off the main power switch. The house went dark.

"That will even the odds a little bit," he told Dennis.

Then he went to the basement window, which was about five feet above the basement floor, and locked. Ron unlocked it and opened it, knocking out the outside cover with the butt of his gun. "They will be here anytime now. I'm going to lift you up. Climb through the window and run as fast as you can to the car. Don't bother waiting for me. I'll find my way back home."

"No. I'm not leaving you behind, Dad," Dennis said.

"Yes, you are. There is no other way. I'll get out of here. Don't worry about me. I just need to know that you are safe."

Dennis could hear the men coming down the basement stairs. They would find them soon. He lifted his foot. His father locked his hands underneath it and lifted Dennis up to the window. He pulled his body the rest of the way through it and onto the ground outside.

"I love you, Dad," Dennis said as he got on his feet.

"I love you too, Dennis. I'll see you soon," he said to his son.

Dennis ran as fast as he could. When he was about two blocks away, he heard three gunshots, followed a few seconds later by four more gunshots. He stopped in his tracks and turned around. Dennis thought about going back, but there was nothing he could do. He had to protect his wife and his mother. Soon, he thought, the Cuneo family would figure out that Dennis was involved. They would come after him and his family. His immediate thought was of Elise in the funeral home. She was in immediate danger. Dennis got to his car, locked the evidence from Lou's safe in his trunk, and drove toward the Pinera Family Funeral Home. He tried to call Elise while he was driving, but her cell phone went to voicemail. He called the funeral home number. The answering service picked up. They often transferred the company phones to an answering service after business hours. Dennis did not leave a message.

Ten minutes later, he pulled into the parking lot of the Pinera Family Funeral Home. The lights were out, and the parking lot was deserted except for Elise's car. It was empty, parked in a space at the back of the lot. He tried calling her cellphone again. There was no answer. He got out of the car and walked to the entrance. The door was locked. Except for a security light in the entrance, the lights inside were off.

Dennis walked to the back of the funeral home and could see some lights on the second floor in the area where Joseph Cuneo had his office. There were also several cars parked in the back lot. "People are working upstairs," he said to himself.

In the back of the building was a driveway that led down to the garage, which was connected with the basement.

He followed the driveway to a large six-car garage. The garage
was connected directly with the embalming room and casket
storeroom. The funeral home had a large storage area where
their excess inventory of caskets, vaults, and cremation urns
were stored. There was a large showroom on the main floor that
displayed their bestselling merchandise. The storage area in the
basement contained extra inventory. Dennis had been given a
tour of the funeral home when he first started working for the
Pinera family. He remembered being amazed at the volume of
merchandise stored in the basement. The Pinera Family Funeral
Home was massive. Families that attended a service at the funeral
home had no idea how large it was. They saw only the offices,
break room, lobby, and parlors that occupied about half of the
main floor. They never saw the second floor, the basement, or
a large portion of the main floor. Those areas were off-limits to
visitors.

There were four garages in the back of the funeral home.
The outside of the garage area resembled a shipping dock. The
driveway was about three feet lower than the dock area containing
the garage for one of the bays. That bay was used for deliveries
of merchandise and supplies. A second bay had a driveway that
was slightly elevated, resulting in only about a two-foot rise in
the dock. That bay was used for body deliveries. It was perfect for
rolling the gurneys out of the pick-up van right into the garage.
The other two driveways ran level with the garage doors to allow
vehicles to enter and park in the garage. On bad weather days,
the hearses and delivery and pick-up vans would be stored in
the garage, protected from the elements. The garages were deep,
which allowed for as many as eight vehicles to be parked inside
at one time.

The garage doors were shut and locked this time of night.

There was a delivery door just to the left of the first garage bay. It would be locked too, but Dennis brought a tire iron with him to pry open the door. He wedged the thin metal edge of the tire iron in between the lock and door frame and pried the door open. There was a single security light inside the delivery door area. Other than that, the area was totally dark.

Dennis shut the door behind him, and with his tire iron in hand, he moved slowly into the garage.

There were two hearses, a family limousine, and a van inside the garage. No one appeared to be around. It was completely quiet. The light from the entrance gave Dennis some visibility into the garage, but the deeper he got into it, the dimmer the light became and the more difficult it was to see. There were several light switches throughout the garage, but he didn't want to turn any on. It was best that no one know he was in the building. He didn't want to explain why he was there.

Near the rear of the garage was a swinging door that opened inward from the middle, creating a large pathway into the embalming room. The door was marked "private." There was no light illuminating underneath the door, so it appeared the embalmer was not working that night. Dennis slowly pushed the door open. It was completely dark inside, as there were no windows in the room. Without light, it was impossible to see more than a few feet in front of him. The smell of embalming fluid was strong, the odor irritating Dennis's nose. He needed to sneeze. He held his hand tightly over his nose and sneezed as softly as possible. The room was cold. It was purposely kept cool to preserve the remains until the embalming process could be completed. He felt chills running down his body. Goosebumps were starting to show on both his arms. Dennis was used to the cold from working in the refrigeration room of the crematorium, but that was different. He wasn't afraid at the crematorium like he was at that moment. Something was wrong. He knew it. It was just too quiet.

The embalming fluid was starting to make him feel sick. "It shouldn't be that strong," he said to himself. "It would only be that strong if it was being prepared for the embalming process or if there were a leak or spill." Dennis wished he could see what was causing the strong odor, but he couldn't take the chance of someone seeing him as he moved slowly through the room, using his hands to guide his way. Dennis had only been in that room once before and tried to remember where the exit was. He needed to find Elise, and he needed to get out of the embalming room as soon as possible. "But, where the hell is the exit door?" he asked himself. Dennis thought it was on the opposite side of the room from the door leading into the garage. But in the dark, he was disoriented. He remembered that the room was large, and he remembered the room had four or five tables used for prepping the bodies. Dennis remembered the shelves of supplies, and he remembered the large machine that was used to drain blood from the bodies before embalming. He remembered that the same machine was used for replacing the blood with embalming fluid. "Maybe that's where the smell is coming from," he told himself. "Maybe one of the tubes has a leak."

As he moved forward, the tire iron he held in his right hand collided with the metal frame of the table and made a loud noise. He stopped and listened, wondering if anyone had heard the noise. Feeling secure that no one was coming, he used his left hand to feel around to find the edge of the table. It was on his right, and he moved forward, reaching out with his left hand to feel the second table. *They are lined up*, he thought. If he continued to move forward in the same direction, he should feel the third table. A few seconds later, he confirmed that it was also just to his right. The fourth table, as he remembered, was the embalming table, the one with the machine and tubes to remove the blood and replace it with embalming fluid. He remembered that table was larger than the others and was against another wall. Above it were the shelves containing supplies and the embalming fluid.

As he moved deeper into the room, the odor became even more intense. The smell was starting to burn his eyes, which began to water. He stopped and wiped his eyes with the sleeve of his shirt, then took two more steps and walked right into the fourth table, which was directly in front of him. His right leg stepped directly into the metal roller on the bottom of the table, its sharp edge penetrating his skin painfully on his right ankle. He could feel the blood soaking through his pant leg. "Damn it," he cursed silently.

He lifted his left hand out in front of him to feel for the corner of the table. The exit door would be close to that table. Then he felt it. With his left hand extended in front of him, he could feel the legs of a still-warm body lying flat on the table. *That's odd*, he thought. *After death, bodies turn cool, and the body temperature lowers. Then, they become stiff.* The body on the embalming table was neither cool nor stiff. *It must have been a very recent death.*

He jerked his hand back. Damn, he wished he could see. He moved his right hand across the base of the table — the edge was less than a foot away. Dennis moved his body in that direction, using his left hand to guide him around the table. A few steps past it, he felt the wall. He ran his hand along the wall until he found the frame of a door — the exit door.

He had just touched the edge of the door frame when it flung open, and the light switch was turned on. It was a shock to his eyes and caused his vision to be blurred for an instant. In his panic, Dennis swung the tire iron with as much force as he could muster. The stranger was caught by surprise as the sharp end of the tire iron penetrated his skin, and he stumbled. Dennis swung the tire iron a second and a third time. The tip of the tire iron began to drip blood, and the stranger fell to the floor. Dennis could hear the moans, then there was silence. As his eyes began to adjust to the light, he saw the body lying in a pool of blood on the concrete floor. He saw the blood and skin tissue drip from the end of the tire iron. The stranger made no noise. He did not move. He lay flat on the floor on his stomach. A large wound at the side of his head was still spitting out blood and some sort of gray substance that Dennis recognized as brain matter. There was no doubt the stranger was dead.

Dennis reached down to roll him over enough so that he could see his face. He didn't recognize the man. He was wearing a white jacket, similar to what a doctor would wear when visiting patients. *He must be one of Joseph Cuneo's people*, he thought. *Or a new embalmer he hired*. It didn't matter. He was dead, and soon the men upstairs would come looking for him. Time was running out.

It was then that a sick feeling struck the pit of his stomach. His thoughts shifted to the body on the embalming table. "Why was it warm?" he asked himself. Dead bodies turned cool rather quickly. Plus, the temperature in the embalming room would expedite the outside temperature of the body. It made no sense that the body he touched was still warm. Unless he rationalized, the person on that embalming table had just died in the last few minutes — or, he further speculated, the person on that embalming table was still alive.

The pain in the pit of his stomach had to know who was on that table. He turned and looked. The body was covered with a white sheet, except for the ankles and legs. The feet were small. The ankles were thin and shaven. Dennis was certain that a woman was underneath that white sheet. He grabbed one edge of the sheet near the top. He closed his eyes for just a second, afraid of what he might see. Then, he pulled the sheet off the body.

The lights went dark. He felt a sharp pain on the side of his neck, a jolt that sent pain throughout his body. Dennis fell to the concrete floor and passed out.

Chapter 14
The Mayor

Ky Cole let his ego get too big. He thought Joseph Cuneo would give him his blessing to seek higher office. Ky had set his sights on becoming governor of Missouri and let others convince him that he could actually get elected. And with Joseph Cuneo's support and money, he probably could become governor. He was smart. He was likable. He could give a good, powerful speech. And he had done what no other major of Kansas City had done in over thirty years—he had dramatically lowered the crime rate. Yes, with Cuneo's support, he could have been governor.

But he wasn't going to get his support. In fact, Cuneo was extremely upset when he found out that Ky had already entered the gubernatorial race.

"You stupid son-of-a-bitch," he yelled. "You don't do anything unless I tell you to do it. I don't want you to be governor. Your job in Kansas City is not finished. We are not finished here. What gave you the fucking idea that you could make this decision without talking to me? I made you what you are, not you. Your ass would be cleaning out toilets or serving hamburgers at McDonald's if it wasn't for me. I made you, and I can break you anytime I want."

Ky Cole stared blankly at Joseph, stunned by his reaction. He had never talked to him like that before. He expected him to be happy with his decision and to offer his support.

Suddenly, Cuneo calmed down and lowered his voice, softening his tone. "I need you to withdraw your name from the election. Do you understand?"

"I'm sorry, but I don't understand. Can't I help you more as governor than I can as mayor?"

"Yes, someday. But not right now. Now I need you in Kansas City. Our work is not done here. We've got to finish what we have started, and that's going to take a while. Maybe in four more years, I can give you my blessing to run. But not now."

"I'm sorry, Joseph, but in four more years, the political climate may be different. I'm popular right now. Governor Bell is not seeking re-election. Now is my window of opportunity. The Republican gubernatorial committee says I need to run for the office now, not in four more years."

Ky could see the anger building up in Cuneo's face. His face tightened. His eyes hardened. He could see the red tint of anger boiling up from his neck to his face to the top of his head. He wanted to run, but he was in Cuneo's office on the second floor of the funeral home. Two large, intimidating men were waiting at the door. There was no way for him to escape.

"This is my final warning, Ky. Withdrawal your name from consideration immediately. And by immediately, I mean tomorrow morning."

"Or what, Joseph?" he said back defiantly, even as his entire body shook in fear.

"Ky, you know me better than that. I don't threaten. I am more of an action guy. Now, if you'll just consider my request logically, you will see that I am right. You and your family have a comfortable life in Kansas City. Thanks to us, you are making more money than you ever dreamed of. Your kids go to the best Catholic schools, and your wife can buy as many shoes and dresses and fine things as she wants. Life is good for you in Kansas City. We keep you safe. Your children don't need to worry about being kidnapped, and your beautiful wife doesn't need to worry about being raped or disfigured or possibly killed. There is no need to watch your back everywhere you go, wondering if the person walking behind you will be your killer. Ky, if you just look at the situation logically, you'll see that Kansas City is where you belong."

Ky lowered his head, defeated. He was not on the same playing field with Joseph. For the first time in his life, he was fearful of him.

"Ky, I don't need your answer right now. It's one in the morning. Why don't you go home, get a little sleep, and come back to my office at eleven in the morning? You can give me your answer then. Just make sure you come back with the right answer."

Ky turned and walked out of the office, down the stairs, and out to his car, then drove to a bar about halfway between the funeral home and his house in Mission Hills. He needed a stiff drink, or two, or three. Drinking helped settle his nerves and relaxed him. It helped him think and gave him courage. It helped him make difficult decisions that a sober, rational mind would never make. Five tall glasses of Royal Crown and ice later, he had made his decision.

He stumbled out of the bar and into his car. Five drinks

gave him the courage to believe he was not afraid of Joseph Cuneo. "Instead, he should be afraid of me," Ky said to himself as he started the car and drove the remaining six blocks to his house. He pulled into his gated driveway and looked up at his massive three-story brick home with the white wood pillars that went from the overhang on his room down to the wood porch that ran the entire length of the front of his house. The mayor was proud of what he had accomplished in life. He had been successful in life without Cuneo's help and had earned everything he had by himself, without anyone else's help.

Who did Cuneo think he was talking to him like that? He was elected mayor, no thanks to him. Cuneo should be thankful to him for giving him the city contract. Cuneo had prospered as a result of it. Ky didn't owe Cuneo anything. It was Cuneo that owed him. Now, that son-of-a-bitch was threatening him and his family. Well, there was no fucking way he was going to stand for that. He was the mayor, after all. Nobody got away with threatening the major.

Ky parked his car and walked into the house. It was dark inside. The door alarm was on. He punched in the code, and the beeping stopped. The mayor turned on a light and walked upstairs. He needed to check on his family, and he needed to know they were safe. His two daughters, Sara and Elizabeth, were ten-year-old twins. Sara was born twenty-five minutes before Elizabeth. She was an easy birth. Elizabeth was not. She had turned in the womb, and her neck was wrapped up in her umbilical cord. She was suffocating. Doctors had to slice open Diane, Ky's wife, to save Elizabeth's life. She was not breathing when the doctors removed her. They rushed her into another room and used small, electrical paddles to resuscitate her. She had gone without oxygen for some time. She was in extensive care for nearly two weeks. But she survived. Her mother was left unable to have additional children.

Diane was a perfect mother that treasured her two daughters. Admittedly though, she gave more of her attention to Elizabeth, whose mind had never been quite right since that difficult birth. She stuttered when she talked, and as a result, she talked more slowly than her sister. Elizabeth was not as smart and struggled in school and in social settings. She had no real friends. Her mother provided her the extra love she needed.

Both girls slept in the same bedroom. There were two additional bedrooms in the house. They could have elected to have their own rooms. But they had slept in the same room their entire lives. They shared a special bond that only other twins could understand.

Ky reached the twins' bedroom door and opened it slowly so as not to wake them. The lights were off except for a night light plugged into the far wall. He walked over to their beds. Elizabeth slept on the right, near the window. She had it cracked slightly to let in the cool, fresh air. It helped her sleep. She was covered from head to foot in her blanket. He leaned down and gave her a gentle kiss on top of her head. Then he moved to the other side of the room where Sara slept. She was lying on her stomach with her head buried underneath her pillow. He moved the pillow from behind her head and reached down and kissed her on the back of her head. She didn't move.

He began to turn and walk away when he noticed a piece of paper lying on top of the sheets that covered Sara's body. He reached down and picked up the note. It was hard to read in the dark, so he walked over to the night light so he could read it.

You should really lock all your windows and doors at night, the note read.

He ran to the master bedroom. Somebody had been in the house. He remembered the threat that Cuneo had made and made a promise to himself. "If anyone harms my wife or kids, I will kill them."

Ky swung open the bedroom door, flipped on the light switch, and ran to the bed. "Diane," he screamed. "Wake up!"

"Ky, what's wrong?" she said in a groggy voice.

"Sorry, honey," he said, reaching down to touch her. "I fell asleep downstairs. I must have had a bad dream. Are you okay?"

"Yes," she said. "I was sound asleep. Come on to bed."

"I will, honey. I just have a little work to do first. I'll come to bed in a few minutes. Go back to sleep."

Ky walked out of the room, still clutching the note in his right hand. His hands were shaking, and he needed a drink. So after kissing his wife goodnight, Ky walked downstairs, went to his den, and poured a stiff drink. It took several sips to calm his nerves, and when he was settled. Ky walked around the lower level to check all the doors and windows. "How did the stranger get in?" he wondered. He found the answer when he reached the sliding glass door leading to the back of the house. It was partially open. Ky shut and locked the door, then went into his den and poured another drink. It was 4 a.m. There was no way he was going to go to sleep now.

Cuneo had sent him a message. He expected his answer in five more hours. Ky picked up the phone on his desk in the den and called Norman Brown, Kansas City's Chief of Police.

"Joseph has no idea who he is messing with. I'm the fucking mayor," he said to himself.

The phone rang eight times before it was answered.

"Do you know what fucking time it is?" Norman said when he finally picked up the phone.

"Norman, it's me, Ky Cole."

"Oh, sorry, Mayor. I thought it was someone else."

"I need you to come to my house as soon as possible. It's very important. Bring Detective Jacks too."

"Okay, Mayor. Can you give me about an hour?"

"Yes, but hurry Chief."

The phone went dead. Ky sat in his chair. He was still shaking, partly from fright and partly from anger. He finished his drink and headed upstairs to take a shower and change his clothes.

Ky was at the front window when the unmarked patrol car approached the gate to his driveway. He pushed the switch, and the gate opened. The car drove up to the front of the house. Norman Brown and Detective Jacks walked up to the front door.

Ky stepped outside. "Can we talk in your car, gentlemen? My wife and the girls are still asleep. I don't want to disturb them."

"Sure," Norman said.

The two men presented a drastic contrast to each other. Detective Jacks was tall, athletic, and all muscle. Norman Brown was short, heavy-set, and twenty years older. He had a huge beer belly that made him nearly as wide as he was tall. He smoked cigars all the time. Ky couldn't ever remember seeing him without a cigar in his mouth.

"What's the matter, Ky?" Norman asked.

"I need your help," he said. "Someone broke into my house tonight, and they left a note on my daughter's bed." Ky reached into his pocket and pulled out the note, and handed it to Norman.

Norman read it and handed it to Detective Jacks to read.

"Chief, I know who left the note. Well, not exactly, but I know who is responsible for it," he said, staring directly at the two men.

"Who?" Norman asked.

"It's my cousin, Joseph Cuneo."

"Why would he do that?" Norman asked.

"I have put my name in the hat to run for governor. He doesn't want me to run."

"That doesn't make any sense, Ky. Why doesn't he want you to run, and why would he threaten you because of it?"

"This is probably going to come as a big shock to both of you, but Joseph has been committing crimes. His side of the family is involved in mob activities. He has been using the funeral home to launder money and destroy evidence of some of his crimes."

Norman Brown began to laugh, starting with a smile, then a soft laugh, and finally, a full belly laugh.

"You're fucking kidding me, right? This is some sort of sick joke. You woke me up in the middle of the night, had me wake the detective up too, got us to drive all the way out here, just to play some fucking practical joke on us," Norman said.

"It's no joke, Chief. Joseph demanded that I meet with him at eleven this morning to tell him I will withdraw my name from the race for governor. He threatened me and my family if I don't withdraw. I'm sure it was one of his associates that broke into my house last night and left that note on my daughter's bed."

"Have you been drinking, Mayor? You smell like you've been drinking."

"What does that have to do with anything, Norman? Yes, I had a couple of drinks last night, but I'm as sober as either of you right now, and what I'm telling you is the truth."

"Mayor Cole, do you have any evidence of the crimes Mr. Cuneo is committing?" asked Detective Jacks.

"Well, no, I don't. But I do know he asked me to rig the bidding for the city burial contract so his funeral home would win the contract."

"He asked you, Mayor?" Detective Jacks asked.

"Yes, that's right."

"And you rigged the bidding as he asked?"

"Yes, but you don't understand. He threatened me. He forced me to do it."

"How did he force you, Mayor? Because right now, it looks like you are the person that committed a felony," Detective Jacks said.

"Listen, boys," Norman said. "Let's not get into a pissing match. Ky, I've got to say that there is really nothing we can do without evidence. I can't arrest him without some proof of a crime. I can't even get a search warrant to check his offices. The only thing I can do is to question him. Do you want me to do that, Ky?"

"No, I don't think that would be a good idea," he said, hanging his head just a little.

"What we can do, Mayor, if you want, is give you some added security. We can have someone stay with you at all times. We can keep a man at your house to keep an eye on your family when you're at work. Do you want us to do that, Mayor?" Detective Jacks asked.

"Yes, I would appreciate that, Detective."

"I'll take care of it right away, Mayor."

"You know, Ky. If you are concerned for you and your family's safety, you should consider hiring security guards. I'm sure the city council would approve the cost," Norman said.

"Maybe I will. Thanks, gentlemen, for getting up so early to come out. I'm sorry I wasted your time."

"It's okay, Mayor. Please let me know if you get any more threats."

"I will. And, Chief, if something should happen to me or my family, I trust that Cuneo will be at the top of your suspect list."

"Yes, he'll be at the very top, Mayor. Enjoy the day. It should be a nice one."

Ky walked onto his front porch and watched the car as it went slowly down the driveway and out of sight. The sun was starting to come over the horizon. It was nearly six—five hours before his meeting with Cuneo.

At 10:45 a.m., the mayor walked into the Pinera Family Funeral Home. He was greeted by Linda Collins. "Hello, Mayor, we've been expecting you. Mr. Cuneo is upstairs. You can go right up."

Ky walked the steps up to the second floor. He saw the cameras hanging from the ceiling and knew he was being watched. At the top of the stairs, he knocked on the door. A large man in a sport coat and tie opened the door.

"Hello, Mayor. The boss is waiting for you in his office. I'll take you to him."

Ky followed the man down the hallway. Out of the corner of his eye, he could see others watching him. He was the show of the day. He was the last man to stand up against Joseph Cuneo and live. But now, everyone expected him to be defeated, for him to fall in line and be a good soldier. They were watching him to see if he would be defiant one last time. He wondered if they wanted that to happen. Maybe they wanted to see him hurt. Maybe they got a kick out of seeing their boss kick someone's ass.

Maybe Ky would decide to put on a good show for them.

The silence upstairs was deafening. The stranger that greeted him at the top of the stairs reached the office door a few feet in front of him. He knocked on the door and then opened it slightly. "Mayor Cole is here to see you, sir."

"Let him in, Lee," Cuneo said. "Come in, Mayor. Take a seat. Can I get you anything to drink—bourbon, scotch, anything? You name it."

"No, I'm fine."

"Okay, then have you made a decision, Mayor?"

"Yes, you've won this time, Joseph. I'll withdraw my name for governor, but I've got one condition."

"What's that, Mayor?"

"You need to promise me that you will never come to my home again and will never threaten me or my family. You have to promise that no harm will come to me or my family."

"That sounds like several promises, Mayor. You know, from the tone you used, it almost sounds like a threat. Are you threatening me, Mayor?"

"No. I would never threaten you, Joseph. I don't believe in ideal threats. I, like you, believe in action, not threats."

"Careful, Mayor, about what you say. Words can come back to hurt you. Okay, Mayor. You've got my word. Nothing will happen to you or your family as long as you don't cause any trouble. You know, like calling the chief of police and telling him to come to your house at 5 a.m. You won't do anything that stupid anymore, will you, Mayor?"

"How did you know about that?" Ky asked with his voice shaking just a bit.

"It doesn't matter, Mayor. All you need to know is that I will know if you do anything like that again, and I won't be as understanding next time. Now, get the hell out of my office. You have a race to drop out of."

Ky Cole was defeated for now. He knew it. Somehow, Joseph knew about his meeting earlier that morning. That meant he knew what he had told Norman and Detective Jacks. *Are both of them on the Cuneo payroll, or just one of them*? he wondered. If only one was on the take, the other would be in danger because of what Ky had told them.

Then he worried about himself and his family. Were they still in danger because of what he said earlier that morning? Cuneo had given his word that he and his family were safe, but could he trust his word?

He reasoned that Cuneo still needed him, and as long as he did, Ky and his family would be safe. He got in his car in the parking lot of the Pinera Family Funeral Home, started the engine, and called his wife.

"Hello, Diane. Honey, I wanted you to know first. I've decided not to run for governor. I just don't think I'm ready yet. Maybe in four more years, we can try again."

"Ky, you know I love you, and I'll support whatever decision you make, but I thought you were absolutely set on running now. You told me that the opportunity was now. You seemed so sure of your decision. What changed your mind?"

"There are just so many things I need to accomplish in Kansas City right now. I want to take care of them first. I can consider running again in four years."

"Okay, honey, you've got my support no matter what you decide to do."

"Thanks, Diane. I love you, honey."

"I love you too. Are you going to be late tonight? I'm getting ready to go out and shop for dinner, so I'm wondering if

I should cook for three or four?"

"Set the table for four tonight. I'll be home around six."

"Will do. By the way, there was an FBI agent that called for you earlier this morning. He left his number. Do you want it?"

"No. I'll get it from you tonight. See you later, honey."

He hung up the phone, started the car, and drove out of the parking lot. *What the hell did the FBI agent want with me*? he thought. Whatever it was could wait. Ky needed to get to city hall to contact the secretary of state in Jefferson City. He needed to withdraw his name from the race for governor. Then he needed to find someone he could trust in city hall, someone that wasn't on the Cuneo payroll. He thought about who he could trust on the drive. Anyone could be on the Cuneo payroll, and he wouldn't know it. It was obvious that either Detective Jacks or his friend, Norman, the chief of police, was working for Cuneo — possibly both of them. Ky hoped it wasn't his friend, Norman. He had always respected Norman and thought of him as being beyond reproach. But until he knew for sure, he couldn't trust either of them. One or both of them had told Cuneo about their meeting with Ky earlier that morning.

Ky thought about people in city hall that had gone against the grain of projects supported by the Cuneo family. One name came to his mind — Councilman Terry Michael. He had opposed the construction of the two new cremation furnaces at the Pinera Family Crematorium. Ky remembered he was not present for the vote to approve their construction. *Did the Cuneo family put pressure on him not to vote*? Ky wondered. He made a mental note to contact Councilman Michael.

A few minutes later, Ky pulled into his parking spot at city hall. He walked upstairs to the top floor where his office was located. He shut the door and called the secretary of state's office, and withdrew his name from the governor's race. Then he called his supporters who had encouraged him to run and explained his decision to withdraw. He told them he had come to this decision for personal reasons. He felt that he still had a lot to accomplish in Kansas City.

A few minutes later, he picked up the phone and called Councilman Michaels. They exchanged a few pleasantries. Terry Michaels was not a supporter of the mayor. He had battled corruption his entire political life. He was certain that Mayor Cole was corrupt and on the Cuneo family payroll. But even though he didn't trust the mayor, he was curious why he would call him out of the blue.

"What can I do for you, Mayor?" he asked.

"Councilman, there is something I would like to discuss with you. It's very important, and I don't want to discuss it over the phone or in either of our offices. Could you meet me at Riley's Bar, 14th & Broadway, at eight tonight?"

"Yes, I'll be there," he said. "I take it that the drinks will be on you, Mayor."

"Yes, I'll even throw in an order of pretzels and beer cheese dip."

"It's a deal. I'll see you at eight."

"Thanks, Councilman. Also, please don't tell anyone about our meeting."

"All right."

Ky hung up the phone and called his wife. "Hello, Diane. Can you have dinner ready at six sharp? I have an appointment at eight. I'll need to leave a few minutes past seven."

"Sure, I can do that. But I was hoping we would have you home tonight."

"I won't be late, honey. I should be home by ten or ten-thirty."

"Okay, Ky. We'll see you at six."

Ky had just hung up from talking to his wife when his secretary rang him.

"Mayor, a Special Agent Bradshaw is waiting for you. He says it is urgent. Do you want me to send him in?"

"Yes, Gloria. Send him in."

A few seconds later, the door opened, and a tall, thin man that looked to be in his late twenties or early thirties walked in.

"Hello, Mayor," he said, holding out his hand to shake. In his other hand, he held out his FBI badge and identification.

"What can I do for you, Agent Bradshaw?" Ky asked.

"I talked to your wife earlier today. Did she tell you I need to talk to you?"

"Yes, she told me. I've been very busy today. I didn't have time to call you, Agent Bradshaw."

"Mayor, you were instrumental in helping the Cuneo family procure the burial contract for the city, weren't you?"

"Well, I wouldn't say I was instrumental. I educated Mr. Cuneo about the steps needed to bid on the contract. I had nothing to do with influencing the selection of his funeral home. I believe that would be illegal, Agent Bradshaw."

"Yes, it would, but I wasn't accusing you of doing anything illegal, Mayor. I was only curious how much you knew about Joseph Cuneo's arrangement with the city."

"Not much, I'm afraid. The city's contract procurement office handles all bids from vendors. I know the Pinera Family Funeral Home won the bid, but that is about all I know."

"Mayor Cole, the FBI is investigating several suspicious deaths in which the bodies were cremated and which the city paid for as part of their contract with the Cuneo family. Are you aware of any body dispositions that have been paid for by the city that were not authorized?"

"No, Agent Bradshaw. And, like I said, the procurement office is the one that authorizes payment for vendor services. It's their job to make sure the invoices they are presented with are accurate and have been authorized."

"Well, that's where I seem to be a little confused, Mayor. I have gone to the city procurement office. They, too, thought the invoices sent in by the Pinera funeral home were excessive. But they showed me your signature giving payment authorization for every invoice the funeral home submitted."

Ky shifted in his seat nervously. He had been caught in a lie. He searched his mind for an explanation. "Well, Special Agent, I don't remember authorizing payment for the Pinera funeral home specifically. A tremendous amount of paperwork comes across my desk every day. If my signature is on the payment authorizations, then I must have signed them. But I just don't remember."

"Okay, Mayor. You and Joseph Cuneo are related, aren't you?"

"Yes, we are cousins. But I don't know why that is relevant, Agent Bradshaw."

"I'm not sure that it is relevant. I was just curious, Mayor." Bradshaw stood up and began to turn to leave. Then he stopped and looked at Ky. "I have just one more question, Mayor. Don't the city burial contracts specifically call for the bodies to be embalmed, placed in a casket, and buried in the city cemetery?"

"Yes, I believe so."

"Then why are the bodies being cremated?"

"I don't know," Ky said. "Maybe you should ask Joseph Cuneo."

"We intend to, but you have been authorizing payments for these burials. Were you aware that the bodies were cremated rather than buried?"

"No. I wasn't aware of that."

Agent Bradshaw left the mayor's office. Ky got up from his desk and closed the door. He went back to his desk and called his secretary.

"Gloria, could you please hold my calls? I don't want to be disturbed this afternoon unless it's something urgent."

"Yes, Mayor."

Ky opened his bottom desk drawer and pulled out a pint of gin that he had stored there for emergencies. He poured a paper cup full of gin, set the bottle on his desk, and took a long drink. Then he picked up the phone and called Cuneo.

"Joe, this is Ky. We may have a problem."

"What is it, Mayor?"

"I received a visit from Special Agent Bradshaw with the FBI a few minutes ago."

"Oh? And what did he want with you, Mayor?"

"He had questions about the contract you have for city burials. He suspects I helped you secure that contract. He also knows about the cremations you are doing to dispose of those bodies."

"Damn it, Mayor. This isn't a conversation you should be having on your office phone. Why don't you meet me in my office in thirty minutes?"

"Okay, Mr. Cuneo."

Ky hung up the phone, took another drink of gin, and headed out the door. "Gloria, I've got an appointment. I doubt that I'll be back today."

A half-hour later, he was sitting in Joseph Cuneo's office.

Cuneo was visibly upset. "What the fuck are you doing talking to me about the FBI on your office phone? Your phones are probably being tapped, you stupid son-of-a-bitch."

"I'm sorry. I guess I wasn't thinking."

"No, you weren't, Ky. You've been drinking too. I can smell it on your breath. You're not the sharpest knife in the drawer, Ky, and alcohol just makes you that much dumber. Now, try to tell me exactly what the FBI agent asked you about."

"He wanted to know if I helped you procure the city burial contract."

"What did you say."

"I told him no. The contract was awarded by the city procurement office. I had nothing to do with it being awarded to you."

"Good, Ky. What else did he ask you?"

"He said he had proof that I had signed the payment authorizations for all your burials. He said the procurement office said the payments to you seemed excessive, and so they requested that I approve them."

"What did you tell him?"

"I said that if he had proof, then I must have signed them, but I did not remember. I have so much paperwork that comes across my desk every week that I don't remember everything I sign."

"So now, Ky, the FBI not only thinks you are corrupt, but they also think you are stupid. Was there anything else that he asked you about, Mayor?"

"Yes, he asked if I knew why the bodies you were supposed to bury were being cremated?"

"What did you say?"

"I told him I didn't know. I told him he should ask you."

"Fuck, Ky. What were you thinking? By answering that way, you made it sound like you did know that bodies were being cremated. The FBI couldn't have possibly known we were cremating the bodies instead of burying them unless someone told them. Did you tell them, Ky? Or maybe your lovely wife? I know she invited Agent Bradshaw into your home earlier this morning. What did they talk about, Ky?"

"Nothing. She would not tell the FBI anything."

"Maybe, but someone told them about the cremations. How else would they know?"

"I don't know, Joseph."

"Ky, we are watching you and your wife. If you or your wife so much as hint that the Cuneo family is involved in anything illegal, I will be extremely upset and trust me, you don't want me to get upset."

"I understand, Joseph."

"Now get the fuck out of here and don't call me again. If you need to see me, come to my office. Also, make sure your wife keeps her mouth shut too, or I'll need to shut it for her."

Ky arrived home a few minutes after six. He expected his wife would have dinner on the table. After all, he told her that he had a meeting at eight. But instead of finding dinner on the table, he found his wife sitting in a chair in the family room, crying.

"Diane, what's wrong, honey?"

"Ky, the FBI came to visit me this afternoon. It was the same agent that came this morning, Agent Bradshaw."

"What did he say that upset you so much?"

"He says you are involved in illegal activities, maybe even murder. He says you are involved with crimes committed by the Cuneo family."

"That's just not true, Diane."

"He says that unless I cooperate, I could be charged as an accessory to your crimes."

"Oh hell, Diane. He is just trying to scare you. He has no evidence because I haven't committed any crimes. You believe me, don't you, honey?"

"Yes, I believe you, but I also know what the Cuneo family is capable of. They are mobsters, and your cousin, Joseph, is the worst. I wouldn't be surprised if he has murdered someone or had one of his thugs do it for him. Is it true he has a contract with the city, and you helped him get it?"

"Yes, he has a burial contract with the city, but I was not involved in helping him get the contract. We are cousins, that's it. I'm not involved in his business, and he's not involved in mine. You've got to believe me, Diane."

"I do believe you, Ky. But Agent Bradshaw is not going to stop until he brings down Joseph Cuneo and anyone else that is involved in his crimes. Right now, he thinks you are involved. He says he has proof, and it won't be long before he is able to issue a warrant for your arrest. He says you are going to go to prison unless you cooperate."

"Please don't worry, Diane. I will take care of everything. I won't go to prison, I promise you. Just, please be strong, and don't talk to Agent Bradshaw again unless I am present. Okay?"

"Okay."

"Diane, where are the girls?"

"I asked my mother to pick them up and keep them at her house tonight. I was hoping we could talk and work things out together. You know, Ky, if you have any information about the Cuneo family's criminal activities, you need to talk to Agent Bradshaw right away. He will protect you."

"I can't do that right now, Diane, even if I did have

information to give him. I don't know who we can trust. Diane, I have a meeting I need to get to. We will talk more when I get back, I promise. Do me a favor. Don't talk to anyone about your visit from Agent Bradshaw. Also, honey, please check in with your mother and make sure the girls are all right."

"Okay."

CHAPTER 15
THE BASEMENT

Ky walked into Riley's Bar a few minutes past eight. There were only a handful of patrons inside. Riley's was a quiet, neighborhood bar, not the type of place that he was likely to be noticed. He looked around and spotted the councilman at a table in the corner of the bar.

"Thanks for meeting me here, Terry. Sorry, I'm running a few minutes late."

"No problem, Mayor. I'm a couple of drinks ahead of you. You'll need to catch up. I've got to admit, Ky, I am more than a little curious why you wanted to meet with me. We haven't exactly been friendly in the past."

"What are you drinking, Councilman?

"A highball."

Ky ordered two doubles of gin on the rocks for himself and another highball for the councilman. They made polite conversation for a few minutes. When the drinks arrived, he downed one of his drinks with three large gulps. Then he explained the purpose of the meeting.

"Terry, why didn't you show up to vote against the additional cremation furnaces for Pinera Funeral Home?"

"I don't see how that is any of your business, Mayor. Besides, I would think you were happy I didn't vote. You wanted the approval of those cremation furnaces, didn't you?"

"Yes, I did then, but I'm not so sure now."

"What do you mean?"

"I mean that Joseph Cuneo pretty much has me by the balls. I mean that I think I am being set up to be blamed for crimes he may be committing that involve that crematorium. Terry, please answer my question. Why didn't you show up to vote against the construction?"

The councilman polished off his third drink. "I think you'd better order us both another drink before I answer that question."

Ky waved for the server to come over again. "Darling, why don't you bring us both another drink, put them in tall glasses, and fill them all the way up with one cube of ice?"

"The reason I didn't show up to vote was that I was threatened. I am sure the threat came from the Cuneo family. I was told that if I voted against the construction, a family member would have an accident. So I chose not to attend the meeting rather than vote in favor of the construction. Joseph Cuneo is a dangerous person. He is a psychopath. If you are mixed up with him, there is no good way that things are going to end for you or your family. You need to go to the police."

"That's just it. I can't. The Cuneo family has the local police in their pockets. They have key people in city hall in their pockets, too. That's why I called you. You're one of the few people I can trust. I know you are not on Cuneo's payroll. I need your help. I need to stop Cuneo before he kills me or my family."

"Wait a second. I'm just as afraid of the Cuneo family as you are. Even if I wasn't concerned for my own life, I have a wife and three children. I can't jeopardize their safety."

"If we are both careful, neither of us will put our families in danger. I am convinced that Cuneo is laundering money for the mob through the Pinera Family Funeral Home. I think Lou Pinera knows about it. No one has seen him lately — they may have killed him. The evidence of the laundering operation must be upstairs in Cuneo's office. There is a safe next to one of the walls. I bet the accounting records that will show his money laundering will be in that safe."

Councilman Michael shook his head. "There is no way you'll be able to get into that safe. He probably has several of his goons watching, and even if he doesn't, I'm sure there are alarms and security cameras that would capture you trying to break in."

"Yes, you're right. I've considered all of that. We need a diversion, something that will get Cuneo and his associates to leave that second floor, something that will force him to put any evidence that could hurt him into that safe."

"So, what do you have in mind, Ky?"

"A fire. We need to start a fire in the funeral home, a large enough fire that they will need to call the fire department. A large enough fire that they will need to evacuate the funeral home. A large enough fire that they will need to put any evidence of their crimes into that fireproof safe in Cuneo's office. I believe I know the combination to his safe. My wife and I have been out with Ellen and Joseph several times. He is my cousin, you know. Ellen had a little too much to drink one night and let it slip to my wife that the combination to his safe was their wedding anniversary. She joked about how, because her husband had trouble remembering their anniversary, so he wouldn't forget, they changed the combination of his safe to that date, 01 13 66."

Councilman Michael put his drink down and stared blankly at Ky. Then, he shook his head.

"No, no, no. I'm not going to commit a felony to try to find evidence of a crime. You're crazy, Mayor. I've got a good life. My family has a good life. I'm not going to throw it all away because of your wild speculation. If you really believe that Cuneo is using the funeral home to launder money and to perpetrate other crimes, you need to go to the FBI. I'm sorry, Mayor, but leave me out of this."

Councilman Michael stood up and walked out.

What was I thinking? Ky thought. Councilman Michaels had no reason to help him. The mayor had no right to ask him to help, particularly when it meant committing a felony. Now, if he did start a fire at the funeral home, Michael would be a key witness for the prosecution if he went to trial. If he did start a fire, he'd better make damn sure that he left the crime scene with evidence of Cuneo's crimes. His drinking had impaired his thinking. He should have never brought that idea up to the councilman. He needed to go home, get a good night's sleep, sober up, and tomorrow morning he'd be thinking a little clearer.

Ky got in his car, started the engine, and drove home slowly and careful. He was drunk and didn't want to get stopped. It probably wouldn't have mattered if he did — he was mayor. No policeman was going to give him a ticket. But Ky didn't want the embarrassment of being stopped, of someone knowing how intoxicated he was.

When he arrived home, he quietly opened the front door. He didn't want to wake up his wife and didn't want her to know how much he had drank. She had wanted to talk. That was the last thing that Ky wanted to do in his condition. Their talk could wait until the morning. The lights were off downstairs. He flipped on a light switch in the foyer. It provided him enough light to see up the stairs.

Ky walked up the steps and opened the door to the girl's room. They weren't there. Then he remembered they were spending the night at his in-laws. He shut their door and walked to the master bedroom. The door was shut, locked from the inside. *Damn, she is upset with me.* "Diane, I'm sorry, honey. Please let me in."

Nothing was said. The house was quiet, too quiet. *What about Murphy?* he thought. Murphy was their golden retriever and usually met Ky at the door. *Even if Diane took Murphy into the bedroom with her, he would surely bark when he heard someone knocking on the door.* There was no sound from him.

Ky knocked even louder on the bedroom door. "Diane, please open the door."

There was nothing but silence. Ky lifted his right leg and, with all his force, kicked at the door just to the right of the lock. It swung open. The room was dark. Ky could make out the covers on the bed. They were pulled up all the way over the pillow where his wife lay.

She must be sound asleep. She must have taken a sleeping pill.

He reached for the edge of the bedsheets and pulled them down, expecting to find Diane sleeping. But underneath the covers was Murphy. His head had nearly been severed with something very sharp — a knife, or perhaps an axe. He was lying in a pool of his own blood. On top of his body was a note.

You've been a bad boy, Mayor. Come and talk with me, now.

Ky drove as fast as he could to the Pinera Funeral Home.

The note wasn't signed, but he knew who it was from. Joseph Cuneo had his wife. Ky knew that. If she was still alive, she wouldn't be for long if Ky didn't come. He pulled into the parking lot of the funeral home. It was early in the morning. The lot was dark. So was the funeral home. There were only two cars in the parking lot, both together and both parked at the far back corner of the lot. He didn't recognize either car. Ky pulled to a parking space near the main entrance. The door was unlocked. A single security light was on in the foyer. It provided just enough light for Ky to find his way to the stairs leading up to his cousin's office.

That's when he heard the noise coming from the basement. It sounded like something had fallen. He looked for the stairs leading to the basement. *Maybe Diane is down there*, he thought. When he reached the top of the stairs leading to the basement, a light suddenly turned on in the basement. He moved slowly down the stairs trying to be as quiet as possible. When he reached the bottom, he stopped to look and listen. Someone was in the embalming room. He could hear them working.

"Help me lift him up and put him on the table," Ky heard someone say. He moved closer to the embalming room. The door was open. Two men, large men were lifting the body of a young man off the concrete floor. Ky did not recognize him. His body was lifeless. It looked like the young man was dead. "Lay him on this gurney, now. We'll need to move the woman off the embalming table so we can work on him," he heard one of the men say.

From his position twenty feet away, Ky had a good view of the embalming table. He watched as the men moved the body that was resting on the table.

Ky nearly passed out. The body on the table was Diane.

Shock ran through his body. It was closely followed by anger.
The anger swelled up inside him. He looked around for any sort
of weapon. On a workbench nearby was what looked like a steel
rod, used to crank the steel gurneys to lift them. It was a tool
similar to a car jack. *It will do the trick*. He reached for the steel
rod, held it securely in his right hand, and moved silently to the
embalming room. Both men had their backs to him as they were
lifting his wife off the embalming table. He lunged at the first
man, swinging the steel rod with all his might. He landed the
first blow to the the stranger's back. The second blow came down
on the man's head. He could hear the cracking of his skull. The
second man reached for a gun in his pocket. Before he could lift
it all the way, Ky pounded him in the face with the steel rod. He
fell to the floor. Ky lost control of himself. He pounded both men
several more times. Their blood splattered everywhere. There
was no doubt. Both of the strangers were dead.

Someone was bound to hear the noise. There wasn't
much time. Ky reached down to check his wife's pulse but felt
nothing. He reached over and gave her a tender kiss on the lips.
Then he grabbed two large plastic containers of embalming fluid
and carried them to the garage. He poured the embalming fluid
throughout the interior of two of the hearses parked in the garage.
He lit a match and threw it in one of the hearses. The fire spread
quickly. Then he threw a match into the other hearse. A small fire
began, but it erupted quickly. The fire intensified. A smoke alarm
near the embalming room went off. Others located around the
basement went off too. The noise from their sirens was almost
deafening. A sprinkler system in the garage and embalmer room
was triggered by the fire, smoke, and heat. Ky stood in stunned
silence. He hadn't thought about the sprinkler system. It was
beginning to slow the progress of the fire. That was until the

fire reached the gas tank of one of the hearses. The explosion rocked the funeral home. It also negated the effectiveness of the sprinkler system. A second explosion took out the sprinkler system altogether.

Ky heard several men coming down the stairs from the second floor. He heard them run through the first floor, checking each area. Then he heard them coming down the stairs to the basement. The fire was blazing now. The smoke was intense. It had encompassed most of the basement and was starting to move upstairs.

"Oh shit," he heard one of the men yell as he saw the smoke. "Get the fire extinguisher."

Ky hid close to the stairway and waited. Finally, six men ran into the basement carrying four fire extinguishers. Sirens could be heard coming closer. The fire department was on its way. The men tried desperately to put out the fire, but it was too large, and it was spreading.

"Boss, you need to get out of the building. There is a fire in the basement, and we are not going to be able to put it out," Ky could hear one of the men say on his cell phone.

After a futile attempt to put out the fire, and with two fire trucks pulling up in the back of the building, the men ran into the embalming room. There were bodies in there — bodies they didn't want the police or the fire department to see. The men carried the bodies into the storage room. They only had a few minutes before the fire department was inside the building. It was not enough time to get rid of the bodies. They would need to hide them. The caskets in the storage room seemed like the perfect hiding place. The men opened caskets and placed the bodies inside. Then they closed the lids. If the fire reached the storage room, the wood caskets would make fine firewood. The bodies would burn just as if they were in a cremation furnace.

With the bodies securely hidden, the men ran up the basement stairs and out the front door. Cuneo and two of his associates that remained upstairs were already outside. The funeral home was vacant except for Ky and the bodies in the caskets. A third explosion shook the building. The fire had spread to more vehicles in the garage.

Ky ran up the stairs toward Joseph's office. "Damn," Ky said to himself as he got to the second floor. "I hope this building lasts long enough for me to escape."

The door at the entrance to the second floor was locked. Ky kicked it several times. Finally, it broke free of the lock. He ran inside. Smoke was beginning to reach the upper level. There wasn't much time. He ran through the hall directly to Cuneo's office. The door was locked. One swift kick, and it opened. He went directly to the safe at the far wall of the office.

He used the numbers of the Cuneo anniversary to open the safe. The first try didn't work. The second try didn't work. "He must have changed the combination," Ky said to himself. Luckily, he had come prepared. Inside his pocket was a hook pick. He ran the end of the hook pick into a small opening at the top of the combination wheel, moving the pick sideways inside the hole until he heard a click. The safe opened up. Ky grabbed everything inside the safe, closed the safe, and ran downstairs to the first floor.

He hurried toward the front door. That's when he saw Joseph Cuneo standing outside. Fearful of what his cousin would do, he turned and ran toward the basement. The smoke was thick, his breathing was labored. He hurried down the stairs into the basement, looking for a window, any possible way to escape. But the smoke was just too thick.

Ky was somewhere within the storage room when he heard the screams for help. He followed the yells to a wooden casket at one corner of the room. The smoke was so dense that he used his hands to guide his way to the sound. He opened the casket. Inside was a young man, coughing, desperately trying to escape. His fingernails were bloodied from trying to open the casket. Ky reached down and pulled him out.

The two of them followed the sounds of the firefighters working in the garage. Every step was a struggle. Both men were weak, desperate for breathable air. Then, a few yards away from the garage, another cry for help could be heard coming from the storage room. It sounded like a woman's voice. The voice sounded weak, the cries softer.

Ky stopped moving. "Was that Diane?" He had to go back. He had to try to save his wife.

He looked directly at the man he had just rescued. Then he handed him the papers he had found in Joseph Cuneo's safe. "Take these," he said. "If I get out of here, give them back to me. But if I don't, contact Special Agent Bradshaw with the FBI. Give the papers to him. He will protect you."

***

Dennis took the papers and walked into the garage. Two firemen grabbed him and carried him outside, where they put an oxygen mask on him. Soon his breathing became less labored. Dennis Glenn was going to be all right.

An ambulance pulled up. Two paramedics climbed out of the ambulance, opened the back, and began to pull out a stretcher. But Dennis was not about to let them take him to the hospital. He had to find Elise. What had Joseph Cuneo done with her? Was she still alive? Had she escaped with him and his thugs? He couldn't let the paramedics take him to the hospital. If she was still alive, she would need his help.

Dennis took one last, deep breath from the oxygen mask, took it off of his face, got to his feet, and ran. In the commotion, nobody chased after him. As he came around the front of the funeral home, he saw Joseph Cuneo and several of his men. They didn't see him. Dennis scanned the crowd out front of the funeral home for Elise, but she wasn't there. *Is she still inside?* he wondered. He couldn't go back in, not now.

Then, he spotted the delivery vehicle in the parking lot of the crematorium. There were several people outside in the lot, watching the scene unfold at the funeral home. He scanned that group.

Most were the new employees that were hired to work in the crematorium. He did not see Michael Cuneo. "Someone must have recently delivered a body to the crematorium. The delivery vehicle was what the funeral home used to transport bodies. Could that be Elise?" he wondered.

He needed to find out. Dennis walked the long way around the block so he wouldn't be spotted. He came up from the backside of the crematorium, carefully watching the crowd for anyone that might see him. When he was confident that no one was looking, Dennis slipped into the front door of the crematorium. The lights were on, but it was quiet inside. "Michael Cuneo must be here," he said. He had not noticed Michael in the crowd that was in the parking lot. Dennis walked quietly, assuming that Michael was somewhere inside.

As he approached the cremation chamber, Dennis could feel the heat of the furnaces. With the additional three cremation furnaces, the room could easily be twenty to thirty degrees warmer than the rest of the building. Dennis walked to the worktable in the cremation chamber. He reached down and grabbed the steel mallet lying on the table. It was the tool used to mash down bones while they were still in the cremation furnace. He walked past the cremation chamber and down the hallway toward the refrigeration room. The door was closed. The light was on. *He must be inside working*, Dennis thought.

He reached the entrance to the room—that's when he heard Michael Cuneo. He was inside. Dennis had no choice. He had to confront him. If Elise was in there, he needed to get to her now. Dennis raised the mallet in his right hand and opened the door with his left.

Elise was on the gurney. Standing over her with his pants completely off was Michael Cuneo. Dennis nearly blacked out with rage. He charged Michael, and with all the force he could muster, he struck him over the back of his head, then again and again and again. Blood shot out of his head, causing splatters on the wall, ceiling, floor, and desk. Michael didn't have a chance to fight back. In all likelihood, the first blow to his head killed him. The rest of the blows were overkill. Dennis's rage had taken control.

He moved quickly to his wife and felt for a pulse. He couldn't find one. He looked at her with tears rolling down his face. She was naked. He covered her with a sheet. Her eyes were wide open, staring into his face. Her pupils were large. Her eyes seemed to glow. She was trying to tell him something. He knew it. "What is it, honey?" he asked.

He waited in silence for a response, any response. There was none. He checked her pulse one more time. There was nothing. Dennis bent over and put his lips on hers. He kissed her one final time.

CHAPTER 16
TALKING EYES

Dennis walked over to his desk, picked up the phone, and called the FBI field office in Kansas City. "May I speak to Special Agent Bradshaw, please."

"I'm afraid he is not in the office, sir. Can I take a message?"

"Tell him that this is Dennis Glenn. Tell him I just killed someone in the refrigeration room of the crematorium. Tell him that Joseph Cuneo will be coming for me soon. If he finds me dead, tell him that I've hidden some evidence in the refrigeration room."

Then he thought about the two detectives that had come to see him and Elise. He had one of their cards in his wallet. He opened it up and pulled the card out. It was the business card for Detective Jacks.

"What was the other detective's name?" he wondered. Dennis could not find his card. He wasn't even sure if he'd left him one. Dennis remembered Lou Pinera's suspicions that members of the local police were on the Cuneo family payroll.

But Dennis had to trust someone. He had to stop Joseph Cuneo.

So he picked up the phone and called Detective Jacks.

"Hello, this is Detective Jacks. How can I help you?" the voice on the other end of the phone said.

"Detective, this is Dennis Glenn."

"Yes, Dennis, what can I do for you?"

"I'm in the crematorium, Detective. I've just killed Michael Cuneo. I have proof of crimes committed by Joseph Cuneo and his crime family. Can you get here as soon as possible? I don't know how much longer I can wait until they discover I'm here."

"I'm leaving now. I'll be there right away. Dennis, does anyone know where you are?"

"No, I don't believe so."

"Hang on. I'll be there in fifteen minutes."

Dennis hung up the phone, then sat down at the desk and looked at the papers that had been in Joseph Cuneo's safe. "Give them to Special Agent Bradshaw," he remembered the mayor saying.

He panned through the papers. Some of what the mayor had handed him were accounting ledgers. Some of the papers listed names with dollar amounts listed next to them. Several of the names listed were police officers. Some were city officials. One of the names sent chills down Dennis's body. Detective Jacks was listed on the paper, with a dollar amount of $5,000 next to the name.

"Oh shit," Dennis said out loud.

Detective Jacks was on the Cuneo family payroll. Dennis picked on the steel mallet with one hand and grabbed the papers with his other. He needed to hide the papers. There wasn't much time. The detective would have notified Cuneo by now. Someone would be coming anytime.

Dennis could hear the front door to the crematorium open. He picked up the phone in an effort to call Special Agent Bradshaw one last time. The phone line was dead. He hid the papers from Joseph Cuneo's safe in the only place he could think of. Then he turned out the lights in the embalming room and waited.

There were several footsteps coming. Detective Jacks had called Joseph Cuneo. He was in the crematorium, and so were several of his thugs. They stopped to search every part of the building as they made their way to the refrigeration room.

Suddenly, all of the power in the building went out. The place went completely dark. Dennis couldn't see more than a few inches in front of his face. The crematorium, for the most part, was underground. There were no windows to let in natural light. With the electricity turned off, it was pitch black inside. Dennis used his ears to listen for any movement of the men that were coming for him. The footsteps had slowed. They were in the hallway now. He could hear their hands running against the side of the wall to guide their way. The dark could be used to Dennis's advantage. He would have the element of surprise. But the surprise wouldn't last long. They would have guns. He only had the mallet.

But Dennis would inflict as much damage as he could before they took him down. In his mind, he had no reason to live. His wife was dead. His father was probably dead. Cuneo had inflicted as much pain on him as was humanly possible already. Death did not matter to Dennis. In fact, he looked forward to it. It would end his suffering, and maybe, just maybe, he would meet up with his wife in the afterlife.

In a way, he was happy. His suffering was about to end, while Cuneo's was about to start. Dennis had killed his son. Soon he would see his lifeless body lying on the cold, concrete floor, his brains splattered on the walls, ceiling, everywhere. He would soon learn all about suffering.

Dennis could hear someone at the door just a few feet away from him. He readied the mallet. The door squeaked as it began to open. Dennis couldn't see a damn thing, but neither could they. Dennis used his ears to determine when to attack. He could hear their heavy breathing, could smell the scent of cigars and bourbon. When the squeaking of the door stopped, Dennis thrust the mallet with all his force. He felt it collide with one person and heard the cries of pain. He brought the mallet back and flung it again and again and again, making contact each time. The screams, groins, and cries intensified. Then he felt a sharp pain in his gut that caused him to lean over in pain, still wildly swinging the steal mallet he held in his right hand. If he was going to die, he was going to take others with him. Then he felt a jolt to his neck. It knocked him backwards into the gurney where his wife lay. He dropped the mallet. As he began to fall, he reached for his wife with his left hand. Dennis wanted to touch her one last time. Then, he fell to the floor.

***

Dennis never expected to wake up, but he did. He was strapped down to a gurney directly across from his wife. He was groggy, in pain, but he was alive. Standing next to him was Joseph Cuneo. His eyes were swollen and red—he had been crying. He had realized the pain of losing someone he loved. Michael was his oldest son, the one that would take over the family business someday. He was so much like his father. Now he was dead, and the person that killed him was lying on a gurney just inches away from Cuneo.

The thought of him suffering brought a smile to Dennis's

face.

"Stop smiling, you son-of-a-bitch. You're going to pay for killing my boy," Cuneo said, glaring down at Dennis. Then, with his right hand, he reared back and slapped Dennis across the face as hard as he could. "Before this night is out, you are going to beg me to end your life. You are going to suffer more in the next hour than you can possibly imagine, and I'm going to enjoy every minute of it."

"Fuck you," Dennis yelled back defiantly.

"You know, Dennis, I had no intention of killing you. All you and your wife had to do was keep your mouths shut and stay out of my business. But you and she just couldn't do that, so here you are lying next to each other, both about to experience pain beyond anything you have ever imagined."

Dennis's eyes got large. He wondered if he had heard him right. Was his wife still alive?

"Well, that got your attention, Dennis. Would it surprise you to know that your wife is still alive? Oh, she doesn't look like it, I know. You probably even checked her pulse. You didn't feel a pulse, did you? You know, you really surprise me, Dennis. I thought you were smart. Didn't you ever, even once, suspect that some of the bodies you were cremating were still alive? You were the one that killed them, Dennis. You put those poor people in the cremation furnace while they were still alive. Can you imagine the incredible suffering they must have gone through? They could see you. They could feel you. They watched in agony as you lifted them into that cremation furnace. Can you imagine the pain they went through when the flames and heat from that furnace boiled them from the inside out? They couldn't scream. They couldn't move. I'm sure they tried to tell you. Couldn't you see it in their eyes? Their eyes—that was the one thing I feared would give it away. The drugs had a weird effect on their eyes. We couldn't close them. They were always open, always looking at you. Couldn't you see them trying to talk to you with their eyes?

"You must have been suspicious. So many bodies in your refrigeration room. So many of them with their eyes wide open. Weren't you the least bit suspicious of all the special orders? You never said anything. Oh, you talked to your wife about it. We listened to your conversation. But you didn't know that those bodies were still alive, did you? How can you live with yourself knowing that you murdered so many people? Now, look at your wife, your lovely, lovely wife. Can you see her trying to talk to you with her eyes? She can hear us right now. She can see you, too. She just can't move or talk. But she is aware of everything happening around her. Tell her you love her, Dennis. She will hear you."

"I love you, Elise."

"Oh, that is so sweet. It's so nice to see true love. I'm sure you couldn't possibly imagine any worse pain than watching someone you love die right in front of you. Unless, of course, you were to watch that person suffer so much that they beg to die."

"You son-of-a-bitch, I would kill you with my bare hands if you'd let me out of these straps."

"Bobby, turn the electricity back on and turn the cremation furnace on."

"Come on, Mr. Cuneo. You don't need to harm her. I'm the person you want. Kill me, torture me as much as you want. Just please don't hurt Elise. I'm the one that killed your son. I'm the one that betrayed you. She had nothing to do with it. She won't talk. She won't go to the police. Please, leave her alone."

"I am afraid I can't do that, Dennis. But I can keep you

from screaming. We'll give you a shot—not a full dose, mind you, just enough to quiet you and keep you from struggling. I want to see the expression on your face when we drop your wife into the cremation furnace."

Dennis felt the shot go into his neck followed by the coolness of the liquid going into his vein. He felt his body go numb, but not all the way. For a while, he could move his fingers and his toes, and he could move his face slightly.

It was a strange feeling to know he was alive, could see, could hear, but could not talk or move. This was the second time he had been injected with something. The first was earlier in the evening in the embalming room. But that was different. That substance knocked him out. It didn't paralyze him. This time he was completely immobilized.

Dennis watched as Cuneo removed the sheet that covered Elise's body. He watched him fondle her breasts and gently kiss her on the lips. He watched as Cuneo got undressed. Dennis knew what was about to happen, but he was powerless to stop it. He tried with all his willpower to move, but he couldn't. So he watched as Cuneo got on top of his wife. When he had finished, he got dressed and turned to Dennis. Cuneo had a sick smile on his face.

"Did you enjoy the show, Dennis? I've never made love to a corpse before. It's really very enjoyable. Oh wait, your wife isn't a corpse. Is she? Not yet, anyway. Still, she was a pretty good fuck—a little unemotional but satisfying. I think she enjoyed it. It was a little hard to tell. She just laid there," Cuneo said with a laugh.

Dennis was dying inside. Outside, he looked emotionless, but inside, his will to live had disappeared. He was shutting down inside. Even his eyes became cloudy. He could no longer see Elise, and he could no longer see the monster in front of him.

Cuneo ordered his men to lift up Dennis and put him on the same gurney as his wife. He laid there next to her, smelled her perfume, and felt the warmness of her body. Dennis strained his eyes to see her one last time. The gurney was small, meant to hold only one person. In order to fit both of them, the men had turned them on their sides. Dennis and Elise were facing each other. She was looking directly into his eyes. He resisted his will to give up long enough to look into her eyes one last time. His wife was talking to him through her eyes. He could see it. She told him that she loved him, that everything was going to be all right, that they would see each other again.

The men rolled the gurney out of the refrigeration room, down the hallway, and into the cremation chamber, stopping directly in front of the furnace. The same furnace where Dennis had cremated so many living bodies. It was so hot next to the furnace. He had never felt that kind of intense heat before. When the furnace door was opened, a blast of heat fell over his body. He had opened that furnace door hundreds of times in the past, but it never felt this hot. Dennis was about to experience what so many of the bodies he had put into that furnace had experienced.

"Dennis, I know you can hear me. Your suffering is not going to end right away. I'm not going to make it that easy for you. I want you to watch for a while," Cuneo said.

He ordered his men to lift Elise off the table. Dennis knew what was about to happen. He used every bit of willpower to shut down the inside of his body. He prayed to God to let him die. On the outside, he was paralyzed. But inside, his brain was still functioning.

It is amazing what a person's brain can do when it has a single purpose. Dennis willed his brain to shut his body down. One by one, his internal organs slowed and then stopped functioning. He was paralyzing the inside of his body. His eyes began to cloud up. His mind lost sight of reality. He was going to a better place in his mind. Then, his eyes began to close. The pain inside of him disappeared.

CHAPTER 17
A LONG SLEEP

It was the drop of water that fell from the ceiling and landed in his left eye that brought him back to reality. His eyes were not closed—they were wide open, staring at the ceiling. Dennis could hear the rain beating down on the room he was in. He could feel the irritation in his eye from the drop of water that fell in it. There was light in the room, natural light. A window could be seen out of one corner of his eye, and he heard a dripping sound, but it didn't sound like rain. It sounded like his heart was beating loudly, but the sound wasn't coming from his chest. It was coming from behind him. Dennis felt a tightness in his right arm. It was an uncomfortable feeling. He tried moving his eye to see. His eyeball began to move. *The drugs that they injected in my neck must be wearing off*, he thought. Dennis could feel the fingers on his left hand begin to move and his toes begin to wiggle. His right hand moved slightly. Dennis turned his head just a few inches. That's when he saw the tubes in his arm. A liquid was flowing through them into his veins. The coolness of the liquid collided with the warmth of his blood.

Dennis turned his head to the right and could see the window. It was raining outside. The sky was dark. The thunder and lightning were electrifying the sky outside. He could see the single water spot on the ceiling. In the center of the spot was a small crack. A small dot of water was forming, slowly getting larger. When its weight could no longer be supported by the ceiling, it fell. Dennis watched until the droplet narrowed, thickened, and released itself from the grasp of the ceiling, and turned his head just in time to feel it drop onto the side of his face.

Dennis wasn't in the refrigeration room of the crematorium—he was certain of that. There were no windows in that room. That room was cold. This room was warm. Dennis tilted his head far enough to see the machines behind him. One machine had a monitor that showed his heartbeat. It was strong and loud. Another monitor showed his blood pressure, his vital signs. Then, there was the IV dripping a liquid substance into a long plastic tube that ran into his left arm.

Dennis was in a hospital. It was obvious to him now. *But why*? he asked himself. *Did someone rescue me from the crematorium? That must be it*, he thought. He was alive and was waking up. The liquid that Joseph Cuneo had put into his veins, the liquid that had paralyzed him, was wearing off. *But, where is Elise*? he wondered. Dennis tried calling for her, but his voice was too weak. His words came out as a soft whisper. He could barely hear himself.

Dennis struggled to move his body. With all his willpower, he lifted his right arm and brought it down on the tubes connected to his left arm. He opened his clenched hand and took hold of the tubes, pulling them out of his veins. The machine behind him beeped, slowly at first and then louder and more frequently. An alert was sent to the nursing station, and a few seconds later, two nurses and a doctor ran into his room.

"Where's my wife?" he hollered. He could hear his voice now. It was loud and strong. "Where's Elise?"

"Settle down, Mr. Glenn," the doctor said. "The nurses need to put the IV back into your arm. Please don't move. Otherwise, we'll need to strap you down."

"What's going on, Doctor? What happened to me? Where is my wife? Is she dead? You've got to tell me."

"Nurse, give Mr. Glenn a sedative."

"No, I'm fine. Please, no more drugs. I'll be quiet. Just tell me what's going on."

"Mr. Glenn, you have been in a coma for nearly six years. We had given up hope that you would ever wake up. The hospital took care of you for six months. But they eventually transferred you here."

"Where's here?"

"Sunnyside Sanitarium. We've been taking care of you for five and a half years. You were in a terrible accident, Mr. Glenn. Do you remember?"

"No, Doctor. I don't remember anything."

"I'm not surprised. It's possible that you will never remember that accident or any of the last six years of your life. It really is a miracle that you came out of your coma. The doctors at the hospital wanted your wife to take you off life support, but she refused, thank God. That's when they forced her to move you."

"Please, just tell me what happened, and tell me about my wife."

"Well, like I said, you were in a terrible car accident. From what I remember from the news reports, your wife received a call from her aunt the night of the accident. She was in a bar. She had been divorced from your father-in-law for several months and was depressed. The drinking numbed her feelings, but too much of it made it impossible for her to drive home. So, she called your wife to come to pick her up and take her home. Your wife had remained friends with her, so she drove to the bar to take her home. You insisted on going with your wife. Do you remember anything about that night?"

"No, I don't."

"It was storming, the temperature near freezing. The rain was turning into ice, so the roads were beginning to get slick. You arrived at the bar and picked up your mother-in-law. You insisted on driving home. The weather was turning nasty. Your wife sat next to you, your mother-in-law in the back seat. The police assumed you hit an icy patch in the road. There were no skid marks. The car veered off the road, down an embankment, and into a tree. Your wife was thrown from the car. Your mother-in-law, Gloria Booker, died in the car. You and your wife were rushed to the hospital, both of you in critical condition. You had a lot of swelling in your brain. The doctors decided to put you in an induced coma. Quite frankly, Mr. Glenn, you weren't expected to live."

"What happened to Elise, Doctor?"

"That's the really strange part, Mr. Glenn. When she was thrown from the car, she sustained life-threatening injuries. She was completely paralyzed. When the paramedics reached her, they thought she was dead. It didn't appear that she was breathing. Her heart rate was almost non-existent. They brought her to the hospital, and she was put on life support. Your father-in-law brought a priest with him to administer the last rites. An hour later, she was taken off life support at the request of your father-in-law and was pronounced dead. He made funeral arrangements for her at his funeral home. She was delivered there a few hours later. You know, the odd thing about your wife's body was her eyes. They never closed. They remained wide open. Doctors tried to close them, but it was as if they were locked open. She just stared at the ceiling. It was Tony Pinera that noticed it. He was the embalmer at the funeral home. Elise was on his table. He was preparing to embalm her when something in her eyes caught his attention. He looked closely, and that's when he saw it—at least, he said he saw it."

"What was it?" Dennis asked.

"A teardrop—a single teardrop in the corner of her eye. He was convinced she was still alive, and thank God, he was right. She was just a few minutes away from being embalmed. He called his father and Andrew Pinera. They rushed down to the embalming room. By then, she was able to force more teardrops to form in her eyes. They rushed her back to the hospital, where she recovered fully."

"Where is she? Can I see her?"

"No, I'm afraid not. As far as I know, she is doing fine, but she had an emotional breakdown recently. She is getting rest and receiving treatment. I'm sure you'll be able to see her soon."

"Doctor, is she still paralyzed?"

"No. Nobody knows what happened or why, but her paralysis was temporary. Your wife is fine, Dennis. She has come to see you nearly every day for the last six years. She has sat in a chair next to you and talked for hours at a time. For a long time, we worried about her. We knew there was no way you could hear her, but she kept right on talking, carrying on a conversation with you, just like everything was completely normal. She's a wonderful woman, Mr. Glenn. You are a lucky man. When you began to come out of the coma, we did notify your parents. They are out in the waiting room. I know they are anxious to see you. Do you want me to send them in?"

"Yes, Doctor, please send them in right away."

Susan and Ron Glenn ran into the hospital room. Susan reached her arms out and hugged and kissed her son, crying. But they were tears of happiness. Her prayers had been answered. She had never given up hope. Dennis held her tight, but she was the one that wouldn't let go. Her tears had left damp spots on his shoulders. The wetness had soaked through his hospital gown and onto his shoulders. He didn't mind. Dennis never thought he would see his mother again. He was crying now, too.

She looked older, more fragile. *Has it really been six years since I last saw her last*? he thought.

Her tears were causing her make-up to run. He lifted his hand to wipe her face.

"I love you so much, Dennis Glenn. Don't you ever try to leave your father or I again."

"I love you too, Mom. Damn, I missed you."

Ron stood back, giving his wife time to comfort her son. Dennis could see the puffiness around his father's eyes. He had been crying too. But Ron wasn't a man that showed emotion. He would never admit that he had been crying. Still, Dennis knew he had. Dennis knew that his father loved him., even though he had difficulty expressing his emotions.

For three more weeks, Dennis remained at Sunnyside. He often asked about Elise, but no one would give him information. The answers his parents gave him were vague. They would only say that she was doing better. He could tell they didn't want to talk about it, that they were hiding something. Whenever he would press his parents, they would say, "She is doing fine. You will see her soon."

The physical therapy was long and difficult. In many ways, he was completely starting over. Dennis had to learn how to walk again, and he had to learn to write. He had to learn to feed himself. Many of his motor skills had to be relearned. Therapy, he was told, would last for a long time. Sunnyside's goal was to reteach him enough of his motor skills so that he could go home. His physical therapy could last for years.

During his time at Sunnyside, his parents never talked about Elise unless Dennis asked about her. In fact, they rarely talked about the last six years at all. When they did, they would talk only about the good things that had happened. They talked about Hillary and Teddy—they were living with Ron and Susan now. They were older, slower, more laid back. Hillary struggled to climb stairs due to arthritis. She never got on the bed anymore. It was too difficult for her, so she laid at the side of the bed. Teddy still climbed on the bed and slept at the foot of the Glenns' bed. But he had slowed down too. Teddy wasn't nearly as fast as he used to be. He could no longer catch birds on the lawn, although he still chased after strangers and small animals just like he had before, but now those chases winded him. He came inside with his head hanging and with labored breathing. Teddy slept more than he played. His bark was still as loud as ever, but his heart was not in the chase.

His parents talked about retirement. Dennis's dad was retired now. He did a little fishing, but mostly he just stayed around the house. They talked about traveling once Dennis was back on his feet. There hadn't been a lot of happiness over the past six years. There wasn't a lot that they could tell Dennis about right now. He needed to get stronger. He needed time to slowly adjust to life again.

As hard as the family tried to keep it hidden, some events

of the last six years were discovered by Dennis through television, radio, newspapers, and conversations he overheard. Dennis was aware of some of what had occurred while he was in a coma.

He learned that the Pinera Family Funeral Home had recently burned down, with arson as the cause. Mayor Cole and his wife were inside. Both died in the fire.

He learned that the crematorium that stood across the street from the funeral home had been the scene of some grisly murders and that it was scheduled to be torn down.

Everything he had heard on the news, he had dreamed while he was in the coma. Those dreams continued when he slept, but they weren't dreams anymore — they were nightmares now. Most of his nightmares involved him working in the crematorium.

In a recurring nightmare, he walked into the refrigeration room. There was one body lying on a gurney, covered in a white sheet except for the toes. On the big toe of the right foot was a red tag. He rolled the body into the cremation chamber, opened the furnace, and removed the white sheet. The body was Gloria Jean Booker, and she was looking directly at him. She was alive, begging him not to kill her. She began to cry. Tears rolled down her cheeks, and she lifted her hand to try to push him away. Dennis lifted the gurney and pulled her onto a conveyor that was attached to the door of the furnace. She begged him to stop and began to scream. The intense heat of the cremation furnace began to cause blisters to immerge on the surface of her legs and arms. Dennis wanted to stop, but he couldn't. He started the conveyor, and her body moved slowly into the furnace. Her screams were horrific, and he watched as she fell into the furnace. Her screams intensified as he watched her skin begin to bubble. She was boiling from the inside out. Her screams were agonizing for him.

Dennis closed the furnace door, hoping he would stop hearing them, but he didn't. He ran to the refrigeration room and closed that door, but the screams continued. They wouldn't stop.

Dennis would wake up in a cold sweat, but her screams continued to echo in his ears. That wasn't the only nightmare, but it was the one that occurred most often. All of his nightmares had one thing in common — they all took place in the refrigeration room of the crematorium. In all the nightmares, there were corpses in that room, and in all those nightmares, their eyes were open. The eyes talked to him and begged him not to cremate them. And all his nightmares ended the same way, with screams of fear. More intense than anything he had heard before, they were screams of unbearable pain. The screams were so horrific that Dennis woke up in a cold sweat at the end of every nightmare.

The day Dennis was released from Sunnyside, his parents were excited. It was a day that nobody thought would happen, a day that Elise and Dennis's parents had dreamed of many times. But that day was also met with anxiety. He would need to be told about Elise. Dennis expected to see her soon. That wasn't going to happen. He would need to be told the truth of what had happened. His mom and dad would sit down with him and tell him about Elise. But not the first night he came home. That night would be for celebrating.

Susan made her son's favorite dinner, spaghetti and meatballs with cheesy garlic bread and roasted Italian potatoes. For dessert, she made a cherry pie. They drank wine and talked about good times. Hillary and Teddy sat by Dennis's side. They had welcomed him home exactly the way they had every morning when he came home from work, wagging their tails and fighting for his attention.

"They looked so different from what I remember. They're

older, grayer, and fatter," Dennis said to his mother.

"Well, it has been six years, honey. The dogs are getting old."

Dennis retired to the basement at a little past ten, the dogs following him. He laid in bed tossing and turning, with Teddy at the foot of the bed and Hillary lying on the floor next to him. He couldn't sleep. He was afraid to sleep. The nightmares were returning almost every night now. Plus, he couldn't stop thinking about Elise. Something was wrong. His parents acted like everything was normal, but it wasn't. Something had happened to Elise, and he planned to confront his parents in the morning.

For days now, he had an uneasiness about the events that occurred in his nightmares. He couldn't help but think of the dreams he had while he was in the coma. Those dreams had turned dark now. They had transformed into nightmares, and they had intensified. They seemed so real and wouldn't end until he woke up. The last few nights, his nightmares centered around the fire at the funeral home. That was the one nightmare he knew was based on a real event. He had seen and heard about it in the news and the newspaper. Mayor Cole was in his nightmare. He was in the basement of the funeral home with Dennis — he'd saved his life. He handed Dennis the evidence before he ran back inside to save his wife. The news stories said that the bodies of the mayor and his wife were found in the basement of the funeral home. Dennis had dreamed that they were in the basement of the funeral home. Dennis had also had nightmares about the murders that took place in the crematorium. That event also occurred. But the timeline of those events meant they happened while he was still in a coma.

Why do I remember events so vividly that happened while I was in a coma?

How could he know about them? His dreams were so vivid. He was convinced that he was there and that he was a part of those events. Dennis had to get answers, and he couldn't wait any longer. He remembered, in his dreams, that he talked to Detective Jacks. It was the middle of the night, but he couldn't wait. He called the police department.

"May I speak to Detective Jacks?"

There was an awkward silence on the phone. "Detective Jacks is deceased."

Dennis hung up the phone. He had seen that in his most recent nightmare. He was murdered in the crematorium the night of the fire at the funeral home.

Dennis went online and googled Detective Jacks of the Kansas City police force. He was killed answering a call at the crematorium. Next, Dennis googled Andrew and Elizabeth Pinera. He read that they had died in a house explosion and fire. That had been in his dreams. Next, Dennis googled Michael Cuneo and discovered that he was bludgeoned to death in the crematorium across from the funeral home. Then he read about his killer. That's when he nearly fell to the floor.

CHAPTER 18
ELISE

Dennis ran upstairs to his parents' bedroom. "We need to talk right now," he said. "I want to know what happened to Elise."

There was no waiting for the morning. They needed to tell Dennis now. Ron led his son into the kitchen while Susan stayed behind for a few minutes. She picked up the phone and called Elise's doctor.

"Dr. Moore, I hope I didn't wake you. This is Mrs. Glenn, Dennis's mother."

"I'm awake, Mrs. Glenn. I was expecting your call, just not this early in the day."

"Sorry, Doctor. But Dennis is demanding to know about his wife. Can you please come over right away?"

"Yes, give me thirty minutes. And Mrs. Glenn, please don't tell Dennis where his wife is or why."

"I won't, Doctor."

Susan hung up the phone and walked to the kitchen, where

she put on a pot of coffee. When it was done, she poured three cups and sat them on the breakfast table. Then she told Dennis the truth, at least as much as she could.

"Dennis, please know that your father and I love you very much, and we love Elise, too, just as if she were our own daughter. This is going to be difficult for you to hear, but you are going to find out sooner or later. The night that Gloria Jean Booker died did not happen the way the news media has said. She had been drinking heavily and was depressed. Her lover had recently broken up with her. She called you that night and asked you to come to pick her up. You did, but you didn't take Elise. You went by yourself. Elise told us that you had an argument that night. She said you confessed that you had an affair with Gloria. You said that it was over, that it was a mistake."

"What?" Dennis looked stunned. "I never had an affair with Gloria Booker. I never cheated on Elise."

"Your father and I didn't think so, Dennis. But in your wife's mind, she believed you did. She told us that you told her you only loved her, and you begged for her forgiveness. When you left the house, she followed you."

"Son, why did you leave Elise home when you went to pick up Gloria?" his dad asked.

"Elise was not herself that night. Gloria called Elise to ask for a ride. They maintained a good relationship even after Lou divorced her. I think Elise was about the only one of her ex-relatives that kept in touch with her. But when Elise answered the phone, she began yelling at her. She accused her of trying to break up her marriage. Elise was convinced she was having an affair with me. I got on the line and told Gloria I would pick her up. She was drunk, and she needed a ride. That infuriated Elise. I asked her to come with me, but she refused. So, I went by myself.

Dad, I have no idea where she got the idea that Gloria and I were having an affair. We barely knew each other. Besides, I would never cheat on Elise. I love her."

Susan continued her story. "Well, Elise said she followed you to the bar and watched you go inside. A few minutes later, she saw you leave the bar with Gloria and get into your car. Elise followed you. She was upset—she thought you were meeting with your lover again. She wanted to hurt both of you. You must have spotted her following you because you sped up. You lost control of your car when you crossed an icy bridge. She was right behind you and couldn't stop. She hit your car and knocked you off the road. You went down a hill and collided with a tree. Then she lost control of her car, and it rolled over several times. She was thrown from the car."

"Yes, I remember her being thrown from the car in my dreams. She was paralyzed, wasn't she?"

"No, she was never paralyzed. She wanted you to believe that. I think she wanted to believe it, too. She felt it would have been just punishment for what she did to you and Gloria. She never got over what she had done. The police said the accident wasn't her fault, but she thought differently. The accident was only the beginning of her nightmare that played out over the last six years. While you were in a coma, her father asked her to take over your job at the crematorium. She was fine with that since it meant working the graveyard shift so she could spend the days at the hospital with you. She wanted to be by your side when you woke up. She was always certain that you would. After six months, the doctors had given up hope of you waking up. You were on life support. They wanted to take you off of it, but Elise insisted that you stay on it. She refused to allow them to unplug you. Finally, the hospital refused to keep you any longer. That's when Elise admitted you to Sunnyside. She sat by your side nearly every day for six years, until three months ago."

"What happen three months ago?"

"That was the night the funeral home burned down. That was the night Elise got her revenge. Honey, I hate to tell you this, but your wife told us that she was raped by a coworker at the crematorium. Elise was traumatized by what happened to her. She began a downward spiral after the attack. Elise told us that she had trouble sleeping. The night of the assault kept playing out her nightmares at night. She became terrified of falling asleep. I begged her to go to the police, begged her to get help. But she refused. She began spending all of her spare time by your side. She talked to you like you could hear every word she said. She carried on regular conversations with you. Your father and I were worried about her — so were some of the nurses and doctors at Sunnyside. I asked her about her conversations with you. She said that she talked into your eyes, that your eyes talked back to her. I'll admit, son, that your eyes did freak a lot of people out. They wouldn't close. The doctors tried to close them, but they seemed to be locked in place. But as weird as your eyes appeared, nobody believed that they talked except for Elise.

"Honey, the police determined that your wife killed Michael Cuneo, the man she said attacked her. They said she bludgeoned him to death with a metal rod. There were three other bodies found in the crematorium that had been bludgeoned to death too. One was a detective. Then she went to the funeral home and set it on fire. Five people were killed in the blaze, two of them the mayor and his wife. No one knows why they were there. They were found in the basement. So were three other bodies. None of them were identified."

"I don't believe Elise is capable of hurting anyone, let

alone killing people," Dennis strongly replied.

"I'm sorry, honey. But it is true. Elise is getting the help she needs now. The doctors say she is improving every day."

"Where is she, Mom?"

"Honey, her doctor will be here any minute. He will explain everything to you."

A few minutes later, the doorbell rang. Ron went to the door while his wife comforted her son.

"Hello, Doctor. We're glad you are here. My wife is in the breakfast room with Dennis. She told him about Gloria Booker, the rape, and the night of the fire, but nothing else."

"How much about the night of the fire did your wife share with Dennis?"

"Not much, Doctor. She only mentioned the bludgeoned bodies in the crematorium and the bodies of the mayor and his wife that were found in the funeral home."

"Good. I'll explain everything else to Dennis."

Ron and Doctor Moore walked back to the breakfast room. Doctor Moore introduced himself to Dennis while Susan poured him a cup of coffee.

"Hello, Dennis. It's good to finally meet you. We were all concerned that you might never come out of that coma. I came to visit you several times at Sunnyside, but you were in the coma, so I'm sure you weren't aware I was there."

"No, Doctor, I don't remember you visiting me."

"That's understandable given your condition. Dennis, do you remember Elise visiting you while you were in a coma?"

"No. I don't have any recollection of anyone visiting me."

"Dennis, what did you dream while you were in a coma?"

"I remembered working in the crematorium. I remembered my family and my dogs."

"Dennis, I need you to tell me everything you remember."

"Why?"

"Trust me. It's important. I need to know everything you remember from your dreams."

"I remember that Gloria Booker died in a car accident. I cremated her. I remember all those bodies, the special orders, with their eyes wide open, staring back at me, trying to talk to me. I remember cremating so many bodies. I remember Elise's parents dying in the house explosion. I remember Lou Pinera taking over the business. He brought in Joseph Cuneo as a partner. That's when everything started going wrong. He was part of the mob. His cousin was the mayor. He signed a contract for body removals with the city. But there were so many bodies coming into the crematorium, many of them with their eyes wide open. I used to think I heard their screams when I dropped them in the cremation furnace.

"I remember wanting to escape, but Joseph Cuneo wouldn't let me. He was a psychopath. I remember the night Lou Pinera was nearly murdered by him. He was left in his car in the garage with the engine running. He barely escaped with his life. He ran to my house. He had papers in a safe in the basement that proved crimes that would send Joseph Cuneo to prison. He asked for my help to get the papers. I went with him to his house — Dad went with us. We found the papers, but Joseph Cuneo's men found us before we could escape. Lou Pinera was killed. I was afraid my dad had died too. I was able to get away with the evidence that was in the safe. Elise was at the funeral home, looking for additional evidence in a safe in Lou's office. I went to the funeral home to find her. I got as far as the embalming room when someone attacked me. The next thing I remember was being inside a casket, pounding on the inside of it, screaming.

Someone heard me and opened the casket. It was the mayor. We both ran to escape the fire, but on the way, the mayor thought he heard his wife in the storage room. He handed me some papers that he said would incriminate Joseph Cuneo. He told me to hold them for him, and if he didn't come out of the fire that I should turn them over to the FBI.

"When I got outside, the paramedics gave me oxygen. They wanted to take me to the hospital, but I had to find Elise. So I ran. When I came around the front of the building, I saw Joseph Cuneo and several of his men. Elise was not with them. The only thing I could think was that Elise must be in the crematorium. I thought they had drugged her and were planning to cremate her, so I ran there. I got inside and worked my way to the refrigeration room. That's when I saw Michael Cuneo on top of my wife. I went crazy. I picked up a metal rod and bashed in his head. Then other men came into the refrigeration room. I swung the metal rod as much as I could and hit several of them before they took me down. The next thing I remember is Joseph Cuneo standing over me. I had killed his son, and he wanted me to suffer. He was going to cremate Elise and me while we were still alive. He gave me a shot of some drug that paralyzed me, but I could still see everything. I could still feel pain. His men took us to the cremation furnace—he wanted me to watch as they cremated Elise. She was still alive. They began to lift her into the furnace. That's when I blacked out. I don't remember anything after that."

Doctor Moore took notes as Dennis talked about his dreams. Then, when he had finished, Doctor Moore took a sip of his coffee, looked up at Dennis, and began to talk.

"Dennis, I don't fully understand how—the mind is very complicated—but somehow your wife talked to you while you were in a coma and your dreams reflected everything she told you. Your wife told me that she spoke into your eyes. She was convinced you understood everything she said. She was convinced that you talked back to her through your eyes. She was even convinced that some of her actions were based on what you told her she should do."

"No, Doctor. That's crazy. That is impossible."

"Maybe, but maybe not. Your wife suffered a traumatic event in her life the night of the car accident. She loved you more than anything in the world. She believed you had just confessed to her that you had an affair with someone she trusted, her ex-aunt. Then she heard you talking to her. You ran out of the house without an explanation. You can imagine what was going through her mind. She followed you, and when she saw you get into your car with Gloria Booker, she was enraged. She followed you, rammed your car, and pushed you off the road. When she saw that she had killed Ms. Booker and thought she had killed you, it sent her mind into a tailspin. That night was the trigger that set in motion the next six years. She even tried to commit suicide after the accident. She took some sort of concoction made up of antifreeze and teardrop solution. It didn't kill her, but the results made it look like she was dead. She was paralyzed. Her breathing was slowed to a point it was nearly undetectable. She fooled the doctors. They pronounced her dead, and she was nearly embalmed. Tony Pinera saved her life. She was lying flat on the embalming table, staring back at him. There was something different about her eyes. He got close to them and saw a small spot in the corner of one of her eyes. It looked like a small drop of blood, no larger than the head of a needle. He looked at it for several seconds, trying to determine what was causing it. He had never seen anything like it before. Then he noticed it slowly expand, getting larger. It was beginning to slide down her face.

If it hadn't been for the teardrop she was able to force out of her eye, she would have been embalmed while she was still alive.

"This will be difficult for you to hear, Dennis, but after that incident, your wife began to invent an alternative life. She believed you could hear and understand everything she told you. And as it turns out, she was right. Those years that she spent by your side, she told you an incredible story. She even told it as if you were the one at the center of everything that was happening, even though, in reality, it was your wife that was at the center of it all. You see, Dennis, none of what you remember in your dreams happened to you. But much of what you remember did happen to your wife."

"No, it can't be. This is crazy, Doctor."

"I assure you, Dennis, everything I am telling you is absolutely true. At some point after the car accident, your wife's mind split into two separate personalities. One was the wife you knew and loved. The other was much different. The two personalities lived side-by-side within her mind. I believe both of her personalities talked to you while you were in a coma. At first, the Elise you knew and loved was the dominant personality. For a long time, that was the only personality that spoke to you. The other personality was rarely seen outside of her work. Even your parents did not realize she was anyone other than Elise. She was able to control and conceal her other personality for a long time.

"Dennis, the police suspect that your wife murdered her parents. I believe that if she did, Elise was not aware of it. I believe her other personality was responsible for her parents' murders. In a way, her other personality committed crimes your wife had only thought about. On the surface, Elise loved her parents. But in the back of her mind, she hated them for making her get an abortion. She not only blamed them for the death of her child, but she also blamed them for not being able to have children. Dennis, the abortion set in motion her downward spiral. She loved you very much, but she was lonely. She wanted a child. Her parents took that opportunity away from her. I believe her other personality first surfaced the day she murdered her parents. I believe it was that other personality that actually killed her parents. Elise was not responsible. In fact, the Elise you knew was completely incapable of murder.

"For a long time, the personality that was the woman you loved remained dominant. Elise was never aware of the actions of her other personality. She invented a person that, in her mind, was responsible for all the evil she told you about while you were in a coma. That imaginary person was Joseph Cuneo. In actuality, there was no Joseph Cuneo. He never existed. He never was partners with Lou Pinera. Elise was Joseph Cuneo. After her parents died in the explosion, Lou Pinera needed help to run the funeral home. He asked Elise to become his new partner. Lou knew very little about the funeral home, nor did he want to. He was content handling the books. He turned the operations of the funeral home and the crematorium over to your wife. She was the one that hired Michael Cuneo. She became very close to him. Eventually, their relationship grew beyond friendship. He fell in love with her, but she stilled loved you. Elise felt enormous guilt, so much so that she invented stories about Michael Cuneo. She told you about terrible things he had done. That guilt manifested itself by giving her other personality more control. The Elise you knew showed herself less often. Joseph Cuneo became her dominant personality."

"So, are you trying to tell me the dreams I had about things that Joseph Cuneo did, were actually things my wife did? That's insane."

"I don't know everything she told you while you were in the coma, only what you have shared with me this morning. I suspect that much of what she told you about Joseph Cuneo was, in fact, things she had done, crimes she had committed. However, some things she told you were likely fiction. She believed you understood everything she told you while you were in the coma. I am certain she shared with you some things she wanted to believe were true or colored some of her stories so you would not think badly of her. Remember, Dennis, she never stopped loving you. She certainly didn't want you to stop loving her. Your wife was a very sick person. As the years went on, she lost grasp of reality. Her other personality became stronger with time. Eventually, it completely took control of her."

"What do you mean by that, Doctor?"

"I mean that Elise no longer exists. The other personality, Joseph Cuneo, has taken control of her. Her mind was barely holding on to some part of herself just before the night of the fire. That day was the anniversary of her abortion. I believe Elise intended to end her life that night. She went to the crematorium and injected herself with some sort of poison. But, Joseph Cuneo wouldn't let her die. He made her believe she was raped that night by Michael Cuneo in the refrigeration room of the crematorium. That imaginary attack resulted in her mind refusing to acknowledge the existence of Elise Glenn. At that moment, she became Joseph Cuneo. He took complete control of her mind."

"Christ, I want to see her, Doctor. I want to see her now."

"That's what I'm trying to explain to you, Dennis. Elise no longer exists. The night of the murders in the crematorium and the fire at the funeral home, he escaped. Joseph came to Sunnyside. He was in your room, Dennis. He blamed you for the murder of his son, Michael, and he also blamed you for your wife wanting to commit suicide. Joseph Cuneo was not ready to die. He couldn't let your wife kill herself, and him too, so he put a substance in your IV, a type of poison. Then he unplugged your life support. If it wasn't for Special Agent Bradshaw with the FBI, you would have died that night. The ironic thing is that it was your wife that called him. She did that from the crematorium just before she lost complete control of her mind.

"Dennis, you can take some comfort in knowing your wife's final act was to try to save your life. When the agent entered your room, he saw a man leaning over you, injecting a substance into your IV. When he wrestled the needle from the man's hand, he saw that the person was a woman, dressed in man's clothes. That person was Elise."

"Oh my God. I can't believe it. Where is she, Doctor?"

"Elise is getting the best treatment possible. She is at Resthaven Psychiatric Hospital."

"I've got to see her, Doctor."

"I'm afraid that would be extremely harmful to her right now, Dennis. Elise no longer exists. Joseph Cuneo occupies her room, and he blames you for the death of his son. I'm afraid his reaction to seeing you would be detrimental to his treatment."

"You are making progress treating her, aren't you?"

"We are making progress treating him. Dennis, as difficult as it will be for you, you must forget about your wife. Do not try to see her. Do not try to contact her. She is gone and may never be back."

"I'm sorry. I just can't accept that, Doctor. Either you take me to her or I will go there on my own. I've got to see her."

"Okay, Dennis. I understand. I would probably feel the same way as you if this had happened to my wife. I will take you to him. But I can't allow him to see you. There is an observation room next to his room. He is being watched and monitored twenty-four hours a day. I will talk to him. You can watch and listen from the observation room. Remember, though, the person in that room is Joseph Cuneo, not your wife. Are you absolutely sure you want to see him?"

"Yes, I am."

The Glenn family followed Dr. Moore back to Resthaven. It was a large five-story brick complex surrounded by a ten-foot-high iron fence. A large gate manned by two security guards was at the front of the complex. Inside, the building was old, gray, and cold. The lighting was poor, and the hallways smelled like a combination of urine and ammonia.

A slow, noisy elevator took the family up to the fifth floor. A security guard sat in front of a large metal door that led into the patient wing. Dr. Moore showed his badge, and the door was opened. Inside, the odor was intense. Screaming could be heard coming from some of the rooms.

At the far end of a long, narrow hallway was room 533. Next to it was the observation room. Dr. Moore summoned a nurse to accompany the Glenn family inside the room. The room was small, maybe twelve by twelve, with four chairs and a large window that ran the complete length and height of one side of the room. A curtain was closed, hiding the other side of the window from view. The Glenn family took seats at the base of the window.

A few seconds later, the nurse that accompanied them into the room touched a button, and sound could be heard coming from the other room. They heard Dr. Moore entering the other room.

"How are you doing today, Joseph?" they heard him say.

There was no response. The nurse pressed another button,

and the curtain opened.

Dennis nearly collapsed. His mother began to cry. His father put his arms around her.

In front of them, strapped down to a bed, was a man. At least, it looked like a man. He was in men's pajamas. He had short, dark hair. His face looked worn and unshaven. His eyebrows were thick and dark. Dennis did not recognize the person in that room until he talked. There was no mistaking the voice. It was Elise.

"Joseph, do you remember Dennis Glenn?"

Joseph's face showed anger. "Yes, that's the son-of-a-bitch that murdered my son and tried to kill me."

"Joseph, do you remember Elise Glenn?"

"Yes, she was the whore that worked in the crematorium with my son. She seduced him. Then she told her husband that he raped her. Dennis Glenn murdered my boy because of what that bitch told him."

Dr. Moore had one more question. "Joseph, what happened to Elise?"

"Oh, I can't tell you that, Doctor. I'm afraid you would think badly of me."

"It's okay, Joseph. I'm your friend. I won't think any differently toward you."

"She got what she deserved. She is at the bottom of the cremation furnace. I'm afraid there is nothing left of her but ashes."

-END-

Alan Brown grew up in the suburbs of Kansas City and graduated from Shawnee Mission East High School in 1973 and Avila University in 1979. Now He lives in a suburb of St. Louis, MO, with my wife and three daughters. He also has four sons that are grown and living outside the home. He enjoys writing about his experiences growing up, examining the fantastical side, the dark side of a person's natural fears. All of his books are based on a reality in his life. He is a fan of Alfred Hitchcock. Like his stories, Alan Brown's will conclude with a twist, something he hopes will take the reader by surprise.

www.ingramcontent.com/pod-product-compliance
Lightning Source LLC
Chambersburg PA
CBHW030136180626
46812CB00002B/706